SILENT
NO MORE

N. E. HENDERSON

Publisher © N. E. Henderson Books
Editor: Charisse Hankins (2020)
Proof Reader: Nikkita McDuffle (2020)
Cover Art: Nancy Henderson (2020)
Paperback ISBN-13:

For Michael

This book is my first just as you are my first and only child. You're the greatest joy in my life and the coolest person in this world. Never forget that. You make me laugh like no one else can. It's a privilege to be your mom. You captured my heart from before I knew you and you'll always have it along with my support in anything you do. I love you to infinity and beyond.

PROLOGUE

NICHOLAS

"What the fuck does he want now?" I huff, glaring down at the name displayed on my cell phone. If I never have to speak to him again it'll be too soon. Jerking my hand off the steering wheel, I reach over, turning the volume down on the stereo that's blasting Avenged Sevenfold's "Nightmare" through the speakers.

My Father. A man I despise.

If God existed, the man's life surely would have ended by now. But that hasn't happened, and I don't see it happening any time soon. I'm the type of guy who prays for his dad to get a brain hemorrhage that will take him straight to Hell—where he belongs.

"Yeah?" I greet him as I turn into the underground parking garage at Lockhart Publishing in my silver Audi R8.

Way to ruin my day, Dad.

"Nicholas, is that the way you normally answer your phone?

You're the CEO of a company for Christ's sake. The least you could do is act like a professional." Two companies to be exact, but what does being a CEO have to do with professionalism when the person on the other end of the line is the sorry excuse I call father? The man should know by now I'm going to do and act any way I want. I've never been the "do as you're told" type, so why start now?

"I wasn't aware this was a professional call." My tone is sarcastic, but I couldn't care less. The dickfuck knows I hate him. Nothing will ever change that fact. We will never drink a beer together. We will never have a strong father/son bond. Hell, the only bond we do have is blood. Just knowing his blood is running through my veins and that it will forever link us disturbs me.

"Son, let's not argue today. I called for a specific reason, so I won't keep you any longer than necessary." I can tell by his clipped tone he doesn't want to be on the phone with me any more than I do with him.

"Fine, then tell me what you do want so I can get back to work." I breathe out in annoyance.

My father was a well-known defense attorney in Los Angeles when I was growing up. He made a living getting criminals out of jail for many years, and now he's a prominent judge. There is some real fucked-up irony in that. The man should be locked up for the things he's done to my mother over the years. Why the woman stays married to him is beyond me. It's not like she needs his money. In fact, my father has benefited from her inheritance more than she has.

Rotten bastard.

"As you know, Thursday is Thanksgiving, and your mother would like you and your sister present for lunch." He knows I'll do anything for my mom. I think I proved that to him a long time ago. "Do you think you can do this for her?" he adds. He knows I'm going to say yes.

"What time?" I ask on a sigh as I open my car door, stepping out into the dark, musky air under my building. To my annoyance, I slam the door harder than I intend. Fuck! Why do I let this man get under my skin so easily? Just the sound of his voice tends to set me off.

"Noon," he responds. A few hours in the company of my father is sure to piss me off along with adding additional renovations to my house for my handyman to fix. Not that I can't repair the damage I create myself, but why go through all that trouble when I can hire someone to do it? I'm sure the guy already thinks I'm a raging alcoholic. I'm not, of course, or at least not yet. If he knew all the damage was the result of my frustration with my father, he would understand.

Yeah, so I have some anger issues.

"Okay, but if you want Nikki there, then perhaps you should call your daughter yourself." I make my way to the elevator, pressing the "up" button. As I wait, I check the time on my Rolex. It's 1:14 p.m. I have plenty of time before my meeting with Teresa. Why I made that woman Vice President of my company, I'm still not sure.

She is great at business and a brilliant editor, but damn, I wish she would stop trying to get into my pants every time we're alone. Now that she's my VP, I see her more often than I'd like. It's not that she isn't attractive, because she is, with blonde hair, big tits, and a tiny waist, but I don't sleep with people who work for me. And well . . . she annoys the shit out of me. Plus she's too bitchy, and that is a big turn off.

The sound of my father's voice brings me back to our conversation. I need to wrap this conversation up. The longer I speak to him, the longer I'll be at *Knocked Out* tonight, kicking the shit out of my best friend.

Jase is one of the few people that know about my relationship with my father and why I loathe him. He and I share a common hatred for our fathers. Everyone who works for my dad thinks he's an outstanding judge and wonderful family man.

What a crock of shit!

"Nicolette is being her usual immature and childish self. It would be easier for all of us if you ask her to come. She listens to you, Nicholas." He sounds annoyed with his last statement, and I silently laugh. My sister isn't immature or childish. She would just rather ignore his calls than deal with the man. She can't stand the heartless bastard any more than I can.

Any man who lays a hand on a woman with the sole intention of hurting her isn't much of a man at all in my book. That is the kind of fucked-up shit my father loves to do to women. We watched him physically and mentally abuse our mother for years. The day I turned twenty-one, I made sure my father never laid a hand on my mom again. That's not to say he has stopped hurting women, because he hasn't. Now he has a mistress to abuse. He doesn't have a clue that I know about her, but I do. Surely my mother does as well.

As the elevator door opens, Matt, my senior editor and good friend, is exiting. I pin him with my signature icy stare. I can tell by the look that crosses his face he knows I'm in one of my moods, so he wisely says nothing and passes me quickly. These moods only occur when I have to communicate with the man on the other end of my phone.

"Nicholas," he stresses, "just call your sister for me. I don't have time for Nicolette right now. I'm walking into court as we speak." He has never had time for Nikki, or me for that matter. Not that I care. I stopped caring about my father before I learned to write my own name.

"Sure, Dad," I force out through clenched teeth. "I'll handle it. We'll be there on Thursday at noon. Is there anything else? I have a meeting to get to." I'm not completely lying. I do have a meeting to attend, but it's not for another hour.

"No, there isn't. I'll see you then." He ends the call, not bothering to say goodbye. This is nothing unusual. He thinks everyone around him is there to serve him.

I enter the elevator and press number eleven. As I ride up to the floor my office is on, I send my sister a quick text, letting her know the plans for Thanksgiving. This is sure to brighten her day as much as it has mine. My sister is the female version of myself. But perhaps Nikki controls her anger a little more than I do.

As I move my hand to store my phone in the breast pocket of my jacket, I hear the alert telling me I have a text message. I look down; it's my sister's reply.

Nikki: FUCK

The corners of my mouth turn up as I shove the phone back

inside my jacket, just as the elevator reaches my destination. My smile fades; I'm not looking forward to the rest of my day. Dealing with Teresa is one thing, but after dealing with Judge James 'Asshole' Lewis, I'm sure I'll take out my anger on her at some point today.

As I exit the elevator, something, or rather someone, catches my eye. She is standing at Rachel, my receptionist's, desk, with her back facing me. The legs catch my attention first. They are toned and her skin is fair. Her body turns a fraction as my eyes travel up, and I'm able to see her side profile. She is slender, but not at all skinny. My eyes continue their path up her body.

Fuck me. She's beautiful.

My eyes land on her hair. It's a stunning shade of red; darker than strawberry-blonde, but lighter than auburn. It's shiny and bright, unique and different from the everyday variety.

I can't see the color of her eyes from where I'm standing, but that mouth . . . Those pink lips are made for sucking cock. I allow my eyes to drop. She's wearing a navy dress that's a little on the short side to be considered business attire, but it looks good on her body.

My eyes glide back up her body, returning to those beautiful drapes that fall down to the middle of her back. She looks like an angel—an angel I'd like to tie down and fuck.

Goddamn, that hair is making my dick hard.

CHAPTER 1

SHANNON

Six months later

It's a cool evening in early May. The sun has begun to set over the Pacific Ocean causing the sky's orange streaks to stretch around the city of Los Angeles. I'm driving down Pacific Avenue in my black 911 Carrera 4S with the windows rolled down, listening to my iPod blaring in the background through the car speakers.

Well, not really. That may be construed as somewhat of a lie. There is music playing, but I haven't the slightest idea what song is coming through the speakers. I couldn't even tell you which song played before the one that is currently screaming words at me. My brain is consumed with too many other thoughts right now.

Music usually helps me relax, and it always puts me in a better mood, but I can't concentrate on it now, nor am I even paying close attention to the road. I probably shouldn't be driving in my current state of shock, but it's a little late for that realization now.

I've been driving through the city for hours.

I'm a photographer with a gallery in the West Hollywood Gateway shopping center. It's a gallery rather than a studio because I don't shoot any photographs on-site. Actually, it's just a place to display my work. Plus, I have to have an office. I don't think I'm the type of person who can work from a home office. Too many distractions and I would go crazy staying in my tiny apartment all day.

My work consists mostly of things such as buildings and outdoor scenery. I don't photograph people. I will, however, occasionally shoot pets at the animal shelter I volunteer at.

I'm friendly, and I have close friends, but I'm not what you would call a people person. I haven't always been like that. But now, I prefer space away from too many people, and when I'm taking photographs, I especially need to be alone. It's when all the built-up tension inside me releases and I feel at peace.

Most people think I'm this way because I'm an only child and because I grew up without a dad. I had one of course, but he died when I was two. I don't even remember the man. I wish I did, but I don't. I even wish I missed him, but you can't miss someone you never knew; at least I can't. The only thing I have as a reminder of him sits in a bank account, mostly unused.

I'm currently working on my second collection of photographs that will be published in book format. At the age of twenty-six, I already have one book published. *Sights of the City of Angels* by me—Shannon Taylor; it's not a novel by any means. The book is full of photographs with my thoughts underneath each picture describing places as I see them. It's a pretty good coffee table book if I say so myself. A conversation book if you will.

Photos are art to me. They are real moments captured in time. Photos never lie and photos don't hold secrets. Photos are real, true, and above all, honest.

My current collection captures photographs of places in the city of San Diego. It's going to be called *Sights of the City of Saint Didacus*. That is "if" the publishing company doesn't change the name. The collection is almost complete and due at 9:00 a.m. on Friday at Lockhart Publishing. I have a meeting with Teresa Matthews to turn in my portfolio.

I finished taking the photos back in late February, and all rounds of editing were completed last month, but my struggle has been with the arrangement of photographs, so they tell the story of the city perfectly—the way I see it and the way I want others to see it. I've changed the layout at least twenty times, and I'm still not satisfied.

Just six short hours ago seems almost like a lifetime ago.

"Ughhh. . . I'm getting nowhere with any of this." I flipped *my portfolio closed in frustration. Taking my hairband off my wrist, I pulled my hair out of my face. I'd had enough and decided that I may as well start the following day with a fresh pair of eyes. I glanced up at the clock hanging on the wall in my office and groaned. The clock read 11:31 a.m. I had only been working for four hours, but I could no longer focus on my work.*

All I wanted to do was go home and crawl into bed with Luke for at least a few hours before he had to be at work. Luke— my fiancé and a third-year resident in the ER at Huntington Memorial Hospital—and I have been together for five years. We started dating during our junior year in college. We got engaged nine months ago, but for the last six months we've seemed more like roommates than a couple.

I couldn't blame that on Luke. The hospital assigned him the night shift, and I worked mostly during the day. We hadn't had a lot of quality time together, which had been weighing on my mind a lot lately. Hell, we probably hadn't had sex in at least four, maybe even five months. For all I knew, it could be longer.

My sex life may as well have been nonexistent. If I was honest with myself, it wasn't like I was missing much. Luke was what I called a "wham bam, thank you, ma'am" kind of man. I had never called him this to his face or to any of my friends. Basically, I got more stimulation from my vibrator than my boyfriend. Perhaps there was something wrong with me, but I hadn't exactly found out what all the excitement was about when it came to intercourse. It was so much work to get to those few seconds of bliss. Sometimes—a lot of times—I never even made it there.

I decided an afternoon surprise was just the type of thing we needed in our relationship.

Locking the door behind me, I double-checked that I'd done it right. Normally, Jenny would lockup at five, but she was off today. Jenny, my personal assistant, runs the gallery daily, except Wednesdays and Sundays.

Jenny kept me on task. If it weren't for her, I'd never get anything accomplished. She kept me organized too and made sure all my bills were paid on time, even my non-business ones. I wouldn't get through one day with anything completed if I didn't have her, which was probably why I was leaving in the middle of the day in the first place.

The drive to my apartment took only twenty minutes from work before I arrived at the front door to our apartment in Glendale. I smiled to myself and inserted the key, making sure I was as quiet as a mouse, hoping this would be a good surprise for him.

The door opened, and my mouth fell to the floor. I was stone-faced, my smile replaced with shock.

What the hell?!

In our living room Luke stood with his back facing the front door. His pants were around his ankles, and he was missing a shirt. His thick, dark hair was ruffled on the top of his head. A pair of tan legs were wrapped firmly around his hips. My eyes drifted to her hands resting on each side of his shoulders. Her nails dug into the skin underneath them, and I could hear her breathy pants as he slammed her into the wall. Neither of them noticed the front door open with me standing in the entryway.

You would think my first thought would have been to yell or scream, but neither happened. The first thing that popped into my head was that he had never done me in that manner. Interesting, I noted as my anger began to finally filter in.

I stood there for what felt like several minutes not saying anything and just watched, witnessing the scene play out in front of me as reality hit hard. I couldn't have stood there more than fifteen-seconds max. My fiancé was cheating on me. And in our apartment no less.

Our apartment? Really?

"You fucking bastard!" I wanted to yell those words at him, but they came out weak. Both bodies froze in place. I couldn't see the woman's face yet; although, I could see straight strands of long, raven hair.

"Oh fuck!" was the first thing that came out of Luke's mouth as he dropped the woman's legs to the floor. His voice was laced with panic, as it should be. He turned slowly, facing me, and my fierce, pale green eyes met his scared emerald ones.

My gaze cut over to the woman who had covered her mouth with a hand. My heart broke in that moment. Standing naked in my living room was my best friend, Allison. Her sky blue eyes were wide with shock. This couldn't be real. This couldn't be happening. Not her. This had to be a sick joke, but it wasn't. It was real all right.

"You bitch!"

It was all I could say as tears immediately sprung to my eyes. I turned my back on them, jerked my keys out of the door and raced the short distance back to my car. As I slowed my pace, I noticed Allison's red metallic BMW Z4 convertible parked out front. The one I passed on the way in. How did I not notice it? I was in her car at least twice a week! I slid into my Porsche while in a daze. I raced out of the parking spot a little faster than I should have, tears spilling from my eyes.

I'm forced back to the present when I hear my iPhone ring for the hundredth time since I left my apartment. That's a bit of an exaggeration, but frankly I don't care. I ignore the display, as I have every time before. Grabbing it, I flip the silent switch on and toss it over into my shotgun seat. It will still vibrate, but I won't have to listen to the annoying ringing sound.

Glancing at the clock on the dash it reads 6:48 p.m. I puff out a breath of air, knowing it's time for me to find a place to crash for the night. My body aches and I have a piercing migraine above my eyes. I know I can call my friends Katelyn and Stacy to stay at their place, but sleeping on their couch does not appeal to me. I need a comfy bed to crawl into, so I let myself forget about *today*. I'm not ready to talk about what happened, and I know if I go there that's exactly what will happen. If I say it aloud, it will make it more real. *My best friend betrayed me.*

Backstabbing bitch!

I see *The Cove* ahead on the right, about a quarter of a mile up the road just as "Burn" by Papa Roach starts to play through my speakers. I decide in a nanosecond that is exactly where I need to be. It is, after all, one of my weekly hangouts for one reason or the other. Not the hotel, but the amenities it offers, such as a luxury spa, bars, and several restaurants.

I love coming to *The Cove.*

Allison and I get pedicures at *Serenity*, the hotel's spa, once a month. Well, not anymore, that whore will have to find someone else to have a spa day with.

God, did I just think that? I can't believe I called my best, no, ex-best friend a whore, and actually meant it. But you know what? That kind of felt good. I've never been the type of person to call people petty, cruel names, but now, I finally understand why people do it.

I whip into the parking lot, pulling up to valet. A young guy saunters over to my car door, opening it for me. Taking his hand,

I swing my left leg out of my car, allowing him to pull me up. He's stronger than he looks. He can't be more than eighteen, but like any teenager his age, he gives me a once-over with his pale blue eyes. Any other time, this might make me smile, or even laugh, but not today. Sliding around him, I mumble a "thank you" as he sinks into the driver's seat of my car. He's pulling away as I make my way inside.

I'm amazed every time I enter this place. Words don't do justice to the grand entrance. It is modern and sleek. I love everything about this hotel. The aroma is something I've never smelled elsewhere. It's inviting and rich, yet warm. I walk up to the receptionist's desk. The cutest blonde girl greets me. I've never seen her before. Maybe she's new. At least, I don't remember seeing her before; then again, I don't usually check-in for a room when I come here. Her face is plastered with a broad smile. It's not the fake smile I get by most people in the customer service industry. She genuinely looks happy to help me.

After checking in, I toss the key card into my purse but don't go up to my room; instead, I head straight for the main hotel bar. This hotel has three bars and two restaurants. The main bar is called *Quaint*, and it's just that. It is charming, dark, and quiet; just the place to drown my sorrows, a place to be alone.

Getting drunk has never been my idea of fun, and not something I do on a regular basis. Don't get me wrong, I love beer and wine or even sometimes the bubbly, but I hate that feeling of no control. In fact, I've only been drunk once in my life, right after I graduated college, and I swore I'd never do it again.

Of course when I made that vow, I never imagined I would

have caught the two most important people in my life screwing— each other. God, I've given him five damn years of my life. Why the hell would he do this to me—to us?

How could Ally, of all people, do this? We have, no, had been best friends since the first day of junior high; over fourteen years ago. We both decided to attend the same college so we wouldn't be apart. We have always been inseparable. She's like the sister I never had. Apparently, I'm the only one who felt that way.

Fucking bitch!

The bartender approaches me as I take a seat at one of the empty bar stools near the end of the bar on the right side. I go for a smile, but I know it doesn't reach my eyes. I don't know if I'll ever smile again. Yeah, I would say I'm a bit depressed right now—if that is, in fact, what this empty, lonely, angry feeling is. I'm not clinical, so I can't exactly go diagnosing myself.

"What's it going to be, pretty lady?" His smile is warm and sincere. It matches his chocolate eyes and dark hair that is peppered with a bit of gray.

"Vodka tonic and *no* questions, Sam," I say, emphasizing the word "no" as I remove the small, round diamond ring from my ring finger. I should have taken it off hours ago. I twirl it around my fingers while I wait for Sam to bring my drink over.

Cripple dick. I think, picturing Luke in my head.

Surprisingly, I'm more hurt by my best friend than I am the man I was supposed to spend the rest of my life with. What does that say about our relationship?

Sam returns, and I place the ring on the counter to take the drink from his hand. He eyes me with concern when he watches me lay the ring on the counter, but doesn't say anything about it. He turns, walking to the other end of the bar to serve two men in business attire who have just sat down.

I'm not one of Sam's regulars, per se, but we are on a first-name basis with each other, and he always recognizes me when I stroll in. I pop in occasionally after work on Friday evenings. I like to have a glass of wine to relax before going home to get ready for a night out with my friends. Friday nights generally consist of Katelyn, Stacy, Ben, Kyle and myself. Luke and Ally always have to work. Plus, Stacy has never gotten along with Luke, so I try to keep them apart as often as possible.

I look at Sam at the other end of the bar as I take my first sip. The liquid doesn't flow smoothly down my throat. It's a bit tart, and normally, I'd want to make a disgusted gag face and stick my tongue out, but I force it down anyway before taking a larger gulp. The bigger the gulp I swallow, the faster I'll be done. The faster I'll be done, the faster I'll forget today ever happened.

I know Sam is probably wondering why I'm here on a Wednesday night, but I'm grateful he doesn't question me. I'm in no mood for conversation. I just want to forget what I saw, and vodka is the way to do that. I lift the lime wedge from the rim of my glass to suck the juices out before tossing it into the liquid.

As I swallow a small sip from my fourth glass of vodka tonic, my phone starts to buzz on the counter. I'm now wondering why I bothered pulling it out of my purse as I grab it, eyeing the display screen. I roll my eyes, and then when I swipe the answer button across the glass screen of my phone, I speak in the harshest voice I can muster, "Go. To. Fucking. Hell." I punctuate each word to get my point across, then press end, and toss it into my purse. Why doesn't he just give it up already? He's the one that messed up, not me. He and I are finished! There is no talking your way out of that shit. There is no apology that can undo it. Our relationship is over!

I hope the bastard's dick falls off. Yeah, that is a bit harsh, but who gives a shit? I certainly do not.

Fuck him.

And fuck her too!

I nearly jump in my seat when I hear the sound of a man's voice. It's a deep, strong, modulated voice; the type of voice that penetrates your ears and demands attention. "He must have fucked up pretty bad to make a beautiful woman sit in a bar, drinking all by herself."

Although the voice is pleasant to my ears, I want to be left alone tonight. Getting hit on is the last thing I need right now. I look in the direction of his voice to glare at him. He's sitting around the corner to my right, only about five feet away from where I'm seated. My eyes automatically soften when they meet bright blue flames. Talk about intense. They look like the blue embers of a roaring fire reflecting back at me.

Daaaamnnnn.

Those might be the most perfect set of eyes I've ever seen, and definitely the most intense. I lean back a little, feeling like I've been knocked back against a wall. Air momentarily leaves my body. How have I not noticed this man before now? It may be dark inside the bar, but those eyes stand out; they're virtually glowing at me from a few feet away. When air returns to my lungs,

I silently ask myself—am I that caught up in myself? Yeah, I am. At least, tonight I am.

The way he's staring at me is unnerving—unraveling. It's as though he's looking inside my head and is really seeing me, seeing the me I don't allow people to see. The last thing I want is for anyone to see that deep inside my soul.

Maybe it's just the alcohol, and I'm only imagining the way he's gazing at me.

As I take in the rest of his face, I notice his hair is dark brown, or it could be black. It's too dark in the bar to tell. It's messy on top, as though he's already run his fingers through it a few times tonight. He has a square jaw with a little stubble on his face that makes him slightly rugged, but sexy as sin. And a mouth that looks like it could devour anything it touches.

Allowing my eyes to dip, I see he's wearing a dark-colored suit jacket with a white shirt, but no tie. The jacket is open with the first two buttons at the top of the shirt undone. There is no hair that I can see poking out, so he probably has a smooth chest. His shoulders are broad. He's not a small man by any means.

This guy is smoking hot and oddly . . . familiar, but I know I've never met him before tonight. I would remember a man like this.

I begin to feel a little off balance, and not because of the alcohol I've consumed. My body heats up, and I feel a flush creeping across my face. Whatever thought washed through my mind is now gone. I can't remember what I was going to say, so I turn back to my drink—taking an even larger sip—not liking this feeling in the pit of my stomach one bit.

I don't know why I'm even drinking a vodka tonic. I hate this drink. Tonic, yuck, but I can't lie to myself; I know exactly why I'm drinking this. Vodka will get me to where I plan on being the quickest. I have a goal, and I intend to get there.

He addresses me again as I'm draining the liquid in my glass down my throat. "You really should slow down. That's your fourth, and I don't want to see that beautiful face of yours hit the floor."

He sounds like he is genuinely concerned. I don't give a shit how concerned he is. I am none of his business, and how much I drink is certainly none of his concern.

Who the hell is he to tell me to slow down? I'm starting to get pissed off. It has been a long day, and an even longer time since anyone has told me what to do. I'm not about to let someone do it again.

Ever.

I look in his direction, giving him my best "fuck off" expression. "I don't believe I asked, nor need your permission to do as I damn well please, so why don't you mind your own business and stay the hell out of mine?" I say this in a calm and controlled tone, hoping that it will shut the fucker up.

It doesn't.

His eyes darken and smolder. I wish he wouldn't look at me the way he does. It makes me squirm in my seat. The look in his eyes screams authority and control. I've seen that look once before, but not exactly like this. He doesn't scare me at all.

"Careful, sweetheart, you may pay for that remark later," he says as he takes a sip of his drink. His eyebrow is arched, and I can see the corner of his lips turn slightly upward behind his glass.

"Are you threatening me?" I ask with what I'm sure is shock

written all over my face.

"No, just a warning," he laughs out. His eyes soften but remain intense. His smile widens as though he's thinking about something, but he never breaks eye contact with me.

So, he's an arrogant fuck! That smile probably gets a lot of women to drop their panties. Sorry, buddy, but I'm not that kind of girl.

I roll my eyes and pick up my drink, knocking the rest back in one gulp. I wave to Sam, ordering my fifth. Sam looks hesitant, but he fixes me another anyway. Blue eyes and I don't say another word to each other, but I notice he orders a gin and tonic with lemon right after Sam brings me a fresh glass.

I reach for my phone inside my purse to check the time. I clear out the ten missed calls, not even bothering to look at the text messages. I'll deal with all of them tomorrow. Finally looking at the time, I see it's almost 9:30 p.m. At least I'm getting drunk early. I'll still be able to get enough sleep before work in the morning.

I'm mid-way through my sixth drink; my head is fuzzy and clouded when I think maybe I should have taken the man's advice and slowed down a little. If anything, his remark made me continue down my path.

Asshole.

I know it's time to go, and God, I hope I can make it to my room. I wave Sam over, asking for my check while reaching into my purse for my credit card. I place the card on the counter, then store my phone in an inside pouch in my purse.

As Sam approaches a few seconds later, I push the barstool backward before standing up and that's when everything starts to spin.

Shit.

Double shit!

I'm dizzy and this is bad. I needed a distraction, but I think I may have pushed myself too far. Why did I do this to myself? I'm going to pay for this tomorrow morning.

"Goddamn it, Shannon!" is what I faintly hear coming from my right as I lose my balance. I try to grip the bar, but it slips from my grasp as I start to fall backward.

Who said my name? I'm surprised my brain can even form a question as it's barely registering that I'm falling to the ground. It wasn't Sam. I'm sure of that, and I never told Mr. Hotness my name, so it couldn't have been him either.

I don't land on the floor like I thought I was going to. Instead, I'm being lifted into warm, strong arms. My eyes are closed and too heavy to open, but I smell him. It's a powerful yet natural male scent. There's no hint of cologne on him. I've never been attracted to the way a man smells, but by God, this fresh, spicy scent is maddening. I'm too far gone to object to his hold on me when I hear Sam's voice. The sound is low and coming from behind me. He mentions something about my room, but I don't hear everything.

I feel warm and safe.

This is everything I wanted to feel since I left my apartment earlier today.

CHAPTER 2

I wake feeling warm, comfortable, and well rested. Slowly, I sit up in my bed but quickly realize this is not the bed in my apartment. Everything from the day before comes rushing back to me. Images of Luke and Ally in my living room flood my mind. I remember coming to *The Cove* last night, but I've stayed here a few nights in the past so I know this bed is plusher and has nicer linen. This isn't the bed in my room, unless I was upgraded and don't remember. I'm a little worried.

As I look around the large room, for the first time in my life I don't know where I am. Light through the sheer white curtains filters into the room, but no one is beside me in the bed . . . or in this room. I pull the covers off and scoot to the edge of the mattress. My eyes widen as I look down. Panic flutters and threatens to rise in my chest.

"What have I done?" I question out loud as I take in the sight of myself. I'm wearing my white panties and matching bra, along with a huge white T-shirt that I know is much too big to belong to me. Plus, I didn't bring any of my clothes, so where the hell did it come from?

Oh no. No no nooooo! The words are echoing inside of my head.

I spot the clothes I was wearing yesterday sitting on a chair in the corner neatly folded. My cream pumps are lying next to the chair on the floor. I can't help but sigh in relief.

Getting out of bed, I quickly change into my white button-down shirt, gray pencil skirt and pumps. I leave the T-shirt on the chair where my clothes were.

I walk to the door, putting my ear against the wood, listening for any sounds in the next room. All is quiet. I take a second trying to recall last night, but the last thing I remember is my conversation with the jerk at the bar. I remember nothing else. I say a silent prayer to God not to let me open this door and see him—then again, maybe I do want it to be him. What's worse? The guy I remember from last night or another man I do not?

Shit!

I can't believe I let this happen. This is *so* not me.

I ease the door open and walk out. Sitting at a desk next to one of the windows is the asshole himself. I'm overcome with relief for some strange reason. That's a weird feeling and one I don't think I should have at this moment. He looks up and our eyes lock. He still has the most amazing eyes I have ever seen. They are very intense. That part I definitely remember. He smiles at me, showing no teeth, but it's definitely a warm smile.

"Good morning," he greets me as he closes the lid on his MacBook. Shutting the door behind me, I continue looking at him, wondering how I ended up here. I try to rationalize everything in my head, but I was in his bed after all. I always think the worst of every situation I'm in. At least I was wearing my underwear. Surely, that's a good sign?

Keep telling yourself that, Shannon.

"Hi," is the only thing out of my mouth as I tuck a stray strand of hair behind my ear. My tone is low and soft. I sound unsure of myself. He has a smirk on his face as he stands up from his desk chair. After he pushes the chair back, he walks around to the side of his desk.

He leans against the desk, crossing his legs. He's dressed very similar to the way he was last night, only his white dress shirt is buttoned all the way and he's sporting a black tie to match his suit. The jacket, however, is open, same as last night's attire.

Wow, the man is hot! No one should be this breathtaking, especially early in the morning. The five o'clock shadow I recall from last night is gone. In its place is the beginning of a goatee. He looks positively scrumptious. I regret not finding a bathroom to make sure I look presentable. I probably look like crap.

Slowly, I ask the question screaming in my head. The question I'm not sure I want to know the answer to. "How did I get here?" My voice is still low.

"I brought you up here last night," he tells me as he picks up a coffee mug from his desk, taking a small sip. He never breaks eye contact with me. He's looking at me the same way he did last night. I feel nervous, and my body warms all over. This is a feeling

I'm not used to, and on top of it, his response annoys me. I ask the question again and I clear my throat. I know he knows what I'm actually asking, but apparently he wants to play games. I hate games and I'm not about to be toyed with.

"Let me rephrase. How did I end up in your bed, half naked, wearing what I assume is your shirt?" I mentally pat myself on the back; I sound stronger. I cross my arms across my chest, waiting for his response. I try to look the part of someone assertive. His smirk turns into an amazing wide smile, showing off perfect white teeth. Is there anything not perfect on this man? He lets out a small laugh, obviously finding this funny.

I don't.

"Well," he starts out, "when you passed out at the bar and nearly fell on your face like I told you would happen, I brought you here where you would be safe and could sleep it off." After a beat, he adds, "To clarify, you weren't in just my T-shirt. I believe you were also wearing a white satin bra and matching panties when I placed you in my bed last night." My mouth falls open. He has a tight smile, but doesn't wait for me to respond. "So how is your head feeling this morning?"

"Fine," I spit out a little too quickly, but it is the truth. I probably should have a nightmare of a headache, but I don't. I'm well rested and that's a little scary. People are supposed to have hangovers from hell when they drink like I did last night.

He rolls his eyes as if he doesn't believe me. "Really?" he asks with a huff, before taking another sip of his drink. Once he swallows the contents from his mug, he sits it back on the desk, and then crosses his arms to match mine.

"Yes . . . really." I hesitate, breaking eye contact to look for the door. "I have to go," I say as I spot it on the far end of the room. Making my way over to the door, I grab my purse sitting on the coffee table, then bolt. Once I have exited, I'm relieved he didn't stop me.

Leaning against the door, I try to calm my nerves. That was awkward, to say the least. I still don't know what happened. . . Did I . . .? If we . . . Ughhh.

What the hell is wrong with me? Why did I get that drunk? Because your boyfriend cheated on you! I remind myself, and your best friend might as well have gutted you with a knife.

Fucking bitch!

I make my way to the elevator and press the down button. As I wait for its arrival, I notice I'm on the top floor, the floor of the penthouse. *Wow, way to pick 'em up, Shannon.* I don't let my mind wander any longer. I get in, pressing the button to the seventh floor. At least I'm still in the hotel.

Once in my room, I place my purse on the bedside table; I need a hot shower. I don't have any clean clothes and putting on the ones I'm currently wearing is not an option. Dirty underwear is gross and something I don't do.

Shit.

I grab my phone from my purse. Taking a seat at the head of the bed, tucking my left leg underneath my butt, I look at the display; I have thirty-plus missed calls and seventeen text messages. A few of the calls are from Luke and Allison, but most are from Katelyn and Stacy.

I press Katelyn's number from my missed call list first. Less than three-seconds after it starts to ring, I hear Stacy's voice screaming at me. "Are you okay? Where the hell are you?"

I smile at my friend's concern. Apparently, she's spoken to Allison, but I don't want to think about that bitch right now. "Slow down, Stacy. One question at a time, please." *Jeez.*

She huffs, and I imagine she is trying to calm herself down. Stacy excites very easily. "Well," she draws out. "Are you okay?" Stacy doesn't pause to let me answer, which is good, because I don't have any intention of getting into a serious conversation over the phone. "Allison called last night. I just don't want to believe it," she sighs out.

I ignore what she just said. I don't want to discuss Allison or what happened yet. I don't even know how I feel. I only want clean clothes, and she is my source of getting them. "Do you have to work today? I need some clean clothes."

Knowing Stacy as well as I do, I can imagine she's getting irritated that I'm dodging what she is after, but I don't care.

"Yes, but not until later this afternoon," she tells me. "You didn't answer my question," she says, stating the obvious.

"Good. Can you bring me some of Katelyn's clothes? We'll talk when you get here. I'm at *The Cove*, room 704," I tell her while adjusting the pillows behind me.

"Sure, but what's wrong with my clothes?" she asks in a tone that tells me I have offended her. I roll my eyes. Like she doesn't know! No one can fit into the tiny pieces of material she wears as clothes.

"Nothing, except everything you own is either a size zero or extra small, you skinny bitch. It's not going to happen when I'm a size eight," I say, adding a playful laugh, trying to lighten the conversation.

"Point taken," Stacy snorts. "It's good to hear you laugh, Shannon. We were worried about you when you didn't answer any of our calls or texts last night."

Finally, I give her the answer she wants, but I keep it short. It's not a conversation I want to have at all. I wish I could make it all disappear. I just don't want to deal with any of this shit today or even tomorrow. God, I hate him for doing what he did. "I'm okay; now put your ass in gear and get over here. Please don't take all day!" I shout in the sternest voice I can muster.

"Okay!" she shouts back. "Is there anything in particular of hers you want me to bring? I can be there in about an hour."

"Jeans if possible, but definitely nothing dressy or sloppy, and thanks," I say and hang up. I still need clean underwear, so I dial the concierge desk asking for the cleaning service to come pick up my clothes for a wash. A nice-sounding man tells me that service will be up in ten minutes. I hang up and quickly strip out of all my clothes. I place them in a garment bag and set them just outside the door. After shutting the door, I head for the bathroom.

Entering the spacious room, I turn the shower on to hot. As I wait for the right temperature, I reach for the new toothbrush resting in its holster. I apply toothpaste and silently say a "thank you" to management for this hotel supplying all the required toiletries one needs to freshen up.

As I begin brushing my teeth, steam from the shower starts to filter into the bathroom; I know the water is perfect. I get in after rinsing the toothpaste out of my mouth.

I stand under the water, letting everything wash away from the previous day. My tense shoulders quickly relax under the heat of the water, and surprisingly, I feel great. I should feel like shit after yesterday and drinking last night, but oddly, I think I'm relieved. I'm not sure why that is or what that means. Seeing Luke and Allison the way I did hurt, a lot, but not in the way I think it should have. Maybe that means I'm not in love with Luke anymore. Was I ever? I don't think two people who are in love can just fall out of love.

They certainly don't cheat.

Two people who are truly made for each other can get through anything life throws at them, except cheating. Perhaps some people might be able to move past something like that, but I can't, and I won't. For me, there are no second chances or forgiveness from that.

I hope his dick gets a flesh-eating rash. It would serve him right. He's a cheating shit, and he deserves everything he gets—twofold! Yet, as the water beats down on me, I have to admit, I'm not heartbroken. *Why aren't I sad over the loss and betrayal of my fiancé?* I am beyond pissed off though.

Five years down the toilet.

I put the thought of him out of my mind and think about Allison as I massage shampoo through my hair. She, on the other hand, I hate. I never thought that was possible. I loved her the way I imagine I would love a sister. That person you tell everything to and never feel ashamed or embarrassed. So why did she do this to me? It's a total mind-fuck. I don't understand.

It's unforgivable.

I shut all thoughts out of my mind and rinse the conditioner out of my hair. I quickly shave before turning the water off. Stepping out of the shower, I grab a towel to dry off.

Fifteen minutes later, I'm showered, shaved, moisturized, and now snuggled in a cozy, plush bathrobe. Again, I thank management. This hotel is amazing.

CHAPTER 3

I'm standing in front of the windowpane, looking out at the Pacific Ocean in the distance. The water is beautiful and serene. It's a scene that always puts me at ease, settles me. That's probably the reason I love taking photographs on the beach. Every wave is different. They come to the shore, cleansing all the imperfections away. There is something peaceful and calming about the ocean. It's my kind of perfect.

A rapid knock at the door takes my gaze from the window. I turn my head to look at the clock on the nightstand. It's been an hour and a half since I got off the phone with Stacy. I'm impressed she didn't take longer. The girl never leaves the apartment looking anything less than immaculate.

I make my way to the entrance of my room. Without looking through the peephole, I swing the door open and I'm immediately enclosed in a vise-like hug from my friend.

"Katelyn would have come too, but she has rehearsal all day." Katelyn is an actress. Not on TV or films. She's in to theater. I've seen her perform a couple of times. She's fantastic.

"Okay, so tell me. How are you holding up?" Stacy continues. I'm getting the most sincere look I've ever seen from her. Emotions aren't her thing. She avoids them at all cost. As I expected, she is dressed to perfection in a purple, fitted, sleeveless dress that comes right above her knee. Her short, blonde hair comes down just below her jaw. Stacy is perfect hair, smooth skin, classic kind of beautiful.

I ignore her question again. Yeah, I'm probably going to piss her off. I don't care.

"Are you hungry? It's almost eleven o'clock and I'm starving. Eat lunch with me at Mint downstairs." I wait for her reply as I take the bag of clothes hanging from her shoulder. Mint is one of my favorite restaurants. It's not expensive and serves great food. I eat there at least twice a month, usually with Allison.

Why did he pick my best friend? Of all the females that populate this world, why her? Of course a better question is why did she screw a man that wasn't hers to take?

Stacy brings me back from my negative thoughts.

"No! I want to know how the hell you're doing. You don't look broken up like someone who walked in on her asshole boyfriend and best friend getting it on twenty-four hours ago. Shannon, I've been worried about you all night. Why didn't you call or come over?" Stacy pouts, placing her hands on her hips. As I look at her, I realize I'm so grateful she is a part of my life.

"I know I could have come over, and maybe I should have."

Maybe then I wouldn't have gotten drunk and ended up in a stranger's bed.

"That's exactly where you should have come. So why didn't you?" she asks, exasperated as I toss the bag on the bed. I turn back to Stacy and shrug. I don't have a plausible excuse; at least not one she'd like. I don't want to talk. I want to be alone and drown in myself. I guess I sort of accomplished that.

"I needed time by myself to think. After driving around for a few hours, I ended up here," I explain, waving my hand around the room. I conveniently leave out the events of last night. Although, knowing my friend, she would have cheered me on. I could smooth things over with her by filling her in on where I really ended up last night. Not that it matters. I'll probably never see him again. That realization disappoints me a little. Jeez, maybe this whole ordeal has pushed me over the edge.

Placing my hand on Stacy's shoulder, I tell her, "I'm fine. Really, I am. I'm not sure what to make of that just yet. I'm mostly pissed and hurt over Allison. I just can't believe she would do that—to me—with Luke."

I remove my hand from her shoulder. "I am hungry, and I haven't eaten since yesterday morning. I'm going to put clean clothes on and go down to *Mint*. Do you want to join me for lunch or not?"

"Fine," she says, sounding resigned. "After that, I have to go to the station to get ready for work."

"Thanks." Only Stacy would need four to five hours to get ready to forecast the weather on the six o'clock news. I don't voice my thoughts out loud. I know she would be offended, as well as get pissed. She didn't speak to Allison for a week once when she called her a "weather girl."

"Are you expecting someone?" Stacy asks as I'm walking to the door.

"I sent my dirty laundry to housekeeping a while ago. Hopefully, they're back with my clean underwear," I tell her as I open the door a fraction and take the garment bag from an older lady, thanking her as I shut the door.

Walking over to the bed, I dump the contents out then grab the bag Stacy brought and do the same. Looking through my options, I grab a black, short-sleeve fitted shirt, a faux fur vest, a pair of skinny jeans, and the pair of black riding boots.

"I only need roughly twenty minutes to make myself presentable. Will you go down to the restaurant, get us a table, and order the drinks?" I ask.

"Absolutely," she replies with a smile, already heading for the door.

HALF AN HOUR LATER, I'M SLIDING INTO the booth across from Stacy while picking up my glass of Diet Coke. Not exactly the drink I would have chosen, but I'm not complaining since I didn't tell her what to order. Diet Coke is her "go to" drink for anything non-alcoholic and she assumes everyone else drinks it too.

"What, no wine?" I joke.

"I have to work, so I can't drink this early, and if I can't drink, I'm certainly not going to sit here while you do," she deadpans. I know she's serious. Stacy is the life of every party and has been since I met her our freshman year of college. She's the person who broke me out of my shell, making me open up and start trusting people again.

I've always been shy, and she likes to force me out of my comfort zone. Stacy can talk me into almost anything, and she's gotten me to do many things I wouldn't normally do on my own. I'll have to thank her for that one day; although, I'll never explain why that means so much to me. People enter our lives for all different types of reasons, and I'm very glad I met the woman sitting across the table from me.

I can't let my mind wander. Nothing good comes from thinking about the past. The past needs to stay in the past.

"I'm just messing with you. I have to go to the gallery after lunch to finish everything for my meeting tomorrow morning at Lockhart Publishing." I pick up the menu, scanning all the food.

Just as the waiter is walking up, I decide on a cheeseburger with fries. Fatty, greasy food is just the pick-me-up I need. I give the waiter my order and he turns to Stacy for hers. She's eying me in disgust.

"I'll have a grilled chicken salad with light ranch dressing. No cheese, please," she says in her soft, flirty voice to the young waiter who is probably five years younger than she is. Not that she's old. She and I are the same age.

The waiter leaves as I'm rolling my eyes at her.

"You know, if you didn't eat shit food, you could probably fit into my clothes," she tells me while lifting her soda to her lips to take a sip.

"Whatever. I like to enjoy food. I'm not going to limit myself to grass." I take a sip of my own drink. Setting mine back down, I continue. "Besides, I'll never be a size two. I don't have the small frame you do, and I'm quite happy with my body the way it is." It's not like I'm overweight, and I do work out four days a week; although, I missed my morning boxing class today.

"Well, didn't you just get over the flu or something? You were sick for like three weeks. Maybe you should be eating something light." Stacy and concern aren't things I'm used to getting from her. She tends to be selfish and self-center. She never once bothered to call me or bring me anything to eat while I was sick. I, on the other hand, have played nursemaid to her on several occasions back in college.

Maybe she's the one getting sick.

"It was two weeks, but I'm fine now, and I'm ready to eat decent food again." I pick up my Diet Coke, taking a large gulp.

Within ten minutes, our food arrives and I sink my teeth into my burger. One bite down, I remove the bun and toss on some fries and a hefty amount of ketchup before taking another bite of the mouthwatering combination.

"That is so disgusting. I don't know how you eat that," she says, staring at my meal with her eyebrows scrunched together.

"It's tasty, that's how. Do you want to try it?" I ask, holding it out in front of her. We both start giggling and finish up our meal. Being here, I feel relaxed and more like myself. I probably should dwell on why I feel so relaxed as an image of the man with the blue eyes flashes before me. Luckily, I don't have to think about it for too long as Stacy brings me back to the here and now.

"So, what do you plan on doing about Ally?" Stacy asks as the waiter brings us both refills of Diet Coke.

What am I going to do? Part of me wants to kick her ass and another part of me . . . well, *I* don't even know. I'm pissed and my heart aches. It's Allison I hate.

Why did it have to be her?

For some reason, I'm not even considering Luke in my hatred. The Band Perry's song "Done" pops into my head. That's exactly the way I feel. I'm just—done.

"I don't know." There is nothing more to say, because frankly, I just don't know what to do when it comes to Allison. This is not a situation I ever thought I would find myself in.

I look across the room at an older couple eating at a table. They look happy. They look like they love each other and could tell each other anything. I don't recall ever having a moment like that with Luke.

"She called Katelyn last night. She's upset that she hurt you, but she confessed she thinks she is in love with him." Stacy grabs my hand and squeezes.

I don't know what to say to that. I pull my hand out of her grasp. "In love . . . with Luke? What's that supposed to mean? Was yesterday not a one-time thing?" I said it aloud, but really I'm hashing it out to myself. I never even considered they were having an affair. Is it an affair if you aren't married yet?

"I can't answer that. I have no idea. Until last night, I had no clue she—they—were, you know, screwing around." Stacy sips her drink. I think she knows more than she is letting on, but I'm not going to push it. I know she's trying to tiptoe around my feelings, but she's usually much more blunt than she is being right now.

We eat the rest of our mean with lighter, casual conversation. After the waiter brings us the check, we both throw down enough cash to cover the meals, drinks, and tip. When we get up, we hug and say our goodbyes, and then we both set out on our way to work.

CHAPTER 4

I t's right at one o'clock in the afternoon when I walk through the door of Art Through a Lens. That is the name of my photography shop. Walking in, I smile and say, "Hi" to Jenny, who's behind the front counter wrapping a large, framed 24x36 photograph of a ten-foot wave I captured in Hawaii last year.

She flashes a bright smile and asks, "Do you need something to drink or help preparing for tomorrow?"

"A bottle of smart water would be great, but no rush," I reply. "I think I have everything covered for tomorrow. I just need to make sure the layout is perfect. I'll be in my office if you need me." I continue making my way to the back.

Placing my purse on my chair in front of my computer, I walk over to the portfolio lying out on the long section of my L-shaped desk. I take a seat on the bench in front, placing my right leg underneath my butt to get comfortable. I know I'm going to be here for a while, dwelling over which photos should be where in this layout. I wasn't this indecisive with the first book I published last year.

A few minutes later, Jenny walks in with my water. I take it from her hand, thanking her. She doesn't linger, and I twist the cap off and take a sip.

The front door chimes, but I ignore it. Jenny can deal with the customer. Today, I don't need any distractions.

The voices are low, but I make out Jenny saying, "Miss Taylor is busy today. Sir, would you like to make an appointment to come back?" There is a pause before she continues. "Excuse me, sir, but you can't go back there. Sir?"

I feel his eyes on me before I see him. It's that same warm, tingling feeling that washed over my body this morning. I look over my left shoulder at the door. There he is, filling the doorframe with his large, hard body and staring at me with those blue flames.

Holy cow, this man is too hot for his own good.

It should be a sin. Perhaps it is and I don't know it. I'm a terrible Catholic who hasn't been to church since my early teens. Now that so many years have passed, I wouldn't dare take communion without confessing my secrets. And well, that just isn't going to happen. You would think if a person could talk to someone, it would be easy to talk to one's priest. It's not. I tried once, but I chickened out before I even walked into the church.

He clears his throat, pulling me out of my thoughts. My eyes roam over him from head to toe on their own accord. He's dressed in the same suit he was wearing this morning, minus the jacket.

The disappointment I felt earlier at the thought of never seeing him again vanishes. My eyes travel back up, locking onto his.

Jenny follows right behind him and tries to push her way into the room, but he doesn't budge.

"Excuse me, sir, but I—"

"It's okay, Jenny. He can stay," I cut her off, but never break eye contact with him. How did he know where to find me? I don't even know who he is, yet he's standing here in my gallery, in my office. I smile on the inside for some reason.

"Okay, but call me if you need anything." Jenny leaves to go back up front and he and I continue to stare at each other.

I turn on the bench so I'm facing him with my hands in my lap, but I remain seated in the same position, my right leg tucked under me. He walks closer, coming inside my office. He's staring down at me.

I'm the first to break eye contact, looking down at my hands. "What are you doing here, and how did you know where I work?" I look back up to him while I wait for an answer.

He reaches into his pocket and retrieves a small object. When he opens his hand, he reveals my ring lying in his palm—the one I had taken off at the bar last night. I hadn't thought about it or even realized it was missing.

What does that tell you?

"I didn't have a chance to give it back this morning before you ran out."

"I didn't run. I walked out," I reply, and stand to take the ring from him. I did run out, but I didn't think it was that obvious. Apparently, I was wrong.

When I reach to take the ring, he gently grabs my hand. The ring between our hands is the only thing keeping us from complete contact.

I look up at him, now standing, but I still have to look up a little to meet his eyes. I'm not short. I'm of average height at five-feet seven. He must be about eight inches taller, putting him at about six-foot-three. His shoulders are broad. His biceps and chest fill out his dress shirt, making creases where I can see his muscles underneath.

"It looked to me like you couldn't get out of there quick enough," he says in a low, steady tone.

God, I wish he would stop looking at me the way he does. I have knots in my stomach. This is not a feeling I'm used to.

I take the ring from his palm and toss it on my desk, before redirecting my vision back to him. "You didn't answer the last part of my question. How did you know where I would be?"

He takes a half step closer. I can feel his breath on my face and I can smell him. He smells fresh and clean. Like he just stepped out of a shower.

I like it.

"Your business card fell out of your purse last night. I didn't know you would be here. I took a chance, and here you are." The way he responds is odd; like it's forced and he tenses slightly as he says it. Plus, my cards are zipped up in my wallet, so it's a stretch that one just fell out. I don't question him or call him on it, though.

I hear a commotion out front. It's Luke. The sound of his voice makes me want to break something. "Great," I say sarcastically with a sigh. Just what I need. I grab the ring from my desk, step around the intoxicating man in front of me, and walk out of my office to the front. Luke and Jenny are talking. He's dressed in blue scrubs for work.

"What the hell are you doing here?" I ask him in a harsh voice.

I feel the stranger from last night coming to stand behind me. I don't know why he's here, but it makes me feel warm again, almost as if he is keeping me safe and protected.

I ignore this and concentrate on Luke. I don't want to see him. Ever again.

Luke walks up to me, looking me in the eyes. He's only an inch taller than I am. "We need to talk," he says, grabbing my arm at my elbow.

I snatch it out of his grasp, taking a step back. The man standing behind me is so close I can feel his breath blowing the back of my hair. I tense. He notices, because he places his hand on my shoulder and it immediately relaxes me.

Luke looks at his hand on my shoulder, and then at the man standing behind me. His eyes land back on mine. He's angry. "Who the hell is he?"

I ignore his question, because I can, and because I don't know who he is, but at the same time, something inside me is glad he's here. I take the ring from my hand and toss it at Luke. He catches it in his right hand.

"That's yours. I don't want it and I never want to see you again. Now get out of here. We. Are. Done."

Jenny is still behind the front counter, looking uncomfortable, but doesn't say anything. I doubt she has ever heard me raise my voice. I'm not usually like this, and I've never brought drama to work before. I feel bad. Maybe I should have told her about yesterday, but we don't have that kind of relationship. She tries to busy herself. I can only imagine what this scene must look like.

"Shut the fuck up, Shannon! You are mine and we are not over!" Luke says in a condescending tone.

Whoa!

He has always been this way, but for some reason I didn't realize it until this moment. *What the hell is wrong with me?* I can totally see why Stacy and Ben have always thought he was a jerk.

My eyes flare and I take a deep breath. "I don't belong to anyone, and I certainly don't belong to your sorry, pathetic, cheating ass!" I yell back. I want to lunge at him and scratch his eyes out, but instead, I'm grabbed at the waist and flipped around by the man I still don't know. His hands warms me. I should be angry at being manhandled, but I'm not. I want him to touch me again.

"I believe she told you to leave, so I suggest you do that before I do it for you," he says in a strong voice filled with authority. I'm stunned. I don't know what to make of this. Luke looks intimidated. I do a little shimmy dance inside.

Take that, asshole.

"Fuck off, Luke. Better yet, go fuck the little tramp you've been banging for God knows how long." I storm off, back in the direction of my office.

"This is far from over, Shannon." I hear Luke say as he's walking out the door.

The hell it isn't.

44

Damn, that felt good.

I enter my office, stripping off the vest I'm wearing. I'm far too hot and my breathing is rapid. I try to calm myself by standing in the middle of my office taking several deep breaths. He walks up behind me and places both of his hands on my shoulders, the proceeds to massage them softly. It feels nice. I want to wrap myself around his touch.

I immediately relax again, and the tension I felt moments ago melts away. Who is he and why do I feel like this every time I'm in the same room with him?

Slowly, I turn so I'm facing him again, looking up into his beautiful flaming-blue eyes. "Mind telling me your name?" My voice is low and calm.

"Nicholas," he replies while bringing his left hand back to my shoulder where he'd previously let go as I turned.

"I take it you already know mine?"

"I do." He confirms.

I pull away and return to the bench in front of my portfolio. My back is now to him as I tuck my right leg under my butt, trying to feign calm. He's getting closer. I can feel it.

He leans down and over me, placing his hands on the desk to cage me in. His front is touching my back, and again that damn heat covers my body from head to toe. I can only imagine how flushed my face is. Redheads can't hide that shit as easily as others.

"What is this?" he asks while looking at the collection of pictures in front of me. I raise my head. It's now touching his shoulder and our faces are parallel to each other.

There's that smell again. Damn, he's intoxicating. *If I turn to sniff him, would he notice?* Probably . . . so I remain looking forward.

"Did we have sex last night?" I don't look at him. That's the question I wanted to ask this morning, but I didn't have the courage.

He tenses, but only a little. "If we'd had sex last night, you would still be feeling it this afternoon," he replies.

What the hell does that mean? Can this man not answer a straightforward question?

I hate games. I want to know; at least, I think I want to know. "Damn it, Nick, stop dodging my questions and just answer me. Did we fuck? It's a yes or no question." My voice is strained and my face is flushed.

"I told you my name is Nicholas. Don't call me Nick, and no, we did not fuck last night." I relax. At least I didn't make that horrible mistake while intoxicated. He turns his head and his mouth is against my right ear.

"But when I do fuck you, your eyes will be wide open and you won't forget it." His voice is barely above a whisper and his breath feels cool against my heated skin. I shiver.

I can't speak. The words aren't coming out of my mouth. I'm shocked. More shocked than I think I've ever been. Did he seriously just say that? And if we didn't have sex, then where the hell did he sleep last night?

"Where did you sleep then?" I ask, sounding a little bolder now that I know I didn't hop in bed with him.

"The couch," he states, like it should have been obvious. He grabs a photo lying on my desk and hands it to me. "You should use this for the cover. It's perfect." And with those last words, he walks out.

Looking at the photo in my hand, I realize he's right. It's a photo of the statue of Saint Didacus, the patron saint of San Diego. This one photo completes everything. I'm done. No more agonizing over what goes where. He's done my job for me. How did he know? I put the photo in its place before closing my portfolio and placing it in my large tote bag.

Getting off the bench, I grab my tote and make my way to my computer. For the next few hours, I check my emails, handle some other business, and forward Jenny invoices and orders.

Come five o'clock, I shut down my computer and grab my purse to leave. It's a miracle I accomplished anything this afternoon considering my inability to concentrate on things that weren't hard muscles and fiery-blue eyes.

Who the hell is this guy? My mind is focused on him as I walk out to the front of my gallery. I decide I don't need to know, pushing all thoughts of Nick out of my mind. I have enough drama in my life already.

I need to go shopping for some new clothes until I can get mine. Luckily, I don't have to go far. My gallery is in a strip mall that has most of my favorite stores. After locking the door, I head straight to *Eve's*. It's a dressy boutique.

I should have made arrangements to pick up my things today, but I don't want to deal with it yet. Seeing Luke earlier only made things worse, and it's not like I know where I'm going yet. How the hell did I get here? Yesterday morning I thought life was peachy. Well, apparently, it wasn't.

Once I enter the store, Melanie greets me with a warm smile that takes me away from my negative thoughts.

"Hey, Shannon, if there is anything I can help you with just let me know," she says as she goes back to helping a blonde with a blue satin dress.

I'm in here multiple times a week, so most of the associates know me by name. As I look around the store, I decide on a pair of jeans and two fitted shirts, a snug, black, strapless dress and a gray, sleeveless dress with a matching jacket. A black belt and lastly a pair of black pumps both call to me. Melanie checks me out and I head to the next store.

Walking into *Dentelle*, I know exactly what I want. I pick out two white, satin bras and a black strapless one, along with three pairs of panties to match. On the way to the checkout counter, I grab a pair of black stockings and a pair of nude-color ones. This stuff should get me by for a few days.

After walking out of the store, I head to my car with a bag in each hand.

CHAPTER 5

Walking into the lobby of The Cove, I head for the elevators. When I arrive in front of the sleek black doors, I press the up button and wait patiently. The door opens a few seconds later and people begin to file out. Nick is the last to step out. He stands just outside the elevator doors holding his arm across the opening so it doesn't close.

I know he's waiting for me to step in, so I walk forward, but he stops me with his right arm before I'm able to enter.

"Hello, Miss Taylor."

I look up into his eyes. "I don't like to be called by my last name. Goodbye, Nick."

He's still holding my arm, so I don't move. He looks down at my bags and eyes the Dentelle bag, granting me a smile as he releases me. *I like sexy undergarments, what can I say?* I move into the elevator, pressing the number seven button.

"I don't like being called Nick." He pauses then adds, "Oh, and, Shannon, I do hope you bought satin." He moves his left arm from the door, allowing them to slide closed. The last thing I see before they shut is his half smile. I'm left stunned and speechless for the second time today. Apparently, this will be a regular occurrence around him.

Don't get your hopes up, buddy. As hot as you are, I don't plan on getting naked with you.

I enter my room and toss all my bags onto the bed. I'm exhausted and in need of a hot shower to help me relax. Walking into the bathroom, I turn on the shower and strip out of my clothes. As I stand under the steamy water, letting it cascade down my body, a sigh escapes me.

Once I've exceeded the normal timeframe for a shower, I hop out and towel off. The oversized, white cotton towel envelops me, and I saunter to the sink to dry my hair. I have long, straight, red locks that come down to the middle of my back. It's fine but thick. I'm lucky. My hair doesn't require a lot of product to look decent. Just a comb through and it falls into place.

I walk out of the bathroom to retrieve my makeup bag from my purse. With a little powder, eye shadow, mascara, and lipstick, I'm done. My makeup routine takes less than five minutes. I don't fuss over myself like a lot of women do. Sometimes, I'll go to work without any makeup on at all. My friends would die if they knew this, but I'm not a "girly girl" in that sense. I never have been.

Returning to the bathroom, I take the black, satin, strapless bra and matching panties out of the bag, reminded of Nick's comment. *I do hope you bought satin*

I laugh to myself. *Does the man not have a filter?*

My mind drifts for a brief moment, and I can't help but wonder what's underneath *his* clothes. He's one of the sexiest men I've ever seen. Months passing with no sex, this god-like man has me all hot and bothered. I *have* to stop thinking about him. I need a drink, but only one. I don't need to end tonight like last night—in a man's bed.

I quickly put my bra and panties on, and then the black stockings, before steeping into the black, strapless, tight-fitting dress, and pull it up. After zipping it, I finish off with the new black pumps. I reach for my purse to take out my spare earrings, which are silver hoops with black diamonds. They complement the dress.

My cell phone beeps. I pull it out of my purse and unlock it to see the message. It's a text from a number I don't recognize.

Come down to Mist and have a drink with me, please. — Nicholas

He has my number?

"How the hell did he get my number?" I stop for a moment, eyeing my phone. I know damn well *I* didn't give it to him and Jenny wouldn't have either. My personal cell number isn't printed on any of my business cards, so how did he get it? Should I be worried about this? He doesn't come off like a dangerous stalker, but it's not like I've ever had one before. I push the thought away and grab my purse, before heading out the door to Mist.

Mist is a popular bar inside The Cove on the first floor. It usually has a live band every night and there's a dance floor. Ben and I love to dance, so we have enjoyed a few Friday nights there in the past.

When I reach the entrance I quickly scan the room, but I don't see Nick in sight. Then again, I didn't reply telling him I was coming down. I walk to the bar and I'm immediately waited on. Service at this hotel is like no other.

"I'll have a glass of Kendall Jackson's Riesling, please," I order, to go easy on the alcohol tonight by keeping my drink light.

The bartender brings my wine as I feel someone step up behind me. I know it's *him* even before he speaks. I'm beginning to like the warmth that tickles my skin when he is present.

Nick places a hand at the small of my back and the other on my shoulder. The hand on my lower back stays in place, but he moves his other one slowly down my arm until he reaches my hand. Lacing his fingers with mine, he says, "Come with me."

He's not asking, nor he doesn't wait for my response before pulling me by the hand and leading me to a small booth in a back corner. It's a circular booth, and from here, the sound from the band isn't so loud. We'll be able to speak normally instead of yelling over the music.

He waits for me to enter the booth and then moves in next to me instead of across from me like a normal person would do.

"Thank you," he says, settling in the booth. We are thigh-to-thigh against each other.

I look at up at him, confused. "For what?" I take a sip of my wine. I have no idea why he's thanking me.

"For not making me come get you." He takes a sip of his dark drink. We are sitting so close I can smell his breath. He's drinking rum and coke; one of my favorites.

"You would have come up to my room?" I cock an eyebrow, eyeing him. "What makes you so sure I would have come ?" I take another sip, the liquid cool and refreshing on my tongue.

A smirk crosses his face. "Oh, I would've convinced you one way or another. I can be very persuasive when I need to be," he says as he sits his drink on the table.

"Thank you for earlier today. If you hadn't stepped in, I don't know what I would have done to him," I say without making eye contact. I feel him tense, but only slightly.

"Dance with me," he commands, as if to change the subject. Once again, he doesn't wait for a response before he stands and reaches for my hand. I don't reply, but I get up and follow him to the dance floor.

I wouldn't say I'm a good dancer, but I'm not horrible either. He, on the other hand, makes me look like an amateur. The second song starts to play and we slow our pace. I put my arms around his neck and he moves his to my waist. He smells divine; clean, mixed with something spicy. It's a heavy cocktail even without the wine I'm drinking. I could certainly get drunk on this man.

His hand moves to the small of my back and the other to my hip. He pulls me closer and bends his head to my neck, kissing me above my collarbone, I don't stop him. His lips send tingles through my body. Goose bumps prickle my skin, and I suck in a deep breath while bowing into him.

"You taste sweet, like the finest candy," he whispers to me before straightening back into position.

Wow. That was unexpected. Do I want to do this? Yesterday, I was engaged—to someone else. Today, this delicious man, whom I don't really know, is kissing me and I like it. I've never experienced an attraction this fast.

The song ends all too quickly and he steers us back to our table where I finish the rest of my wine in one gulp. I go to take a seat, but he reaches for my hand, halting me. I look up at him.

"I think we should get you out of here. I know what too much alcohol does to you and I don't want a repeat of last night," he says, smiling and leading me out of the bar.

When we reach the elevator, I notice the clock. 9:46 p.m. It isn't too late on a Thursday night, but I could use some sleep. I need to be well rested for my meeting tomorrow morning.

As we enter, I press the button for my floor and he swipes his keycard for the penthouse. When it reaches the seventh floor, the doors open and I go to walk out, but he has other plans. He moves forward, grabbing my waist, and pins me in the front corner while holding the door open.

"Come up with me and have one more drink?" He phrases it in a question. "I'll even feed you."

I look up into his blue gaze and grab the lapels from his jacket with both hands for something to hold on to. If I don't hold myself back, there is no telling what I could do to this man.

"I can't," I reply, although at this every moment, I really want to. Luckily, my brain knows better. "I have an early meeting tomorrow morning and I need as much sleep as possible." It's the truth, and I know if I go up with him, I may not stop things from progressing. It's been far too long since I've been underneath anyone, and I find myself wanting just that.

Releasing his jacket, I duck under his arm and walk out of the elevator. "Goodnight, Nick," I say breathily as I'm walking to my room.

My phone beeps just as I'm opening the door and I check the text. It's from him, making me smile. I think this is the first real smile I've had in over twenty-four hours.

Nick: Goodnight, Shannon.

Walking through the door, I kick off my pumps and place my purse on the bedside table, but keep my phone in my hand as I walk over to the window and look out. The beautiful, dark sky is scattered with stars and a bright, full moon. I take a seat on the window pillow and continue looking out it. With my back to the wall and my side against the window, I reply.

Me: I could call you Nicky. Which do you prefer?

I smile joyfully and it reaches my eyes. This just might be a fun game and I don't want to stop talking to him.

Nick: I prefer Nicholas, since that's my name. Nikki is my little sister, so you can't call me that OR NICK.

I'm laughing as I type out anther response.

Me: I'll stick with Nick then. I prefer it anyway.

It's not five-seconds later before my phone beeps once again and I'm smiling even bigger.

Nick: You're obviously not going to sleep anytime soon, so come up here. The code is 7480.

Me: You're bothering me, so stop, and then I'll be able to sleep.

I continue looking out the window for a few more minutes. I do need to go to sleep, though. A knock raps on the door. *You've got to be kidding me. I tell him he's bothering me and he shows up*. I quickly send him a reply as I'm standing up.

Me: I was kidding. You're not bothering me. You didn't have to come back down. When I open my door, I'm still not coming up with you. GOODNIGHT, Nick.

I roll my eyes as I toss my cell phone onto the bed. A few seconds later, it's ringing. I'm already halfway to the door, so whoever it is will have to wait. Even though I'm a little annoyed—okay, so that's a lie—a wide smile creeps across my face knowing I'm about to see Nick again.

I turn the knob to open the door when it flies past my face, only missing me by an inch. Someone's hand pressing against my chest is the first sense that registers before I'm shoved backward. My smile leaves in an instant.

"What the hell?!" I shout as I look up. Luke is staggering in, slamming the door behind him. He's drunk off his ass. *Great*. This is exactly how I need to end the nice night I was having.

"How did you know where I was?" I demand, but don't wait for his response. "You need to get out of here. NOW!" I shout. I'm pissed. I've seen him long enough for one day. What doesn't he get? We're over. I hear my phone from behind me ringing again, but I can't be bothered with it right now. I have to deal with Luke's shit.

"I told you this wasn't over! We. Are not over." He grabs both of my shoulders in a vise-like grip while pushing me backward. My calves touch the base of the footboard.

"Ow! That hurts." I may be a decent boxer, but Luke is much stronger than I am. I'm pushed down onto the bed and he quickly moves on top of me, straddling me to hold me in place.

"Get off, Lucas!" I shout. I only call him by this full name when I'm mad. Right now, I'm beyond pissed. How dare he barge into my room like this?

"Allison might be the fuckable kind, but you, my love, are the marrying kind. Do you hear me, Shannon?" he shouts.

What the fuck? I've never seen him like this—deranged and out of control. Hell, I don't think I've ever seen him *this* drunk before. He's usually the sober one when we go out. And that makes me pause, wondering if there's a reason for that.

I hear the door open and it slams hard against the wall behind it. A few seconds later, Luke is ripped off me and thrown against the wall, breaking the glass mirror hanging there. I look up and see Nick standing over him. His eyes are full of rage. I swear I can see a trace of red beneath the blue flames.

A moment later, a larger man enters the room. He's dressed in all black and sports a shaved head. He looks intimidating as hell. I'd feel sorry for Luke if I wasn't so pissed off at him.

"Get him the fuck out of my hotel and make sure he doesn't return!" Nick orders the man. Nick's eyes are dark and burning with fury. I'm more scared of that look than I was when Luke was on top of me.

The man picks Luke up as if he weighs no more than a few pounds and tosses him out the door into the hall. He turns, looking at Nick. "Yes, sir." It's all he says before they're both gone. I slowly sit up, trying to make sense of what just happened, but nothing is making any sense.

I can feel him looking at me. I bring my hands up to cover my face as I start to cry. I'm usually not a crier, but everything over the last two days surfaces all at once, and I can't stop myself. I'm bawling uncontrollably. I haven't cried like this in a very long time.

Nick gathers me into his arms. I put my hands around his shoulders, pressing my face against his neck. I still can't stop crying. He doesn't say anything as he walks out of the room, carrying me. I hear the elevator door open and he steps in. I don't lift my head, but I know he enters the code to the penthouse.

When we exit, he doesn't set me down to open his door. Once he walks through, he kicks it closed behind him. It's a loud thud, causing me to jump in his arms.

"Sorry. I didn't mean to startle you." His voice is a soothing balm on an emotional wound. Entering his kitchen, he sets me on the granite island countertop of the island in the center of the room. The stone is cold and the room dark.

Turning on his heels, he fetches me a glass of cool water. I take a small sip. It feels cool and refreshing as I swallow, relaxing and calming me a little. I hand it back to him. After placing it in the sink, he returns.

What am I doing here? I don't know this man, but for the strangest reason, I want to be here. I feel safe.

Nick positions himself between my thighs. My tight-fitted, black dress rides up a few inches. We're eye level as he wraps his hands around my waist, pulling me closer, making my dress ride up another inch or two.

Enclosing me in a tight embrace, he whispers, "I'm sorry. I knew I shouldn't have left you alone." He pulls back, looking me over with his eyes more intense than I've seen before, like he's the one in pain. He turns his face away.

Why is he sorry?

"Nick, look at me, please." I cup his face. *Why am I doing this?* It's too intimate and we barely know each other, but shit, my hand instinctively reaches out to comfort him.

"You couldn't have known that was going to happen, but I'm glad you came when you did. Thank you." I'm going to kill Luke if I see him again. Nick looks at my shoulders. Both are still red from the grip Luke had on me.

"I should have. I saw it in his eyes earlier today. I've seen that same look too many times not to know what it means." He moves a hand to my left shoulder and rubs soothingly. His eyes reveal he's angry. I don't understand, and I briefly wonder what he means. He continues before I have a chance to ask.

"That's why I did what I did. That's the reason I moved you behind me today." The rage comes back into his eyes the longer he stares at the red marks. He doesn't like them, so I do the only thing I can think of to make that look go away—I kiss him.

Grabbing his shoulders, I pull him closer to me, and our lips meet for the first time. I must have startled him, because he jumps, but the tension he's holding starts to expel from his body as he kisses me back. His lips are warm and soft against mine. My lips part, and his tongue dives into my mouth, intertwining with mine. He bites my lower lip softly. I'm lost in the sensation. I finally understand what people mean when they talk about earth-shattering kisses.

Wow . . . I mean, WOW! The man could win a talent award for this. It's like he's drinking me in through his lips and tongue.

He pulls away far too quickly, both of us already breathless, but I want more. I need more of him.

"You've had a long night and need to get some sleep," he says, his voice husky.

Screw that.

I wrap my legs around his waist as he starts to back up. Using my calves to pull him back to me causes my dress to ride up farther, rewarding him with a peek of my black, satin panties. He looks down, between us, at the apex of my legs. He places his hands on each side of my thighs, touching my bare skin. It feels incredible. It makes me want him even more.

"Please, don't stop." My voice is low and I sound needy. I can feel the hardness in his pants against my now moist center. It's straining against those pants, wanting to be released. He wants this too. He wants me as much as I want him. Lust replaces the anger in his eyes.

"We have to stop now or I won't be able to. I don't have that kind of willpower. I've wanted you for far too fucking long." He rubs his thumbs over my heated skin.

"Don't make me beg," I whisper. I want this more than anything I've ever wanted. I can't explain it, and to be honest, I don't give a shit at this point. I want to be filled and I will beg him if I have to. I need him inside me. There is an ache between my legs that needs the relief only he can provide me.

He looks at me through dark, hooded eyes. "Oh, baby," he says as he lifts me onto his waist, pulling me into a deep kiss. Holding me with one hand under my butt and the other at the small of my back, he walks us out of the kitchen. As he's walking through the living area, his hand moves up my back, finding my zipper, before pulling it down to its end.

I unbutton his dress shirt at a rapid pace. Damn buttons. As we reach the door to the bedroom, he doesn't take his mouth from mine and he doesn't move his hands. He kicks the door open and takes us through. I think I hear the sound of wood breaking as the door swings open, hitting the wall behind it.

When he nears the bed, he stops, and I unwrap my legs as he slowly stands me up, breaking our kiss. I look up at him again as I pull the bottom of his shirt out of his pants, then slide it off his shoulders. It falls somewhere on the floor, but he doesn't care. As I grab for his belt, he reaches for my hand, stopping my progress.

Why is he stopping?

"Baby, slow down. I plan on enjoying every moment of this, and every inch of you. I've waited too long for this to rush to the finish line now," he says as he pushes my dress down slowly until it pools on the floor. I step out of it.

"What do you mean you've waited too long? We've only known each other a little over twenty-four hours. That's the second time you've said that tonight," I tell him as I stand on my tiptoes, kissing his neck. As I speak, I return my hands to the buckle on his belt, tugging it out of his pants.

I, on the other hand, am in a bit of a rush. This is completely out of character for me. If I give myself too long to think about this, I may end it, and right now, that is the last thing I want to do. I'm still curious, though.

I place my heels back on the floor and look up at him, waiting for an answer. He drops to his knees in front of me, his hands on my hips. He looks up at me when he responds. "Six months. I've wanted you for six long months. The first time I saw you I knew I had to have you."

He trails kisses all over my stomach.

Huh?

His lips feel so good against my skin. "Where did you see me? Here at The Cove?" I ask as he starts lowers each stocking, one at a time. I don't want to ruin the mood, but I need to know. Why has he never said anything to me? Why have I never seen him? I would remember meeting Nick.

Right?

I should probably be creeped out by him admitting he's been watching me for six months, but I'm not.

"No, my office." He starts kissing the top of my left thigh, moving up to my hipbone, and then across my belly.

I wrack my brain trying to think, but I've been in lots of offices in the last six months. Now, he's kissing down the other side until he reaches my right thigh. I lose my train of thought. Those damn lips of his. I run my finger through his hair. It's soft and feels like silk gliding through my fingers. I tug softly.

"Woman, you are going to be the fucking end of me," he says, hooking his thumbs into my panties, pulling them down. I step out and he tosses them off to the side.

He stands and I pop the button on his pants open, sliding the zipper down. I push his pants to the floor. They pool around his ankles, and he steps out of them while pulling me closer to him.

I take a moment to eye him from top to bottom. He has an array of tattoos I didn't expect. Wrapped from the top of his right shoulder all the way down to his forearm, a wide chain cuts through his flesh. It almost looks like it's holding him back, but from what, I do not know. His left arm has even more ink. It's almost a whole sleeve starting from his shoulder and stopping right past his elbow.

There is small black script written across his left rib cage that says, "What's past is prologue." If this were any other scenario, I might laugh at the William Shakespeare quote. His torso is hard and muscular. His muscles ripple down his stomach. His ever-so-glorious "V" shape travels down into his boxer shorts and turns my mind to mush. There is more ink peeping out. It's colorful and I can't wait to see it. Nick reminds me of a beautiful piece of artwork standing before me.

He leans down, his lips landing on my neck and blocking my view of the rest of his body. I lean my head back to give him better access. My back arches, bowing into him for a second time tonight. He has one hand on my butt and the other covering the back of my bra.

Nick unhooks my strapless bra and tosses it to the side. Moving his hand from the center of my back up to the back of my neck, his fingers find their way into my hair. His hair tugging is slightly more aggressive than when I did it to him, but I like it.

He moves his lips to my collarbone, continuing kissing my skin, tasting me as if he can't get enough. He tightens his hold on my hair, forcing my head farther back, and I bite down on my bottom lip.

This . . . him . . . it feels incredible.

He releases my hair, pushing me backward until I feel the bed touch the back of my calves. I sit on the mattress, looking down at his boxers. The bulge he had earlier has increased in size. My eyes widen as he hooks his thumbs in the waistband, pushing them down. His cock springs free. It's larger than any other I've taken. Not that I've taken a lot. I've only been with two other men sexually, one of which I never want to think about; especially right now.

He notices the concern on my face and smiles. "I'll take it easy. I promise," he says. I scoot farther back on the bed and he follows, taking his place on top of me. He straddles me as I lay back on the bed and lowers his face, kissing me on the lips while both of his hands palm my breasts. My lips part, allowing his tongue to enter my mouth and tangle with mine. He pinches both nipples simultaneously, a moan escaping my mouth.

He smiles as he moves from my mouth to my neck, trailing gentle kisses down to my left breast, caresses one while twirling his tongue around my other nipple. Parting my legs, he moves between them, continuing to trail kisses down my stomach until he reaches my aching center.

Oh, yes, please.

He looks up at me and then smiles, a big, boyish grin as he parts the lips of my wet sex with his fingers. I throw my head back, moaning out loud when he licks up the center. His tongue moves to my clit and I grab the duvet, fisting it in both hands.

"Oh, God!" I scream as he pushes a finger inside me, then adds another. I'm already on the edge and the man's just started.

"I like that you're so fucking wet for me." I hear him say through tingles of pleasure as I cry out. He's sucking my clit hard, causing me to scream out again in pleasure, my head thrashing from side to side. He continues his assault until the last of my shudders slow down, and then he removes his fingers. My legs shake from the best orgasm of my life. Damn, I don't think I've ever come so hard, or that fast.

He crawls back up my body until we are face-to-face and I'm panting. He kisses me, hard, like I'm his life raft and he's holding on for dear life. I taste my arousal on his lips and it makes me hot and hungry for more. When he releases my mouth, I'm panting even more than after my mind-blowing orgasm.

He presses his forehead to mine, trying to slow his breathing. "I don't have a condom," he admits with pain in his eyes. I realize he wants this, just as much as I do. I can feel how hard he is and I want that hardness inside me. I've never had sex with a guy without protection, but I don't want this to end. Ending this now isn't an option.

"I'm on the pill," I say in a low, breathy voice, silently praying he doesn't stop. I need more. I need him inside me—now. I can't think clearly.

He raises his head and looks at me, his expression surprised. "Are you sure? You don't have to do this. We can wait."

"Nick, please fuck me," I say, almost begging him to screw me. He takes that as his green light, because he sits up and guides himself to my entrance. Using my wetness to lube himself, he slowly presses forward until he's a few inches inside me. He waits the length of a heartbeat before continuing. But when he does, he fills me until I'm full; full of him.

My breath catches in my throat and pleasure washes through

my body. It overwhelms me as moisture pools in my eyes. I blink the tears away, rapidly, afraid he will notice. If he does, he doesn't say anything.

Nice girl moment, Shannon. But I'm too caught up in the moment to feel embarrassed. That is sure to come later. He moves slowly at first. It's incredible, but I want more. Just as the thought crosses my mind, he begins to increase his speed, and before I realize it, he's driving into me, fervently. I fist my hands in his hair, pulling hard. He grabs my ass, holding me in place. I feel the pressure rising within me. I don't remember ever having more than one orgasm in a day before. Damn, this feels good . . . too good to be real.

"Give it to me, baby." I hear him whisper into my ear, and with his command, I fall over the edge into a sea of the best kind of pleasure.

He comes almost as soon as I do, spilling himself inside me. It's warm and like nothing I've ever felt before. He falls on top of me, still deep inside me. He stills himself, trying to catch his breath. Pulling out slowly, he rolls onto his back, taking a deep breath.

A second later, he stands and strides across the room.

"Don't move. I'm going to grab a cloth to get you cleaned up," he says as he walks into what I assume is a bathroom. I'm content and happy, finally letting out a breath I didn't know I was holding.

CHAPTER 6

"Wake up, beautiful." I hear a soft, soothing voice say to my left, and then I feel a dip in the bed. I'm lying on my front with my hands snuggled underneath the pillow. I'm comfortable and I don't want to move. The sheet is pulled over my bottom, but my back is bare.

Nick's fingers feel like feathers gliding up and down my spine. My eyes flutter open to see him staring down at me, wearing a gray suit with a white shirt and black tie underneath his jacket. His hand comes to rest on the small of my back. His simple touch warms me. "I have to leave for work and I don't have an alarm clock to set for you."

Panic washes over me, but not because I'm in a man's bed whom I don't know well. I might be late for my meeting at Lockhart Publishing. "What time is it?"

He smiles at me. It's warm and sweet and makes me melt a

little. Nick leans down, giving me a light kiss on my cheek. "It's early. Only six in the morning, but don't go back to sleep." I start to rise, but his hand applies pressure so I can't move. "Just don't get out of bed until I'm gone." My confusion must be evident on my face. "If I see any more of this beautiful skin, I'm not going to make it to work today, and neither will you." I sense his sincerity, so I smile and stay snuggled with the pillow as he walks out of the room.

I hear the jingle of keys from the living room, and then a door closes. A minute later, I'm getting out of bed, stunned and stopping in my tracks.

Hanging from the knob of the top dresser drawer is my gray dress, black belt, and jacket. Sitting on top is my new, white satin bra and matching panties, along with my nude stockings. My black pumps are sitting neatly on the floor next to the dresser.

"When did my things get here? And how did the man know what I had planned to wear this outfit today?" I say out loud, one hand covering my mouth.

I look around the rest of the room. Neatly sitting on a soft bench in front of the window are the rest of my things from my own room.

What the he . . .? Oh, I can't think about this right now. I need a shower and I have to get ready. I turn on my heel and head to the door that I assume is the bathroom. Upon opening the door, I confirm my assumption is right as I walk straight to the shower and turn the water on hot. While I wait for the desired temperature, I pee and brush my teeth. My toothbrush from my room has made it up here too. I guess he doesn't want me using his.

Rinsing off my toothbrush, I remember the broken mirror

from last night. Things start to make more sense. They will have to clean the mess up and replace it, but why didn't he just move me to a different room?

"Apparently, this is his hotel," I mumble as I remember his orders to the big, scary guy, who I assume is security.

Stepping into the shower, the water feels good against my skin. I'm not tired. In fact, I feel thoroughly rested. I don't remember the last time I felt this good, if ever. *Is this what great sex does to a girl?*

I hurry through my shower, marveling at how many of my things are here. Unfortunately, not everything arrived, forcing me to use some of his stuff. I hope he doesn't mind, but I don't have the time to dwell on it or to ask him.

As I continue getting ready, I notice a small bruise on my left shoulder, and my mind drifts back to Luke. He's never acted like that in the six years I've known him, but I quickly try to push all of that out of my mind. Today is too important and I need to keep my focus.

Finally, as I'm leaving, I stop and look at the door he kicked in last night. Splinters of wood litter the floor. I glance at my phone and see it's now 7:30. I have to hurry in order to get my portfolio from my office and make it to Lockhart Publishing on time.

Once on the road, I drive over the speed limit to get to my office quicker. This isn't rare for me. Even when there is no fear of being late, I still speed. I don't do it on purpose. I just can't stand driving at what I consider a slow pace.

I unlock the door to my gallery seconds after arrival and rush to the back. I grab my portfolio from the tote I left it in and hear the door chime. I know it's not Jenny. We don't open until 9:00. Walking back out front with my portfolio tucked under my arm, I see Luke closing the door.

"Get out. Now!" I scream as anger washes over me. I can't believe this. He has some nerve showing up here after the stunt he pulled last night.

"Shannon, I'm sorry. Baby, I lost control last night. I didn't mean to act that way, but we have to talk about us. That's all I was trying to get through to you," he says with a solemn voice as he approaches me.

I ignore the "baby" remark.

"Luke," I hold my hand out to stop him from getting any closer, "I don't have time for this. You know I have a meeting at LP this morning. Leave." My hand is touching his chest and I push him backward. "Now!"

He grabs my left arm hard and I'm pulled forward into his embrace. Then his lips are on mine. There is nothing tender about it, and I don't kiss him back. Instead, I bring my knee up to meet his crotch, causing him to double over, but not before he scratches my arm beside my elbow. It hurt and I know it's going to leave another mark.

"Get out!" I shout. "We are over. I never want to see you again. I'll be getting my things from the apartment tomorrow, so don't be there when I come by." I hiss at him.

Luke glares at me in disbelief, but doesn't say anything else as he rights himself and walks out the door. I wait a moment to calm myself, and then I leave too, locking the door behind me.

I will not let this prick ruin my day.

CHAPTER 7

Walking off the East elevator on the eleventh floor of the LP building, I have two minutes to spare. I'm wearing my jacket now. Not because I'm cold, but because Luke left a nasty scratch on my left arm. The same arm where there is still a small bruise. My fair, sensitive skin does not need any more damage.

I walk up to the receptionist and she greets me with a warm, sweet smile. "Hello, Miss Taylor. How are you today?"

"Please, stop calling me Miss Taylor," I say, smiling brightly at the sweet woman who I've come to know as Rachel.

"Okay, Shannon, if you insist," she says, shaking her head. "Mr. Lockhart is ready to see you now."

"Mr. Lockhart?" I question, confused. "I thought I was meeting with Teresa." This is a change I would have liked to been prepared for.

"Miss Matthews couldn't be here this morning, so Mr. Lockhart is handling all her appointments today." She gestures for me to follow her. My nerves sky rocket. I've never met him before, but I know he's the president of Lockhart Publishing. I've heard Mr. Lockhart has a brutal business reputation. I do not need this much pressure today.

I follow Rachel into his office. She announces my arrival and walks out of the door while closing it. I see him standing behind his desk, looking out the window, his back facing me.

We're on the West side of the building, so I assume he has a view of the ocean. His desk is large with two plush chairs sitting in front. There is a large couch and coffee table off to my left and a conference-style table with chairs to my right.

My nerves have just started to calm down when I barely hear him say, "Please, take a seat, Shannon."

His voice is soft and . . . familiar. I walk farther into the room as he turns around to face me. My feet halt and I know my face gives away my shock. A moment passes and my portfolio slips from my grasp, landing with a thud on the floor.

"Nick." It's all that comes out of my mouth. *What the hell?* He rounds the corner of his desk and bends down to retrieves my binder. Standing back up, he gestures towards the couch.

"Why don't we sit?" Everything washes over me and reality sinks in. This is where he saw me months ago. He knew I was going to be here this morning, yet he said nothing. The nervousness I felt only a moment ago is replaced by bitchiness.

"No," I say, taking a step back. I know if he touches me, my anger will dissipate after spending last night with him, a really shitty night that turned out spectacular.

"Would you please take a seat? It's going to be difficult enough getting through this meeting knowing what's underneath that dress." His warm eyes glide down my body and his lips turn up into a small smile. Warmth washes over me as his eyes rise to meet mine. I am determined not to give in to him so easily, so I place my hands on my hips and continue to look at him. I can't believe he is Nicholas Lockhart! He's my damn publisher. This can't be real.

"Did you know I was coming here this morning? Nick, why didn't you tell me who you are?" I demand to know.

He takes my hand, pulling me to the area with the couch and coffee table, but I catch the eye roll he does as he turns. Not letting my hand go, he places my portfolio on the table and turns back to me. My strength is slipping the longer he holds my hand. He pulls me into an embrace. Wrapping his left hand around my back, he continues to hold my left hand in his right.

Ughhh. Since when did I become this weak person? *So much for not giving in to him so easily.*

"I didn't tell you who I was because I wasn't sure you would let things go as far as it did last night, and I couldn't take that chance." He has a point. I probably wouldn't have been *that* unprofessional. His hand glides up my arm. When he reaches the top, he pushes my jacket off my shoulder. Seeing the small bruise causes his eyes to harden for a brief moment.

"I didn't know until I got here that your meeting would be with me. Teresa's sister went into labor several weeks early." He gently kisses the area where the bruise is located. Although I'm still upset he didn't tell me who he is, I don't protest. He pushes my jacket completely off and it falls to the ground. I close my eyes. My mind is clouded and I can't think straight. His lips, his hands, his everything feels so good.

"What the fuck is this?" I'm brought out of my haze.

Huh?

He's still holding my arm and has me around the waist with his other hand, staring at the fresh red scratch. "This wasn't here this morning. Where did it come from?"

"It's not important," I say, turning my back to his front. I know I'm a shitty liar, so I can't let him see my face, but I just don't want to think about my ex. The sooner I'm done with him, the sooner I'll never have to think about him again. Besides, I saw the way Nick reacted last night. He was so angry at the sight of the marks on my body. He looked as if he could murder someone.

"The hell it isn't," he says, turning me to face him. "You're withholding something from me. He did this, didn't he?" He lifts my chin to look at him. He's mad. I can see it in his eyes.

"Yes," I say in a shallow voice. Damn me and my inability to think fast enough to come up with something better.

"Goddamn it! I can't leave you alone for two fucking seconds." He runs both hands through his hair. He's angry. *Is he angry with me?*

"This isn't my fault!" I shout. Does he think I go around letting men hurt me? God, I'm certainly not someone who willingly takes abuse. Well, not that kind. Luke isn't normally physically abusive. At least, he wasn't for the five years we were together. He never showed any signs of aggression.

"I didn't mean it like that, Shannon." He sighs as his face relaxes. But it doesn't last long before his eyes darken and his eyebrows knit together. "I'm going to kill that shit-fuck." He voice is deadly. I need to get his mind on something else.

"Calm down, Sparky," I retort, backing him toward the couch. "You need to relax so we can get on with this meeting."

"Sparky?" His sarcasm hints that he doesn't likes that name, but his expression changes.

"You get worked up and sparks start flying," I tell him as he lowers himself onto the couch. He grabs the back of my thighs, pulling me onto his lap. My pumps fall off my feet and onto the floor. My knee-length dress rides up just under my bottom to accommodate his lap. I can feel the bulge in his pants prodding me through our clothes and the muscle between my thighs starts to pulsate.

He has one hand wrapped around my waist and the other moving up the back of my thigh, underneath my dress, until he cups one of my butt cheeks. He pulls my stomach closer to his face, the fabric of my dress separating my skin and his mouth. He inhales deeply.

"You are perfect," he says, and moves his hand from my waist to the top of my dress where the zipper is. Slowly, he slides it down as he looks up at me.

"I have to see all of you. I *need* to see all of you." I don't stop him. I want this too. I shouldn't, but I do. Last night wasn't enough. There's been an empty void since he withdrew from me last night. I should still be mad at him for keeping his identity from me, but I can't think about that now. I need him inside of me. If he had told me who he was, last night wouldn't have happen and I thoroughly enjoyed it.

He lifts the dress over my head and I rest my hands on his shoulders, watching him as he unhooks my satiny white bra before tossing it to the side. He's still fully dressed. His face goes between my breasts, kissing me there. I bend down, bringing his face to meet mine and kiss him while loosening his tie.

I'm sitting on his lap in nude stockings and white satin panties. He looks down at my sex with hungry eyes. "Stand up," he commands, and I do as I'm told. His eyes hold their position. "Take off your panties but leave the stockings on."

Hooking my thumbs into each side, I slowly slide them to the floor and step out. Then he pulls me back onto his lap.

I go for his belt, unbuckling and pulling it from the loops of his pants, and then toss it to my right. I reach for the button on his pants and it pops open, giving me a peek. After pulling his zipper down, he lifts so that I can slide his pants and boxer briefs to the floor. He kicks them off along with his shoes. His cock is rock-hard, and the length is touching my pussy lips, making me want more.

I push his jacket off his arms and remove it from behind him. He's watching me and rubbing the sides of my thighs. The contact between us is electric. One second his hands are touching the skin above my stockings, and the next, they are gliding down them and back up again.

I remove his tie and unbutton his shirt, pushing it off his shoulders and down his back. He reaches for his cock, stroking it as I lift myself from his lap. He guides himself to my opening, waiting for me to ease back down slowly, and he enters me. The emptiness inside me is gone and I'm filled with him to the hilt.

"Fuck you're hot in there, and so tight. I don't know how much more of you I can take before I explode," he says. I smile, liking that I'm a turn-on for him, because he is certainly one for me.

I start to slide up and down on him, arching my back as he takes a nipple into his mouth, his hands holding on to my back. My head falls backward as he bites down hard and I let out a scream of pleasure. He quickly covers my mouth and I look at him.

"Be quiet. The room isn't soundproof," he informs me as he tries not to laugh. I still and look to the door, wondering if someone is going to come in.

He picks up on my fear. "No one can come in without me pressing a button to let them in." I turn and look at him confused. "The door automatically locks when it shuts. I have to press a button on my desk to unlock it. Safety precaution," he adds.

"We should stop. This isn't why I'm here," I whisper. As I'm about to get off him, he grabs me and flips me onto my back, all without removing his cock from inside me. His lips are on mine before I can protest, and he starts thrusting in and out, hard, hard and fast. I moan into his mouth when I feel myself building inside. I'm going to lose it. I can't hold it back.

"I'm going to fucking explode if you don't come," he grunts and my orgasm ruptures before the sentence is fully out. As I'm crashing, he reaches his climax and spills himself inside me. It's warm, and my cries are muffled with his mouth covering mine.

Both of us pant, he places his forehead to mine.

"Have dinner with me tonight." It's not a question, but I don't think he means it as a command either.

"I can't. I'm going out with my friends tonight," I answer, still breathless. He pulls out of me and I sit up, looking for my clothes. "I'll probably stay at their apartment tonight," I continue. I've already spent the last two nights in his bed. He's bound to want me out of there by now.

It doesn't take him long before he has his pants on and zipped up. "Will I see you tomorrow?" he asks, as he walks over to help me zip up my dress. He plants a soft kiss on the back of my shoulder. It's warm and sends electric currents through my body. How can he do this to me with just a simple touch?

"Yes, I need to get my things from your room," I say, and immediately recognize the look in his eyes as pain. I ignore it and slide my feet into my pumps as he helps me into my jacket. He turns and reaches for his, slipping into it. He looks perfect and too put together; not like he just had sex in his office.

He's strong and in control.

I can only imagine the way I must look, and now I have to walk back through the front office. *Oh God, will they know? Did anyone hear me? Does he do this often? Am I just another client he fucked?* Everything is going through my mind at once. It's too much. I need to get on with our meeting and get out of here.

"Fine. Call or text me when you need to come by." He sounds upset or mad. I'm not sure which.

"You didn't look at my portfolio." I eye it sitting on the table while he is walks to his desk.

"I saw enough yesterday. Did you use the photo I suggested?" I nod, not sure what to make of this.

"Good, then everything is complete. I'll make sure Teresa starts on it Monday morning. I'll have her set up another meeting with you in a few weeks to talk about logistics." He presses a button on his desk, and the sound of the lock confirms it's the unlock button to his door.

He presses another button, this time on his phone, and a second later, I hear Rachel's voice. "Yes, Mr. Lockhart?"

"Please show Miss Taylor out," he tells her. No more than five seconds later, Rachel is at the door to collect me. Reality hits hard. That's all this is—an office fuck—and now he's dismissing me.

Unbelievable.

CHAPTER 8

I didn't go back to work. I need time to think. I can't believe I let all this happen. *What is wrong with me? Nothing is wrong with you,* I tell myself, answering my own question. I'm just frustrated.

I've gone months without sex. And my God, sex with Nick is incredible. Both times were beyond amazing, but I know I have to end this. If I keep this up, I'm going to fall in love with him. I know I can't handle another heartbreak. Besides, now that he's my publisher, it's inappropriate.

The strangest thing is, I'm heartbroken over Allison, not Luke. It hits me, the light bulb flicks on, burning bright. *Luke was a convenience.* I wasn't in love with him the way I should have been. If it wasn't for Allison's involvement, I may have welcomed the betrayal. It was an eye-opener, but still . . . how the hell could she do this to me?

Bitch!

Yeah, I'm nowhere close to being over it.

I end up parked outside of Bella's. When I'm stressed or having a bad day, I shop. It's my second favorite store, and I do need a dress for tonight. My friends and I are going to Club Blue.

As I walk in, I immediately see the dress I've been eyeing for two weeks. I know it fits my curves perfectly. I've only tried it on at least five times. White satin underneath with a white lace overlay. It's sleeveless, showing the right amount of cleavage and it ends four inches above my knee.

I grab the size eight from the rack and walk to the lingerie section in the back where I find a white, strapless, satiny smooth pushup bra and matching panties from the rack, and then head to the checkout counter.

"It's about time you bought this dress," the lady says. I don't know her, but she has obviously seen me in here a few times. I smile warmly and hand her my credit card to complete the purchase.

I toss the bags into the passenger seat of my car and slide into my seat, wasting no time before I take a left out of the parking lot and head to The Cove. I have to get my stuff from Nick's place before he gets home. I can't see him again. If I do, I'll want him again. Who am I kidding? I want him right now. I'm sure he won't be too upset. Men like him don't have trouble finding a woman to fall into their bed.

Stepping into the elevator, I retrieve my cell phone to bring up the text from last night with the code for the penthouse. I quickly type it in and ride up.

When I enter the living room area, I walk straight to the bedroom and grab all my belongings. On the way out, I notice the doorframe has already been fixed. I sigh. I'm going to miss him; not just the sex, but him. How can I be so affected by a man I just met two days ago? I've never felt this way for another person, and that's scary.

I shake my head—like that's going to help me forget him—and make my exit. I reach my car and toss everything in my small trunk. When I settle into the driver's seat, I take my phone out of my purse and see I have a missed call from Katelyn. I quickly call her back.

"Hey, chickie. Are we still on for tonight?" I can hear the excitement in her voice. Katelyn loves our Friday nights together. She's not a big drinker like me, but we both love to dance.

"Absolutely," I say, returning the same excitement in my voice. "I need a fun night out, and the welcomed distraction." I leave out that the distraction I need is from Nick, not Luke and Ally.

"Are you okay? Stace claims you are, but I need to hear it from you," she says. Her excitement has turned to concern.

"I am," I reply, because truthfully, I really am. I don't miss Luke. Allison is a different story. She was supposed to be my best friend. I'm hurt and angry by what she did. I don't know if I'll ever be able to forgive her.

"Can I come over to get dressed at your place and crash on your couch tonight?"

"Of course you can. You should know by now you don't have to ask. Get your ass over here. I need to see you, so I can make sure for myself that you really are good." She has worry in her tone.

Katelyn, just like Stacy, is a good friend.

"In fact, there is no reason you should be staying alone in a hotel. Bring all your stuff and you can stay with us for a while," she adds.

This is why I love my friends. I smile against the phone. "Okay, thanks, Be there in thirty." I don't acknowledge the last part. Staying one night is fine, but I have no intention of staying longer. I end our call, toss my cell phone on the passenger seat, and then leave The Cove's parking lot, heading to Katelyn and Stacy's apartment.

TRAFFIC IS HEAVY THIS AFTERNOON, AND IT's taken me forty minutes to get from The Cove to Katelyn and Stacy's apartment in Pasadena. Walking up the stairs, I see Ben locking his door. He and Kyle, his roommate and best friend, live next door to Katelyn and Stacy, which is how we met them one night. It's been a blast ever since.

"Hey, sweetness," Ben greets me halfway up the steps as he's jogging down. "Stacy told me what happened. I can't say I'm sorry you aren't with that dick-face anymore, but I never wanted to see you hurt. How are you?"

I hug him, already laughing. "A better question is what's with the douche-stash, Ben?" I can't stop laughing. It's awful. He starts laughing too.

"What? You don't like?" he asks through chuckles as he rubs his mustache with two fingers. He has no sense of style, apparently.

"No, I don't. It looks really bad. I thought all gay men were born with great fashion sense. What happened to yours?" I ask him, still laughing uncontrollably.

"Quit with that stereotypical shit. Kyle gets on my damn nerves enough with comments like that. Besides, I don't have time for fashion, and I like my douche-stash as you call it. I think it looks fab," he says in a serious, but playful tone. Ben is gay, but his best friend isn't, and Kyle loves to rag on Ben.

"I can assure you it does not," I reply. "Didn't mustaches go out of style in the eighties? The only person I can think of who can rock a mustache these days is Tom Selleck, the actor." Ben rolls his eyes, which is not unlike him, and then kisses me lightly on the cheek.

"Look, babe, I gotta run. I'll see you in a few hours," he says and jogs down the rest of the stairs as I walk up the last three steps.

Before I have time to knock, the door opens and I'm greeted with a big smile from Stacy and a glass of white wine. I take it from her hand. "I do love you. You know exactly what I need." I take a sip and the cool liquid slides down my throat with ease. It's sweet and fruity, just the way I like my wine.

"Please tell me you have food in this apartment. I skipped lunch," I say to Katelyn, who is walking out of the kitchen with her own glass of wine as Stacy is closing the door behind me.

"There are a few slices of my leftover pizza from an hour ago. It's on the kitchen on the counter. You're welcome to it," she offers, gesturing to their small kitchen area.

I round the corner and place my glass on the black granite counter. Picking up a piece of cold pepperoni pizza, I tear a piece off with my teeth. It's delicious. I look out into the living room from the kitchen and Stacy is once again giving me a disgusted look.

"You two are gross," she says as she starts walking down the hall to her bedroom. I know it's going to take her a few hours to get ready. It will probably take her an hour just to decide what to wear.

"No, we just know how to eat unlike you, who is skinnier than a rail!" I shout so she can hear me. *I mean really, who doesn't like pizza?* I mentally ask as I walk out of the kitchen and take a seat on the couch next to Katelyn with my glass of wine and slice of pizza in hand.

"Do you ever wonder how guys don't split her in two during sex?" Katelyn asks while changing the channel with the remote.

I laugh, spitting out my wine. Katelyn has the sense of humor of most men and can speak their language. "Often," I say, and take another bite of pizza.

"So what's our plan tonight?" Katelyn asks me while leaning over and taking a bite of my pizza.

"I was thinking Charro for dinner, and we can head to Club Blue about nine-ish," I suggest, snatching my pizza out of her mouth and taking the last bite.

"Works for me," she says as she settles on a movie and places the remote down. Its *Pulp Fiction* and it's about midway through. This is a classic and one of my favorites. John Travolta is the man, and I love his movies—most of them. I cannot sit through any part of *Michael*.

A few hours later, I'm getting off the couch to find Stacy when I hear my iPhone chime, the sound of a text message. I retrieve my purse and pull out my phone. It's Nick. I read the time on my phone and it's 5:53 p.m. Opening the text I read his message.

Nick: Why is all your stuff gone?

Why does he care? He should be glad I'm gone. I really don't want to deal with this right now, but I reply.

Shannon: I had time on my hands. I decided to get everything today instead of tomorrow.

I start to set my phone down when it starts ringing. It's him. What the hell is his problem? I figured he would be glad to get rid of me after his dismissal earlier this morning.

"Hello?" My anger from this morning starts to filter in. I think I'm madder at myself for giving into my desires than I am at him.

"Where the hell are you?" he questions in an angry tone.

What the hell?

What business is it of his where I am? The last time I checked, I don't belong to him either. What is it with men in the last few days, thinking women are their property? This woman belongs to no-fucking-body!

"At a friend's apartment. What's your problem?" I snap at him, remembering why I thought he was a jerk two nights ago. He has no right to demand to know my whereabouts, and why the hell am I telling him anything? I should hang up on him.

"You said you were coming tomorrow to pick your things up. Why the change of plans? And why when I wasn't here?" His voice is still full of anger. Apparently, this time, his anger is directed at me.

"What does it matter?" I ask, but I don't wait for his answer. "Look Nick . . . maybe we shouldn't see each other again. I have to go, bye," I say quickly and then hang up. Depression crawls down my spine as I set the phone on the table.

I need another glass of wine. Alcohol seems to be my fix for everything these days. Walking into the kitchen, I pour another glass as Stacy walks in.

"Pour me one too, please," she says as she thrusts her glass in my face. She is dressed to kill in a red, strapless, skintight dress that shows way too much leg. She went with matching red sandals with a two-inch heel and a strap around the ankle.

"You look hot. Whose pants are you trying to get into tonight?" I ask as I'm walking out of the kitchen and back into the living room to wake up Katelyn, who fell asleep twenty minutes into the movie.

"No one in particular—now will you two lazy bums get up and get dressed? I'm going over to Ben and Kyle's. Come get us when you're ready to leave," she says in a Stacy-like fashion.

Pouncing on Katelyn, I say, "Time to get up. I'm going to use Stacy's bathroom. Be ready in forty."

She grabs a throw pillow and covers her head. "It's only 6:05 p.m. Can I have another hour?" she whines.

"No, you can't," I say as I stand and steal the pillow from her. As I'm walking to Stacy's room, I toss the pillow into a chair.

"You suck." I hear her say as I'm walking down the hall.

CHAPTER 9

An hour later, I'm sitting on a bar stool in Ben and Kyle's apartment, drinking yet another glass of wine while waiting on Katelyn to emerge from her apartment. Ben peeks his head out of the front door of his apartment. "She's finally ready. Let's roll." He's since shaved off the hideous mustache. Apparently, enough people ragged on him about it at the gym.

We make our way down the stairs and into the parking lot and pile into Ben's dark blue Ford Explorer, Ben and Kyle up front while my two girlfriends and me are in the back. Ben starts the ignition and Katy Perry's "Hot N Cold" is playing. Kyle quickly switches the station to 95.5 KLOS. He and I have the same taste in music, and like me, he hates pop. Ben, on the other hand, doesn't know what genre he likes. It's different every damn month. Apparently, he's into pop right now.

"Dude, stop touching my fucking radio." Ben huffs out, but

doesn't turn it back. Kyle doesn't respond. He knows if he makes a smart-ass remark, then Ben will force him to listen to pop music for the remainder of the drive. He's not stupid.

Once we arrive at Charro, Ben whips the SUV into the only free space available. We made it just in time. Otherwise, we would be finding another restaurant tonight. There is no way I would be walking the half-mile back to this popular eatery.

When we get out of the SUV, I smooth out my dress. I borrowed Stacy's two-inch white heels. We may not share clothes, but we are the same foot size, so we're able to raid each other's shoe closet.

I order a ground beef taco salad with extra cheese sauce and a margarita on the rocks. You can't eat Mexican food without a margarita, and my friends share the same philosophy as we all order the same drink.

"So, Shannon," Kyle starts, "has the douchebag tried to get you back yet?" All heads turn in my direction, waiting for a response.

"Yeah," I sigh, wondering if I should divulge everything that's happened over the last few days. The last two people I want to even think about, let alone talk about, are Luke and Allison, but then what kind of friend would I be if I kept them all in the dark? A pretty shitty friend I would imagine.

"Well?" Ben draws out in a long breath. I guess the conversation with myself in my head was a lot longer than I thought.

"Well, um . . ." I hesitate, searching for the right words to say. "Luke came by work yesterday, caused a small scene, and then showed up drunk last night at the hotel." I leave out the even bigger scene he caused last night. I still can't wrap my head around what he did. "He caught me before my meeting this morning and tried to apologize for his behavior," I finish, thinking I've told them plenty.

"Why did you just hesitate like you didn't want to tell us? Did the shithead do anything?" Stacy questions. Yes, he did, but I don't want to think about that now, let alone discuss it. Surely, they get that.

"I wasn't, and guys, I really want to just forget about him and never have to deal with him again," I say before taking a large sip through the straw of my margarita.

For the last two hours, we've ate, drank, laughed, and called each other on our bullshit. It's already a fun night; I needed this, along with the alcohol to take my mind off Nick. My friends may think I need a distraction from Luke and my former best friend, but the truth is, I need to forget about the best sex I've ever had with a man I don't even know.

After paying the bill, we all walk to Club Blue. It's 9:45 and the doorman lets us pass without waiting in line. It's great having a friend that's on TV sometimes, even if it is only the news. Stacy's face gets us in a lot of places, and we use it to our advantage.

Finding a table that will accommodate the five of us, I take a seat at the end of the high-top table on a barstool.

Ben and Kyle are walking up with our drinks when Ben pulls me off the stool and says, "We are going to dance, sweetness."

The pop song "Mirrors" is playing in the background, causing me to think about Nick momentarily. I think it's a Justin Timberlake song. It's not my type of music, but I know Katelyn and Stacy love it, and I can usually roll with whatever. I may not fully appreciate JT's music, but I love his performances on

Saturday Night Live. The guy is funnier than shit.

Ben is really into it and he's dancing us all over the floor. We are having a blast. After fifteen minutes and burning valves from dancing in heels, I squeeze him on the shoulders and shout into his ear over the music saying, "It's time for me to sit down. I need more alcohol."

He stays on the dance floor when I exit, making my way back to our table. Katelyn hands me a glass of white wine as I take a seat. "I got you a fresh one," she says as she takes a sip of hers.

"Holy hell! If that isn't the hottest piece of ass I've ever seen," she says, looking over my shoulder.

I go to turn around and she grabs my arm to stop me. "Don't look. He's walking this way."

A few seconds later, warm hands wrap around me, and my friend's eyes look like they are about to pop out of their sockets. It's him—Nick. I know by the way he feels, the intoxicating smell of him, and the way my body has little tingles of electricity running through it.

"Pardon me, but I need to borrow this one for a moment," he says, pulling me off the stool by my waist. My friends do not protest, sitting there, stunned with their mouths on the table.

He guides me to a corner by the wall, turning me around to face him. My back is against the cold concrete and he's towering over me with his hands placed on the wall above me.

"Your friend is lucky he's gay," he says with a serious expression. The anger that was in his voice on the phone isn't present.

"What is that supposed to mean?" I ask, clearly not

understanding his point.

"Had he not been gay with his hands all over you on the dance floor, his face would have come in contact with my fist. That's what that means," he tells me through dark, intense, hooded eyes.

My anger is building and I'm about to lash out at him when he grabs the back of my neck, pulling me into a kiss. The anger subdues as I kiss him back, fisting the lapels of his jacket in my hands. All my built up tension from today leaves my body, and I begin to relax.

I do enjoy the affect he has on me.

He breaks away too quickly for my liking, but I continue holding him by the lapels of his jacket. Easing my grip, I look up. "Mind telling me what I did wrong? And why you at it, why did you choose to leave without saying goodbye?" Hurt reflects in his eyes, making my chest ache. I'm getting tired of seeing this pained expression. I don't understand it. I release him and glance down. "Talk to me, damn it." He sounds frustrated.

I look back up, giving Nick all of my attention. "Earlier today, in your office, you dismissed me like I was only there for you to fuck." I say it in a low voice and it feels awful saying it out loud. I look back down. My good night I was having is turning to shit.

He bends his head down and rests his forehead against mine. "That's what you thought?"

"That's what it felt like, and I didn't like it." I grab his lapels again, just holding on to them. He lifts my chin, forcing me to look him in the eyes once again.

"I'm sorry. I wasn't dismissing you. I had another meeting to get to and you brought your portfolio, so I thought we were done."

He has a sincere look on his face. I believe him.

Don't get me wrong, a goodbye kiss would have been nice, but shit. This whole thing that's going on between us is confusing. "Okay," I whisper.

How did I misread the situation?

"Okay, as in, we're good?" he asks, and I nod. He kisses my cheek softly, and then moves to that spot on my neck he likes so much and kisses me again. He trails kisses up my neck until he reaches my ear.

"Introduce me to your friends," he whispers. I nod again, and he steps back, taking my hand. I lead him to our table where my friends are staring in disbelief with dropped jaws. My guess they were watching us. *Nosey bunch, they are.*

When we arrive back at the table, Nick is standing behind me. I pick my wine glass up and finish the contents in one gulp.

"Guys, this is Nick . . . I mean Nicholas," I correct myself. I don't need my friends messing up his name even though I refuse to call him by it. They all introduce themselves to Nick.

Stacy is the last when Nick asks, "Aren't you the weather girl from Channel 5?"

There is silence as Stacy is glares at him. "Meteorologist," she spits outs, and I laugh. I can't help myself. I know Stacy hates being referred to as a 'weather girl.' We all say it to her face, but only when we want to piss her off.

"Chief Meteorologist to be exact," she adds in an angry tone.

I laugh again, thinking about how she slept with the executive producer of Channel 5 news to get that spot. It's not like she wasn't the most qualified; she was. It's the fact she did it to ensure she would get it over anyone else. I love her dearly, but she will sleep with anyone to get what she wants.

Nick doesn't apologize. Clasping my hand in his, he announces, "I'm taking Shannon upstairs with me. Would you all like to join us?"

He is?

My friends' eyes light up and they simultaneously shout, "YES!"

None of us have been on the second level. Most clubbers from level one never have and never will. Level two is the private area of Club Blue. I assume it's where CEOs and celebrities hang out; although, I've never seen a celebrity here.

Making our way out of the elevator and into the room, it seems bigger than down below. A tall railing circles the center. It's open and you can look down on level one. The tables are spaced out more with booths and couches lining the wall. In the back is another dance floor. It's a little smaller than the floor on level one, probably because there aren't as many people up here.

"Follow me," Nick says as he leads us to a private table off to the side. He hasn't let go of my hand since we were downstairs. When we reach a large table, there are three men already sitting at it, but it's big enough to accommodate everyone.

My friends take a seat and Nick gestures for me to follow him to the end of the table. The chairs are a lot nicer up here. They're large black stools, similar to the ones down below, but these have cushioned backs that wrap around, which I like.

I take my seat and Nick stands next to me with his arm draped over the back of the chair behind my head. Without taking his eyes off me, he says, "the guy with a scowl is Jase, the big one is Shane, and the old one is Matt."

"Fuck you, Lockhart," the three say in unison.

Nick looks up and across the table at who I assume are his friends. "I just call it like I see it," he says with a smile.

Matt—the old guy as Nick called him—doesn't look that old to me, maybe late thirties. He has dusty-gray hair mixed with dark black, and a goatee to match. He's wearing a business suit and is drinking what looks to be whiskey.

Shane has milk chocolate, flawless skin, and perfect white teeth. He's wearing a white T-shirt and blue jeans with a Shemar Moore look about him, and I immediately take notice that Katelyn appears to be in awe. Yeah, he's hot, and she isn't blind. My friend takes a seat right next to him. Looking at both of them, they look somewhat exotic. Katelyn has long, curly, jet-black hair, green eyes, and olive skin. They just look right sitting next to each other.

Jase has a similar build to Nick's. I'm guessing they're about the same height and overall size. He has dirty-blond hair that's short on both sides and longer on top, and he has piercing sky-blue eyes. He has tattoo sleeves covering each arm, and lettering across the top of his right fingers. The room is dim and he's standing at the other end of the long table, so I can't make out the word. Colorful ink is poking out of the collar of his T-shirt. I shouldn't be staring at him this long, but he reminds me of Jacoby Shaddix, the lead singer of my favorite band, and in my opinion, the hottest man in the world. At least, he was two days ago, before I laid eyes on Nick.

Nick guides my chin in his direction until I'm now looking at him. He hasn't left his position next to me. His arm is still draped over the back of my chair. "Pay attention to me, please."

"How did you know I was here?" I question him. It's a bit odd how I told him I didn't think we should see each other again, yet we end up at the same club.

"I didn't, but you're not hard to pick out in a room full of blondes and brunettes," he says, running a hand through my red hair. He turns my chair slightly so my side is facing the others, my front toward a black, painted, concrete wall, and he's on the other side of me. He starts to kiss me and places his hand on my knee, the one that isn't resting behind my head.

"White looks stunning on you," he tells me through our kiss while moving his hand up my leg. I think I've died and gone to heaven. His touch feels so good. I'm relaxed again, like I was earlier today in his office. He continues inching his hand up my leg as we kiss, sliding it underneath the hem of my dress, causing me to freeze.

"What are you doing?" I flush with embarrassment and heat, looking to the side to make sure no one is watching. My friends are in full-conversation mode with Nick's friends.

"No one is watching us, and if they were, they wouldn't see anything except me kissing you. The sides of the chair and the height of the table block everything below your tits, babe." He goes back to kissing me. He deepens the kiss, pushing me back into the seat. His tongue pries my lips farther apart and begins to massage my tongue.

He continues to move his hand slowly up my thigh underneath my dress. Surely, my friends can see this. Why aren't they stopping me? Why am I not stopping myself? I don't do public displays of affection. I move my hand on top of his to protest his movement.

"Relax, baby, and let this happen. No one can see us. I promise. But be quiet," he says in a whisper through our kiss. I'm losing myself in him. I retract my hand and my legs widen on their own accord.

His scent is intoxicating and overpowering. His taste is divine, and I can't get enough. His hand reaches the fabric of my panties, and he pushes the material to the side, baring my pussy. With his thumb, he finds my clit and he presses it against me, applying full pressure.

I grab the sleeve of his jacket, biting down on his bottom lip so I don't scream. I need to stop this, but then he starts to rotate his thumb, and with another finger, he enters me, slowly driving his digit in and out of me repeatedly.

"I love how wet I make you almost as much as I love fucking you with my fingers." He adds another, pushing inside a bit harder this time. The rhythm of his thumb remains steady while the pressure inside builds. My head is spinning. Holy shit, he's going to make me come in a room full of people.

My friends and his friends are at the other end of the table only a few feet away. I can't hold back. He's driving me over the edge. The circling of his thumb increases in speed and now he has three fingers deep inside of me. My legs shake a little and he deepens the kiss even more.

I have no idea how I'm not screaming out. All I want to do is moan his name as the heat in my stomach becomes fierce.

"Give in, Shannon. Let go," he says into my mouth. I grip

his shirt tighter, pulling on it as hard as I can. His arm doesn't move from its place and I crash harder than I ever have before. His mouth covers my cries. He steadies his thumb, pressing hard against my clit until the last of my shudders still. I don't feel him when he removes his hand from underneath my dress. I'm still lost somewhere in what is Nicholas Lockhart.

When I open my eyes, he's staring down at me. His face is only a few inches from mine. "Feel better?" he asks with a knowing grin as he inserts his middle finger into his mouth, quickly sucking it clean.

Damn, that is hot!

I nod; it's all I can do. I'm slowly recovering, but I can't move yet. He leans down, his lips touching my ear softly. "I don't think there's anything sexier than watching you come all over my fingers. You taste sweet," he says, then kisses along my jaw until he reaches my mouth.

"Are you two going to continue sucking face all night, or do you plan on joining the rest of us?" Stacy remarks. I release his lips, casting a glare in her direction. I'm not ready to come off the rollercoaster Nick put me on a few moments ago.

I can see she is still fuming over the 'weather girl' comment, but I don't care. She is a weather girl. And she *needs* to get over it.

Nick kisses my temple and I stop glaring at her. "Shannon is tired. I'm going to take her home," he announces. I don't question him, but I'm not tired. We've only been here maybe two hours max. Plus, I'm currently without a home.

"She doesn't look tired," Stacy chimes, lifting her wine to take a sip. She isn't going to let his comment go.

"But she will be. Trust me," Nick replies with a smirk. Everyone heard him.

Did he really just say that?

Stacy chokes on her wine as the rest of my friends burst out laughing. Nick's friends just smile at him.

"I like him," Katelyn declares. She finishes off her drink, turning her attention back to Shane. Nick pulls me off the stool and looks across the room. He makes some type of hand gesture, and then a man in a business suit nods.

"It was nice meeting you all, and ladies, those two are up for grabs," he says gesturing to Shane and Matt, "but Jase is off-limits," he says. I eye him and then Jase. *What the hell is that about?* I wonder. He isn't wearing a ring.

"Thanks, bro, because I needed that," Jase says sarcastically.

"Let's go. There's somewhere I want to take you," he says, guiding me in the direction of the elevator.

Once we're in the car, he pulls out of the parking lot heading west on Ocean Avenue. I figure he is heading to The Cove, but he doesn't make the turn south. Instead, he continues until he reaches Pacific Coast Highway. Taking the exit, he heads north for about ten minutes. Before I know it, he exits off the highway, and then proceeds through a neighborhood. Soon, he pulls into a driveway outside of someone's house. My curiosity is piqued.

Just where has he taken me?

It's a medium-sized brick house with a small porch on the front and a rattan hanging chair on the end. "Let's go inside," he says as he turns off the ignition, opens the car door, and steps out.

I follow, stepping out of the car into the warm night air.

Walking up behind him to the front door, I'm wondering why we're here, and even though I don't know whose house this is, I like it. It's not too big but smells like the ocean. I don't think we're that far from the beach.

He unlocks the door with a key from his key ring, which strikes me as odd. Nick lets me walk in first and as I step inside the lights automatically come on. After door closes behind me, I hear a dog bark.

Could this house belong to a friend of his? Perhaps he's here to feed and water their pet or pets. No one's home.

"Whose house is this?" I ask, following him through the foyer, past the stairs and into the kitchen.

"Mine," he replies as he places his keys on the granite kitchen island.

"I thought you lived at The Cove?" I ask, confused. Why has he been staying at The Cove if he has a house not far away?

"No, I was just staying there while my house was having some renovation work done," he says and walks to the back door. Upon opening it, two dogs barrel in and start jumping on Nick, begging for attention.

I smile, because I love dogs, and his are beautiful. They are both German shepherds. The big one is black and tan, while the small one, who looks to be a young puppy, is solid white. The puppy jumps off Nick and runs toward me, but ends up sliding into my legs as it tries to stop because of the slick hardwood floor. Bending down, I scoop the little furry ball up into my arms.

"I hope you like dogs," Nick says as he closes the door leading out to the backyard and moves to a large plastic container holding their dog food. He scoops food into two bowls, placing them underneath the granite island. I place the puppy down on the floor. She takes her place next to the bigger dog.

"I love dogs," I inform him. "I've never gotten one because I can't stand the thought of it cramped in a small place, but I volunteer occasionally at an animal shelter so I can play with them," I say, coming to stand next to Nick in the kitchen.

"The big guy is Niko and she's Charmin," he states, and I raise an eyebrow. Surely not. "What's that look for?"

"Um, her name," I say as I gesture to his puppy. "It's not after the toilet paper is it?" No way would someone name their pet after that.

"Yeah." Nick laughs. "She's white, soft, and definitely fluffy." He has an amused look on his face.

"And Niko? Where did he get his name from?" I inquire.

"A character from a video game," he responds and I almost burst out laughing.

"You play video games?" The question falls from my lips. He does not look like a man who plays video games.

"Not often, but they can be entertaining, and hell, I'm guy, so yeah." He laughs as he picks me up and sits me on the island. I smile. "Do you like my house?" he asks as he positions himself between my thighs. My dress rides up to accommodate him. I could get used to him constantly between my thighs.

Wrapping my arms around his neck, I answer him, "I don't know yet. I haven't had a tour," hinting for him to show me the rest. I can already tell I like his house.

With that, he scoops me into his arms and turns. "This is the kitchen. Over there is the living room," he says while gesturing off the side of the kitchen. The kitchen and living room are open to each other, both on the backside of the house. There is a large couch in the center of the room facing the biggest flat screen TV I've ever seen.

Turning again, he walks out of the living room and back into the foyer. Pointing to the left of the front door, he says, "That is the downstairs bathroom," and then to the right he tells me, "and that is the formal dining room, although not so formal as you can see." I laugh a little. He has a pool table where there would typically be a large table.

He turns around and gestures up the stairs. "There are two guest bedrooms up there. They're empty, so there is no need to show you." He walks past the stairs into another room. When he flips the switch on the wall, dim lights come on.

"This is the master bedroom," he explains as he sets my feet on the floor. *His room.*

It's warm but modern. The walls are gray, the furniture is black, and the bedding is all white atop a king size bed—the only thing white in the room. I like the look and feel of his house.

"I wouldn't have pictured you in what most consider a normal-sized house," I admit, turning to take everything in.

"I grew up in a huge house and *hated* it," he says. He takes his jacket off, placing it across the back of a chair in the corner. He closes the bedroom door. I assume because he doesn't want the dogs to come in here after they've finished their meal.

"What, no dogs in the bedroom?" I ask as he walks to me.

"They're allowed in here, just not at this very moment," he

says with a knowing grin as he runs both hands down my arms. "Right now, the only thing I want to play with is you." His smile is wicked. My heart rate increases at the possibility.

He kneels on the floor and lifts my foot to rest on his knee as he unbuckles the strap on my heel, then tosses it to the floor, and repeats the step with the other foot. Once I'm barefoot, he stands back up and looks down at me.

His eyes are hooded, but his face is playful. I smile at him and reach for his tie to loosen it. The way he looks at me causes goose bumps to form all over my skin. Once I have it untied and pulled out of his shirt, I toss it in the direction of the chair.

Working his shirt out of his pants, I start unbuttoning it from top to bottom until the last button is undone. It falls open, revealing his tan skin. I place my hands on his torso and rub upward until I reach his shoulders, his smooth flesh heating my fingers. Pushing his shirt off, it pools on the floor behind him.

He kicks his shoes off, lowers his head down to my neck, and kisses that spot he likes so much. "You look like heaven dressed in white," he tells me as he reaches behind my back to unzip my dress. "If you didn't feel like heaven, I couldn't bear to take it off." The things this man says makes me weak in the knees.

The bulge in his pants is hard and aching to be released. I feel it pressing against my stomach. I want to touch it, to taste it, to have it in my mouth.

I undo the buckle of his belt and pull it from the loops of his pants, letting it fall to the floor to go for the button on his pants as he unclasps my bra. My bra gets tossed and his pants unzipped.

Kneeling on the floor in front of him, I grab his pants and

boxer briefs and yank them down, freeing his hard length. The only item of clothing remaining between us is my panties. I want nothing more than to worship his cock with my mouth.

He's looking down at me with a look in his eyes I've never seen before, showing power and strength, radiating lust and need.

I grab his dick, fisting my hand around the base as I bring my lips to it. I dart my tongue out and twirl it around the tip, rewarded with a quick intake of air and a deep moan when I run my tongue along the underside of him, coming back to the tip and twirling my tongue again. His cock is wet, well lubricated from my saliva.

I take him all the way in my mouth, clasping my hand tighter around his cock. He grabs ahold of my hair, fisting my red locks in his hands. "Fuck, Shannon, God, that feels good," he says, breathlessly.

I glide up and down, my mouth and hand working in unison, continuing this rhythm for a few seconds longer, then I quicken my pace. My hand goes for his testicles, cupping and lightly massaging them as I take him farther in my mouth. "Jesus fucking Christ, woman." His motivation makes me go deeper and suck faster. I take him to the back of my throat, swallowing as I continue the pace. "I'm going to come," he says through pants as he tightens the grip on my hair.

Strands are pulled taut and it's painful, but I don't slow my speed. I don't care how hard he pulls. The harder he pulls the more turned on I'm getting. He spills himself into my mouth and I swallow, letting it run down my throat. I don't waste a drop. I find myself liking the salty taste.

"Fuck," he says breathlessly, releasing his hold around my hair.

"Feel better?" I repeat the same question he asked me only an hour earlier.

"Yes," he says, and holds out his hand for me, wearing a smirk I don't mind seeing on his handsome face.

When I stand, he leans down, capturing my lips with his, kisses me passionately. He cups both butt cheeks, lifting my legs off the ground, wrapping them around his waist. "Thank you, baby," he says, walking over to the bed.

He gently places me in the center of the mattress and pulls a pillow underneath my head for comfort. Then he settles between my legs and pulls my panties off slowly while planting soft kisses down the center of my right thigh. He tosses aside and continues laying more kisses up the inside of the same thigh. A devilish grin plays across his face.

He grabs the flesh of my ass cheek in his right hand and squeezes. "I want to fuck this beautiful ass, baby. Will you let me?" he asks, and I'm caught off guard. Nothing has ever entered me there, and I never plan for it to.

Where did that come from?

I shake my head. I can only imagine the terrified look I must be giving him. He moves to my left thigh and plants soft kisses along the inside.

"I want a part of you that's never been had. Will you give this to me?" he asks. His grin has morphed into a serious stare.

I sit up on my elbows. "What makes you think I've never don—"

He cuts me off before I finish my sentence.

"Because the truth was written all over your beautiful face when I asked," he cut me off before I finish my question.

Oh.

Giving it serious consideration, I contemplate what he's told me he wants to do to my ass. *Could I go through with it? Do I even want to do it?* I don't think I do. I shake my head from left to right again, giving him my final answer.

"Fine, not tonight, but, Shannon . . ." He pauses and smiles at me. He's not mad that I just told him no to something he really wanted. "I will have this," he finishes, squeezing my bottom again. "Close your eyes, baby."

I comply, but I feel the mattress expand and I know Nick got out of the bed. Moments later, he straddles my stomach. "Don't open those beautiful eyes unless I say so." What is this man planning? At least he isn't still trying to enter the back door.

With my eyes shut, my sense of hearing hitches up a notch or two. I feel him above me, but I can't tell what he is doing. I'm intrigued.

Nick gathers my arms and pulls them over and above my head, placing them together on the pillow, and then bends down, kissing me starting with my neck, then moves up to my ear before he is trailing feather-like kisses along my jaw. Finally, he reaches my lips.

He sucks the bottom one between his teeth and bites down. I gasp, giving him full access to my mouth, where he takes the kiss to the deepest depth, alternating mingling his tongue with mine, and sucking on it. God, I love every way this man kisses.

He moves from my mouth to the other side of my face; again,

with the feather-like kisses, until he reaches my earlobe, where he bites, pulling it in a downward motion.

"Ahhh." I can't keep quiet.

"You remember the other night when I told you that you might regret what you said to me?" Nick says, his voice is soft and seductive.

"Huh?" I say, as I try to recall what's he's talking about, but I'm coming up blank. With his lips on me, I can't seem to concentrate.

He releases my hand and I feel his lips form into a smile, before he trails more kisses down my neck. "Baby, this is going to be my form of retribution," he states.

What is he going on about?

His hands skim down each side of my body. I want to wrap my own hands around his shoulders, but I can't. I tug, but my wrists won't move. Unease starts to sink in. "Be still."

I open my eyes to see what's keeping me from moving them. My wrists are bound together with the tie he was wearing earlier. My mind flashes back to a dark memory.

No. No. No.

I start to struggle.

"Get it off! Stop! No." I gasp, a sob forming in my chest. I'm yanking on the material, tightening it against my flesh, but I'm not getting anywhere. I'm only making my wrists hurt.

"Baby, stop. I'm just having fun with you," Nick says. I can barely register his words from the panic filling my chest.

This isn't fun. Nothing about this is okay. I want to scream, to struggle. The sound catches in my throat, yet I continue to struggle and try bucking him off me. "Shannon!" Nick calls my name as he reaches over me, releasing me from the binds.

"Get off!" I yell. Once my wrists are free and I can move my arms, I reach up and try to shove Nick off me. I half-succeed, knocking him on the bed on his side.

He's wearing an expression of shock. "What the fuck?" he asks, sitting up. He's looking at me through caution-filled eyes. My breathing is heavy. I sit up, reaching behind me quickly to snatch a pillow and hug it to my chest.

I'm okay.

My wrists hurt, but I'm okay. I've never freaked out like this before.

What's wrong with me?

"Are you okay?"

"Yeah, I—I'm sorry. You should tell a girl before you do that," I respond, my voice just a whisper. *Shit. He probably thinks I'm crazy. Maybe I am. No, I'm not,* I remind myself.

"Are you sure? You just freaked the fuck out on me. What happened?" he asks.

What can I tell him?

I look over at him standing next to the bed in all of his naked gloriousness. His wide eyes look down at me like he doesn't understand but wants to.

"I don't know. I—I wasn't expecting it, that's all." That sounded believable, right?

"You don't know or you don't want to tell me?" he questions in an accusing tone. Maybe it didn't come out as believable as it sounded in my head.

Please, just let it go.

"I said I wasn't expecting it, so just leave it alone, okay?"

"Fine. I'm sorry. Can I at least get back in bed, now?" he asks as he reaches for the blanket to pull the covers back. I nod. I mean, this is his bed, not mine. I don't have a right to tell him either way. He's reluctant for a brief moment, but then shakes his head and slides under the covers. He opens his arms and I leap into them. I can't believe I did that. Nick pulls the covers out from under me and yanks them over us.

"I'm sorry," I whisper into his chest.

"It's fine. I shouldn't have tied you up without asking you first. It won't happen again. Let's just go to sleep."

It sounds like a wonderful plan. I don't know if I'll manage to sleep, but I'll try. I inhale deeply and blow the air back out. I relax in his arms, forcing myself not to remember. Eventually, I fall asleep.

CHAPTER 10

I wake up in the center of the bed, lying on my stomach. Rising up, I twist my head to look at the clock on the bedside table. It reads 8:49 a.m. This is a typical time for me on a Saturday morning. I'm pretty lazy on the weekends.

I roll out of bed and walk over to his dresser drawers to borrow some clothes. I settle on a black Ralph Lauren T-shirt and his black boxer briefs. The shirt is big and swallows me. I roll the band on the boxer briefs so they don't fall off and I go into the bathroom to pee and brush my teeth.

I feel a little stiff. After rinsing my mouth out, I leave the bathroom to find Nick. Walking into the kitchen, I see him on the back deck throwing a ball for the dogs. As I walk out the door, he turns to me. He looks happy and relaxed.

"Good morning, beautiful." He walks up to me and gives me the softest and sweetest kiss on my lips. "Someone used my toothbrush," he says while chuckling. I reach for the ball in his hand.

"Sorry, I hope you don't mind," I say, taking the ball from him. The dogs are waiting patiently. I throw it and they both run for it. Charmin is not nearly as fast as Niko. Poor girl probably never gets the ball.

"You can use anything of mine, and wear anything of mine," he says as Niko brings the ball back to him, bypassing me. My feelings aren't hurt. Taking the ball from Niko's mouth, Nick tosses it into the yard and the dogs take off after it again.

Nick comes up behind me and wraps his arms around me. "You look good in my underwear," he says, and I look back at him over my shoulder and smile.

"You don't look half bad yourself in your workout shirt and gym shorts," I say as he hugs me tightly. Nick is wearing a black sleeveless Under Armor shirt and matching black gym shorts. Man, he has nice big arms. The ink wrapped around his biceps only helps to enhance the bulging muscles.

"Are you planning on working out this morning?" I ask.

"Yes, I'm meeting Jase and Nikki at Knocked Out in about thirty. Do you want to come?" he asks while moving my hair out of the way to kiss my neck.

"Isn't that a gym for MMA fighters?" I ask, recalling him telling me his sister's name is Nikki.

I like it when he kisses that spot.

"Yeah. Do you want to come with me? You can meet my sister," he says while bending down and picking Charmin up off the ground.

"No, I have a few errands to run today. Would you drop me off at my car? I left it at Katelyn and Stacy's apartment yesterday," I say, remembering I have to pick up my stuff from my old apartment. I'm dreading going there.

"Actually, it's already in the driveway. Shane and your friend Katelyn brought it by an hour ago," he replies while petting Charmin. She is a beautiful puppy.

So, Katelyn made nice with Nick's friend? I snicker to myself.

"So why is your sister going to be there?" I ask.

He chuckles. "She's an amateur fighter so she's there more than I am," he replies while sitting the puppy on the ground next to Niko.

"Do you fight too?" I follow him inside the house, closing the door behind me. The dogs stay on the deck playing with each other.

"Not in the sense you're probably thinking. I mainly train with only Jase. He's dating my sister, so getting to kick his ass five days out of the week is how I deal with him dating her," he replies with a smile. He doesn't seem uneasy about it at all. Now the odd comment from last night makes sense. Jase really is off-limits. I don't have any brothers or sisters, but I imagine it's weird for a sibling to be dating one's friend.

"Where are my keys?" I ask. "I need to get my clothes out of my car and change," I tell him.

"I already got your things out. Everything is lying on the counter in the laundry room," he says, pointing to a room off the side of the kitchen.

"Thanks." I walk up to him and wrap my arms around his neck.

He bends down and kisses me on my lips. This man could kiss me for the rest of my life and I don't think I would tire of them.

Mmm . . .

"I'll be at Knocked Out for most of the day. Come by when you get done." He isn't asking, but I don't care. I want to see him in action, and I want to spend more time with him. I don't know where this is going, but I like him.

He releases me and heads for the front door. He turns back to face me. "There's a spare key under one of the cushions in the chair out front. Take it and lock up before you leave. Later, babe," he says, closing the door behind him.

I walk into the laundry room to find the bag with my blue jeans and fitted white shirt. I grab them along with my bra and panties, and head for the master bathroom to take a shower.

Walking in the bedroom, I lay my clothes out on the bed and walk into the bathroom. After turning the handle on the shower faucet to hot, I strip and toss Nick's clothes in the hamper while I wait for the water to reach the right temperature.

Stepping in, the water feels heavenly; I stand there, letting the heat wash over my stressed body.

My mind replays last night. I can't believe I freaked out like that. I can only imagine what Nick must think. I'm thankful he didn't bring it up this morning. That isn't a conversation I can have with him, or anybody else for that matter. Some things need to stay wrapped up for forever, and that's one of them.

Once I'm clean and toweled off from head to toe, I quickly get dressed. I still have Katelyn's riding boots, so I make my way back toward the laundry room for them. Once I have them on, I head to the front entrance of Nick's house. After locating the spare key, I exit and lock door.

Getting into my car, I start the ignition. It's obvious that Shane drove my car over; the seat is pushed all the way back and I have to adjust it.

I pull out of the driveway and head to the apartment I shared with Luke. The life I had only a few days ago. I'm dreading this and I'm praying he's not home. I'm hoping he did the one thing I told him to do and isn't there.

This is unlikely since it's only 9:30 a.m. He's probably asleep. He usually goes out with his friends on Fridays after his rounds are over.

It takes thirty minutes to reach the apartment. His car is not in the parking lot and I say a silent prayer, thanking God. I turn the ignition off and head in. Unlocking the door, I walk in and all seems quiet.

I walk into the bedroom and confirm he isn't there. "God does love me," I say out loud. I quickly go to the closet and pull out my large luggage bag.

I grab all of my clothes first, leaving the hangers on them, and toss them in the luggage case before taking it out to my car. Once it's shoved into my backseat, I head back in and finish packing the rest. It takes both of my gym bags to pack all my shoes. From the bathroom, I only grab my makeup, hair dryer and jewelry. My essentials and accessories are in their own containers, so I quickly tote everything to my car, placing them in the front seat and floorboard.

I go back inside the apartment, grabbing my two cameras

and a black and white photograph hanging on the wall. Looking behind me, I take in the apartment one last time. Luke can keep all the furniture, dishes, and bed. I hate all this traditional-style crap he picked out. I'm going to enjoy decorating a new place.

I leave my key on the coffee table and head out the door. Walking around to the front of my car, I open the trunk. I know it's called a boot, but I just can't call it that. Once I have my equipment stored away, I hear a voice yelling my name close behind me. I already know who it is before I turn around.

"What do you want, Allison?" I ask through clenched teeth. I hate her and I've never hated anyone in my life. I really don't like this feeling.

"Shannon, please talk to me. I'm sorry. I am. You're my best friend. Please talk to me," she pleads.

Is this bitch for real?

"We are no longer best friends! Hell, we are no longer friends! Of all the people to do this, I never would have imagined it would have been you!" I shout a little too loudly. I really don't like this. My neighbors can probably hear.

"I wanted to tell you about what happened. I did, honest. I just didn't know how, and then it just continued. . ."

"It was more than a one-time thing?" I ask with a dazed look, bile making its way toward my throat. I'm shocked. Yeah, Stacy made me question this for a brief moment, but Allison just confirmed it.

"I love him, Shannon, but I never meant to hurt you. I swear I didn't. I love you too. We're like sisters," she says with tears forming in the bottom of her eyes. Now, I'm pissed off. I don't care if she cries. She needs to cry. She needs to hurt the way she hurt me.

"A sister wouldn't have done this," I yell. "You two can go fuck yourselves! I don't care about Luke. You can have him. In fact, it was pretty eye-opening, walking in on him cheating, but you. . .I'll never forgive you," I say, feeling all the hurt coming back up to the surface as I yank the driver's door open. I jump in and slam the door in her face. She is lucky I'm not beating her ass right now. I shove the key into the ignition; I turn it with a quick flick of my wrist before I change my mind. One last look at her, and I see Allison is still crying. I hear her ask me not to leave, to stay and talk to her. She is whimpering out an "I'm sorry," as I pull out of the parking lock. What she doesn't understand is that what she did, what they did together is unforgivable!

It's only 11:30, still morning, and I don't want to go see Nick angry, so I decide to go shopping for a few hours. Buying new things always brightens my day. I head to the strip mall. The same one my gallery is in.

I buy more lingerie at Dentelle. A girl can never have too many panties. I walk past a trendy dog store and decide to go in, thinking I might get a few treats for Niko and Charmin. I walk down each aisle, grabbing things I like.

I leave, having purchased a bag of dog treats, another ball—so they each have one—two huge, plush dog pillows and two new collars. I noticed Niko's looked old and Charmin doesn't even have one. How is he going to take her on a walk if she doesn't have a collar?

After stopping by Starbucks to get a Mocha Frappuccino

Grande, I go by the gallery to check on Jenny. I walk in carrying all my bags and coffee.

I see her helping Mr. Chaney with his order. I think it's the framed photograph she was wrapping up on Thursday afternoon. He's been a client of mine for a few months now. He has at least three of my photos in his home, and one in his office. This will make his fifth.

He and Jenny look at me when I walk in through the door. Jenny is surprised to see me, and it's showing across her face. I'm never here on Saturday unless she's sick or on vacation. "What are you doing here?" she asks.

"I was shopping. Decided to stop by," I reply with a shrug of my shoulders. "Hello, Mr. Chaney." I turn, greeting the customer. "How are you today?" I ask as I set my heavy bags on the counter.

"Shannon, will you please call me Jeffery? I hate it when you call me Mr. Chaney. It's too formal. You make me think we aren't friends," he says while walking up to me and giving me a tight hug. Awkward. I pat him on the back, like I would a dog. I didn't realize we were friends. He is always sweet to me, probably only a few years older too, but as a client, I prefer to call him by this surname. Plus, he's always a little too touchy-feely, so I don't want him to get the wrong impression.

"Sorry, Jeffery, I'll remember next time," I say, taking a step back from him. I turn my attention to Jenny. "So is everything good? Do you need anything from me while I'm here?"

"No. I have it covered. You go and enjoy your day off," she says while handing Jeffery a receipt.

I grab my bags from the counter and Jeffery takes them from

me. "Let me help you with those," he says, but doesn't wait for my okay before he is walking out the door.

I follow him, waving bye to Jenny behind me. "Jeff, really I can tote them. My car is only parked over there," I say, pointing straight down the parking aisle in front of my gallery. He gives me a questionable look. I don't think he likes me calling him Jeff. Oh, well, what's a girl to do! It's what I do. I shorten everyone's name, everyone except Katelyn. She is not a fan of "Katie," or any version thereof. He opens the door for me.

"Nonsense, it wouldn't be gentlemanly of me if I didn't carry them to your car," he says while stepping off the sidewalk and walking in the direction of my car.

"I'm in the black Porsche," I say as I unlock the passenger side door, and let him put everything in the seat. There is no room in my trunk or back seat. "Thank you for your help," I say, shutting the door.

"What are all your things doing in your car? Are you moving?" he asks as he follows me around to the driver's side. *Hmm. . .personal much!*

"I moved out of my apartment this morning," I reply without going into detail.

"Oh? I noticed you aren't wearing an engagement ring any longer. Did you and what's his name. . .it starts with an 'L' I think—" he says, but I finish his sentence because I want to get out of here quickly.

He's being too friendly and getting too personal for my liking. He's attractive, but not my type. Although, no one else is my type since Nick came into the picture. Jeffery is tall and lean with blond hair and deep gray eyes. I don't like his eyes. There chilling color sends a shiver down my spine when I look into them. They make me remember things I've pretended didn't happen for a very long time.

"It's Luke," I finally tell him. "And yes, we broke up a few days ago," I finish while opening my door.

"Shannon," he coos my name as he places his hand on my shoulder. I turn around to face him. And here's that uncomfortable feeling I get when I'm in his presence alone. "When you get over him, I'd like to take you out for dinner," he states, rather than asks. What he doesn't know is that I'm already over Luke.

"I'm kind of seeing someone already," I say because it's somewhat true and I'm currently staying with him. I really have to get an apartment quickly. Nick is going to get tired of seeing so much of me.

"Already?" he draws out. "Is it serious?" he asks, still touching my shoulder, and still making me uncomfortable. I start to squirm. I hate these types of situations. Especially when the guy isn't taking no for an answer, but I can't lie. Nick and I aren't serious. At least, I don't think so. We just met.

"No, it's not, but I want to see where it's going," I say, sounding like I'm making excuses for myself. In a way, I am, but I wouldn't want to go to dinner with him even if there was no Nick.

"Well, the offer is on the table," he says and pulls out a card and hands it to me. "My cell number is on the back should you reconsider. Have a lovely day, Shannon," he tells me right before he turns on his heel and walks away. I take his card and stick it in the back pocket of my jeans.

I rush inside my car and take a deep breath. Those eyes give me the creeps. There's no chance in hell I'd go on a date with him. I push him out of my mind and start the ignition.

Pulling out of the parking lot, I head in the direction of Knocked Out. The drive is only about twenty minutes from my gallery. I'm hungry. I hope Nick hasn't had lunch yet.

I arrive, get out of my car, and walk into the building. The gym is large and the main area is open. There is a boxing ring, a steel cage, lots of weights, and punching bags scattered around.

"You must be Shannon." I hear a soft feminine voice say from behind me. When I turn around, I find an attractive woman with long, wet, dark-brown hair standing in front of me. She has intense, fiery blue eyes; the same eyes Nick has. In fact, she looks just like him, only the female version. I assume this must be his sister, Nikki.

"What gave that away?" I ask as she approaches me. Her smile matches Nick's. She's about my height and size. She's wearing a tight-fitted, white, sleeveless shirt and long, black gym pants. On her wrists, I notice some ink, but I don't want to come off as staring so I don't try to read what the tattoo says. I do, however, catch the ink on her right upper arm. It's a beautiful scene of small and medium-size black birds. They look like they are flying away. I get the sense of freedom and peace etched on her arm.

"He told me to come get him if a hot redhead walked in." She places her hands on her hips. "I'm Nikki by the way."

"Nice to meet you, Nikki. So where's your brother?"

"He's over there, beating the shit out of my boyfriend." She smirks, pointing to the cage with two men inside.

Fuck, that's hot! Nikki starts to walk in the direction of the cage and I follow.

"Hey, Nick, your girl's here," Nikki yells as we approach the cage. Nick looks in my direction and smiles. He immediately receives a punch in the mouth from Jase.

"Thanks, baby," Jase says without taking his eyes off Nick. Jase and Nick stop and exit the cage. Nick immediately comes up to me and pulls me into a passionate kiss. His kiss has a metallic taste. There's a small amount of blood in the corner of his mouth. I'm guessing this is where Jase hit him. He has a little blood on his bicep too, but I don't think it's his. Jase is bleeding a little from the side of his eyebrow.

"Nick, get off the girl. You're going to get her sweaty and bloody," Nikki says, throwing a disgusted look at her brother.

He releases me and grabs a towel. "It's my sweat and blood, so who gives a fuck," he says to his sister.

"Maybe she does," Nikki retorts.

"She doesn't," he replies, walking up to me to towel off the small amount of blood he left from the kiss. Strangely, I don't mind. His sweat and blood taste rather good. *Why does this not gross me out?*

"Nick, have you eaten lunch yet? I'm starving," I say when he removes the towel from my mouth.

"Holy shit, he lets you call him Nick?" she asks, looking at me and laughing hysterically. "He's never let anyone get away with that except me," she says, continuing to laugh uncontrollably.

"Fuck off, Nikki." Nick glares at his sister.

"Get off the man's back, Nikki. He can't help it if he's pussy whipped after two days," Jase says, taking the towel Nikki is holding out for him.

"Fuck you," Nick responds, eyeing Jase. Jase and Nikki laugh. He turns to me. "Yes, I could eat. Let me shower and we'll get out of here," he says, and leans down to kiss my forehead. He walks off in the direction of the back of the building.

Fifteen minutes later, he emerges and looks killer wearing a white Ralph Lauren polo shirt, jeans that fit perfectly, and sneakers. This man is hot.

Hot like sin I tell you.

"Let's go, babe," he says while guiding me to the door.

FIFTEEN MINUTES LATER, WE ARE SETTLING INTO a booth in a small pub. He orders a Heineken and I go with a Red Stripe. He hands me a menu and I scan it deciding on a grilled chicken club sandwich with honey mustard and chips.

The waiter returns with our drinks and I tell him my order. Nick orders the same thing, but without honey mustard. "So what did you have to do today?" he asks after taking a long pull of his beer.

"Did some shopping, stopped by work to check on Jenny, and then I got all my things from my apartment...or former apartment I guess I should say," I reply with a small laugh and take a small sip of my own beer. It's cold and feels nice sliding down my throat.

"You what?" he says, looking concerned. "You didn't go there alone, did you?" A look of shock forms across his face.

"Yes, of course I did. I used to live there and needed my things," I say and take another sip. Maybe I should have left the last part out of my story. No, it would have come up later when he saw all the stuff in my car.

"Why didn't you fucking tell me? I would have gone with you," he barks. I think he's getting angry with me.

Really?

"I didn't need anyone's help. What's the big effin' deal?" I ask. My tone is a bit of a bark too, but I want him to get my point. I'm an adult and I don't need a bodyguard.

"What's the big deal? Are you serious? That asshole assaulted you—twice. That's the big fucking deal." The last part is said through clenched teeth.

"Calm down and drink your beer. You look like you need it." I can't believe he's acting like this, but then again, I really don't know him all that well. "Luke didn't assault me. Well, not really, or at least not intentionally. The first night he was pretty drunk, and yesterday, well, I wouldn't call a scratch an assault."

"I'm not going to calm down, and yes, he did assault you," he says as he's balling a fist.

"Fine, next time I'll ask you to go with me so you can hold my hand." I don't hold back my sarcasm.

"There won't be a next time," he says as he tosses the entire half a glass of beer down his throat.

The waiter brings our food and we eat in silence. Nick seems to be calming down, so I'm going to keep quiet. I would probably say something smart-mouthed and piss him off.

I finish my meal and down the last of my second beer. Nick pays the bill and we walk out. Or rather, I walk out and he follows behind me. When I get to the car and reach for the door, he stops me and turns me to face him.

"I'm sorry, okay? I just don't want you to get hurt. The thought makes me crazy," he says. He pushes the hair off my shoulder and bends to kiss right below my ear. He can't reach his favorite spot on my neck because my T-shirt comes up too high, but he seems to like this spot just fine.

"Forgive me?" he asks.

"Yes," I murmur, closing my eyes, letting his kisses wash over me. It's warm and heavenly, and I want to melt into his arms. All is forgotten. He pulls away and opens the door for me. I get in. He closes the door and walks to the driver's seat. Once inside, he starts the ignition.

"I'm going to drop you off at Knocked Out so you can get your car, then let's go home," he says, and I nod in agreement.

Home? His home. Not mine. But I feel so comfortable in his home and that's a little scary. I don't need to stay there too much longer. I need a place to call my own. It will be good for me. I've never lived alone. I went from living at my mother's, to a college dorm, and then moving in with Luke. I like to think I'm an independent person, but am I?

ARRIVING BACK AT HIS HOUSE, I PARK next to his car. I get out and grab the stuff from the passenger seat. Nick walks over to take my belongings from the back seat.

"You can leave that stuff in there. There's no point in pulling it out just to put it back when I move into a new apartment next week," I say while walking to the front door.

"Who says you're going anywhere?" he replies while coming up behind me and unlocking the front door.

Following him inside, I walk to the kitchen to place the bags on the counter. He doesn't follow; instead, he takes my bags to his bedroom. I unpack where I am, just my few bits and pieces I've brought in with me. I put my clothes on the counter in the laundry room. I need to wash all my things. I need to get the scent of my old life off my clothes.

I let the dogs in and sit on the couch, waiting for Nick. Niko jumps on one end of the couch and curls up. I pick Charmin up, place her in my lap and start petting her. It's only about five o'clock in the afternoon, but it's already been a long day.

First dealing with Allison's drama, then being hit on and asked out by a client who weirds me out every time he's around, and then Nick freaking out at the pub.

What next?

Four days ago, my life seemed simple and free of drama. A picture-perfect life, or so I thought. How wrong I was.

I lie back on the comfy couch with Charmin in my arms. I shut my eyes while I wait on Nick who seems to be taking forever in his bedroom.

When I open my eyes back up and look out the window, it's dark. I must have fallen asleep for at least a few hours. When I sit up, I see Nick sitting in a chair, staring at me. He's holding a small glass of amber liquid. I look to my right and Charmin is now curled up with Niko on the other end of the couch. I beam from ear-to-ear. They are so cute. Beautiful really.

"How long was I asleep?" I ask, placing one leg underneath

my butt, getting comfortable on the couch. The way he's watching me makes me nervous, much like the first night I met him.

"About three hours," he says, still looking at me. He downs the rest of his drink, but he doesn't stop watching me with his intense blue eyes.

"What have you been doing?" I ask as he stands and walks to the couch. He kicks off his shoes and takes a seat in the corner of the couch. He gets completely on the couch, feet and all.

"Watching you," he says as he pulls me back to lean against his chest. I lay my head back against his shoulder and inhale his scent. I could overdose on this man.

"For three hours?" I question, not believing him. Who in the hell watches someone that long, and why?

"No. Only about half an hour." I can tell he's not joking. It's a bit weird. I don't think I've ever just watched someone. Then again, I've never been around someone this beautiful, so maybe I'll give it a try. Yeah, probably not. I just don't get it.

"Glad I could be your entertainment," I say. I turn on my side and wrap my arms around his waist. I snuggle into him and get comfortable. His body is hard and his arms wrap around me tightly. I know he's only squeezing me a fraction of his strength, but it's like he is holding me and never going to let go. I don't want him to.

"Oh, I'm always entertained when you're around," he says, kissing the top of my forehead. "So what's all the stuff on the island about?" he asks and I glance over the couch to the kitchen.

All the dog stuff I bought is laid neatly out, covering the entire kitchen island. I rise up off Nick, get off the couch, and walk into the kitchen. "I'm sorry. I probably should have asked first. I didn't think when I bought these," I say apologetically.

He walks up behind me, wrapping his around arms around my neck, looking down at everything. "It's fine. I'm just not sure why it's all needed," he says, gesturing to the pet items.

I pick up the large black dog collar and fiddle with it. "I walked past a dog store and decided to go in and buy treats. Then I remembered Charmin isn't wearing a collar, and Niko's is a bit old, so I bought them. Then when I passed the beds, I remembered I didn't see any in your bedroom and got those too," I say, taking the tag off.

Touching one of the pillows, Nick laughs a little. "They've never complained about the carpet in there," he says. He seems amused.

"Now they never will," I reply with a smile as Nick removes the tag from Charmin's collar.

"Pink—not exactly the color I would have picked out," he says sarcastically as he walks to the living room where the dogs are still on the couch.

I follow, taking Niko's collar with me. "She's a girl," I point out. "The color will stand out next to her white fur. She's going to look pretty."

"Yeah, well, now she is officially your dog. I'm not claiming her while she's wrapped in pink," he says seriously while fastening the collar around her neck. She jumps off the couch and starts scratching at it. She doesn't like it.

I laugh at her. She looks so cute trying to get it off. "She can't be taken away from Niko. He loves her."

"She's not going anywhere." I look up at his remark. What does he mean by that? He couldn't possibly be insinuating I'm not leaving either. No, that is just crazy.

I change the subject. I don't want to get into this, nor think about what I think he means. "I'm going to get my pajamas out of my car." I grab my keys from the counter.

"Your pajamas aren't in your car. They're in the bottom drawer of my dresser," he says casually. *Did he just move me in?* No, he wouldn't; he couldn't.

I turn on my heel to face him. "What else did you bring in?" I place my hands on my hips, waiting for his answer.

"Everything that was in your car," he says as he walks to the refrigerator and gets a beer out. After opening it, he tosses the top in the trash and takes a long sip.

Does he not realize I'm going to have to repack everything in a few days when I move into an apartment? Perhaps a condo? An investment isn't a bad idea while rates are so low.

"Nick, I didn't want to repack everything next week." I sound a little harsh.

"Why would you have to repack anything next week?" He takes another long sip and finishes his beer. Tossing it in the trash, he gets another one.

"Bringing all my stuff in your house was pointless. I have to find an apartment on Monday. I don't live here." I pass by him, going to the refrigerator. I need a beer after this conversation.

"Now you do," he says, opening his second beer; he tosses the cap in the trash. I freeze for a moment, standing in front of the refrigerator with the door open.

"Now I do what?" I ask, not so sure I want his answer. Shit, I'm pretty damn sure what he is insinuating, but I have no idea why.

"Now you live here, so go shower and change. The pizza I ordered while you were asleep will be here shortly." He takes another sip of his beer. He looks a little annoyed that I'm questioning him.

"Excuse me?" It's all I can manage to say. He's lost his damn mind. That has to be it. Why would he move me in? We've known each other for two seconds.

"Shannon, I don't want to argue. Just go shower or change, or do both, but hurry up." He is definitely annoyed. This is too much, but I'm too tired to fight him on it. I want normal, sexy Nick back, not crazy, sexy Nick.

"Fine, I'll be back in fifteen minutes," I huff as I exit the kitchen walking to his bedroom.

CHAPTER 11

The shower was needed and felt so good on my tired body. Walking out of the bathroom into his bedroom, I head for the dresser to retrieve some clothes.

I open the drawer and pull out my black Victoria's Secret crop pants that have PINK spelled out across my butt in pink font and a pink, solid racer-back tank top. I find my underwear in the top drawer. I let my towel pool to the floor and I dress, but I don't bother with a bra. I hate wearing them at night and I want to be comfy.

Hearing the doorbell, I assume the pizza has arrived. I walk back into the bathroom and brush my hair into a ponytail. All my bathroom products have been put into their place. I'm still in shock. I just don't understand the man.

Nick is calling my name as I make my way to the kitchen. As I enter, Nikki and Jase are both sitting Indian-style on top of the granite island. Jase is sipping on a beer and Nikki is taking her first bite of pizza. Suddenly, I remember I'm not wearing a bra. I grab my boobs.

"Oh, shit," I say, announcing my arrival. They both turn to look at me as Nick is walking in the back door.

"Sorry, I didn't realize other people were here. I'm going to go put on more clothes."

"Don't change on my account. I think you look great," Jase laughs out. I hear Nick curse under his breath, but loud enough for everyone to hear. I turn on my heel and head back to the bedroom, embarrassed.

Walking into the bedroom, I quickly grab my only bra out of the top drawer and put it on. I walk into the closet and find a pair of flip-flops on the shoe rack.

Walking back into the kitchen, I head straight for the pizza. I'm hungry. Once I take my first bite, I get a beer out of the refrigerator and hand it to Nick to open. My hands are full with my pizza and I have no intention of setting it down.

"I thought you were going to put on more clothes," Nick says, eyeing me up and down. He's barking up the wrong tree if he thinks I'm going to change to appease him. If there was approved attire for hanging out, then he should have told me his best friend and sister were coming over.

"I did." I take my beer from him and take a sip. Nothing is better than pizza and beer. I stand in front of him and he wraps his arm around my shoulders. The tension I felt from our earlier conversation is gone. It feels like heaven when his skin touches mine.

"Get off her case, Nick. She looks hot." Nikki kicks his leg from the granite island where she is sitting. She barely grazes his.

Jase hops off, tosses his empty bottle of beer in the trash, and grabs another from the refrigerator. "Dude, let's go play pool. I owe you an ass kicking." He walks out of the kitchen.

Nick releases his arms from my shoulder, leans down, and kisses my neck. "Come watch?" It's more of a question than a demand.

"She's staying with me. There's finally another girl I want to be around. You and Jase run along." Nikki is shooing her brother out of the kitchen with a hand motion.

Nick laughs as he walks down the hall. *Damn, his ass looks fine in those jeans.* Maybe I *could* watch a person for hours, if that person is him. I smile as he rounds the corner and is out of sight. I take another piece of pizza from the box. The pepperoni and cheese melt in my mouth.

"So, has he moved you in yet?" I stop mid-chew and look at Nikki. She crosses her legs Indian-style on the island countertop and looking at me with a devious wide smile.

I finish chewing my pizza and swallow. I know my face must match the color of my hair. Does he do this often with women he's sleeping with?

"No, of course not. I have a couple of appointments next week to look at apartments." This is a lie, but I don't want his sister thinking I'm some kind of leach. Come Monday, I will be looking for a new place.

I grab my beer and down the rest of the contents in one gulp. I must steer this conversation in another direction. I think she senses the awkwardness in the room.

"So I hear your second book will be out soon," she says while hopping off the countertop to grab the pizza box; she tosses it in the trash.

"There isn't a release date yet, but it's complete. I turned everything in yesterday."

How does she know about my book?

Nikki and I continue talking. I have a great conversation with her. We learn we're both addicted to Starbucks. We share the same love for music. Papa Roach being my favorite band and Metallica being hers. We both agree *Pulp Fiction* is the best movie ever made. But my fun is short-lived.

"What the hell is this?" Nick asks as he's walking back into the kitchen. I look over at him to see he's holding something small and thin between his fingers. It looks like a card. As he nears, I see it's the business card Jeffery gave me earlier today.

What the hell!

It seems like he blows a gasket every time I turn around. Apparently, Sparky is making another appearance. He holds the card out and in front of my face.

"It's nothing," I tell him. And really, it's not, or at least it's not his business. "A client of mine gave it to me earlier today."

"Jeffery fucking Chaney is a client?" His voice is one of disbelief. "And why the hell did he need to give you his cell phone number?" Nikki's eyes widen with concern when Nick pronounces Jeffery's name, making me curious about Nick's beef with the man. Nick is furiously mad. I can see written on his face. The veins in his neck are straining against his tight, olive skin. I'm hoping this is about

Jeffery himself and nothing more. I won't deal with a jealous man.

"Nick, calm down. It's nothing, really. He was at the gallery when I stopped by today. He noticed I wasn't wearing an engagement ring any longer and asked me to dinner. It's not a big deal."

His eyes darken and he crushes the card in his hand.

"What the fuck did you tell him?" He steps closer, caging me in with his arms. He places both hands palm down on the granite behind me and looks down at me. He's searching my eyes for something.

"I politely turned him down. There is no reason for you to get this mad."

Nikki hops off the counter giving me a sympathetic look. Jase walks in the kitchen and grabs Nikki by the elbow.

"Nikki, I think we should go." Jase is lightly pulling her by the arm.

"Jeez, Nick, maybe you should just let this go. Jeffery isn't worth your time of day," Nikki tells him while yanking her arm free from Jase's grasp. She glares at her boyfriend briefly before turning her attention back toward Nick.

"And maybe you should do what your boyfriend says and get out of my house." Nick doesn't look at his sister as he says this. He continues to stare down at me. His eyes are full of anger.

"I'm going to pretend you didn't say that to me and leave, jerk off." If eyes could throw daggers, Nick would have plenty in the back of his head the way Nikki is looking at him. She storms off past Jase, and I hear the door slam a few seconds later.

"There is no reason to get this mad," I repeat. What's his

problem with Jeffery?

"Oh, I'm far past mad right now." He takes a half a step back and reaches into his pocket, pulling out his cell.

"What are you doing?" I'm pretty sure I know exactly what he's about to do, and I can't let him do this. Jeffery is a client, a really good client, if I ignore the "too friendly" side of him.

"I'm taking care of this. He needs to know who the fuck you belong to." He is dialing the number already.

Oh, no. He didn't just go there.

Now, I'm way past mad. Who the hell does he think he is! "I'm not a piece of property, Nick. You don't own me." I try to reach for his phone, but it's useless. He holds me back.

"It's Lockhart. Stay the fuck away from Shannon. Is. That. Clear?" His breathing is heavy and his eyes widen. I can't hear the other half of his conversation.

"Because she is mine, so stay away from her, Chaney." He ends the call.

Shocked doesn't even begin to cover what I'm feeling. I don't know what to say or do. What the hell was that about? "You care to explain that?"

I cross my arms over my chest and glare at him, waiting for an answer. I take a couple calming breaths. Maybe there's a reasonable explanation. I'm not seeing one at the moment, but I'm going to give him the benefit of the doubt.

"Because you are mine, and if he comes near you again, I will break his fucking neck." He slams his phone on the counter and storms off to his bedroom.

Yep, still standing here in shock. What the hell just happened?

This is beyond crazy. This is something completely different. I'm not sure I want or need to be around this man. I hear the water from the shower come on as I make my way into his room. The bathroom door is closed so I don't see him.

Should I stay, should I go? I could go to Stacy and Katelyn's, but I don't know where he's put all my things, and by the time I pack, he'll probably be out of the shower. I need time to think, and I can't think here with him.

I grab my tennis shoes and decide to go for a walk. Walking or running always clears my head and I definitely need a clear head right now.

BY THE TIME I MAKE IT BACK, I know I've been gone awhile, maybe even an hour. The walk helped calm me down, but did nothing to help me decide anything about Nick's behavior. The only thing that will help that is talking with him, but I have no idea what to say.

I walk in the front door and come face-to-face with a hole the size of a fist punched in the wall in the foyer. Oh, my God. Did he seriously do that? A shit load of red flags go up.

I shut the door and I turn to see Nick walking toward me from the living room. He looks panicked and worried. Guess I should have left a note.

"Where have you been? I've been going out of my Goddamn mind for almost an hour. I called your cell, but it was here. Your car is here. Everything is here, except you." He grabs me, pulling my head to his chest and takes a deep sigh. It's like he's relieved.

"I just went for a walk to think and clear my head." I wrap my arms around his waist. I know I should be mad, but when he's holding me or touching me, I just seem to relax; this is where I want to be. I don't know why. I've known him less than a week, but I don't want to leave. I'm letting myself grow too accustomed to him and his damn touch.

"Please, don't leave without telling me where you're going. I was worried. Really. Worried." He tightens his hold on me.

"Did you punch a hole in the wall because you're mad at me?" Please say it wasn't me, but even I know that's wishful thinking. He loosens his grip and places his hands on both sides of my face. He leans down and kisses my forehead.

"Yes, I punched a hole in the wall, but I'm not mad at you. I came out and I couldn't find you. I thought you left and the wall was there. I'm sorry. I—"

"It's okay." No, it's not okay, but I cut him off anyway. I don't want him to finish explaining. What have I gotten myself into?

"Why don't we go to bed and forget this happened? Deal?" I ask, sighing. I look up at him, waiting for a response. He takes a deep breath.

"Sure." His lips turn up in a small smile, but it looks forced. He grabs my hand and leads me to his bedroom. The talk I want to have isn't much of a talk at all. I walk to the closet and remove my bra, tennis shoes and socks.

Walking back to the bed, I remove my sweatpants and climb in. Nick is already in the bed naked. I realize this when I lift the covers, sliding under. He grabs my waist, pulling me closer to him so my back is to his front. He slides his arm under my tank top, but doesn't move farther up than my ribs. He kisses my ear lightly while holding me tightly against his chest.

"I know I overreacted and I'm sorry." He tightens his hold on me and inhales a deep breath in my hair.

I hesitate for a second, not sure I should push him, but I want to know why. "Why don't you like Jeffery Chaney?"

He's quiet for a long time, and I don't think he's going to answer. "I've known him a long time. He's a lunatic."

"Meaning what exactly?" I ask.

He's quiet again, but after a few seconds, he sighs deeply. "Just let it go, and promise me you won't see him again. I don't care that he's a client."

"Nick, you aren't telling me anything. I can't just drop a client. I mean, it's not like I'm a friend of the man. This shouldn't be a big deal."

I feel his body go tight. He doesn't like what I said, but he isn't telling me anything. I don't want to argue again. I need to distract him so he will let this go. I rise up on my hands and knees, and then crawl on top of him. He places his hands on my hips and gives me a sinister look.

"I think you will look a lot better out of this tank top," he says as he's gathering the bottom and pushing it up. I pull it over my head and toss it behind me. I lean forward and kiss him on the mouth.

"Panties off, now," he demands.

Jackpot.

It worked.

CHAPTER 12

I wake up to a puppy whining beside the bed. *Ughhh, hush please.* I need more sleep after Nick thoroughly worked me over last night, and then a second time. I lift my head a little and look over to Nick's side of the bed; he is still asleep, lightly snoring. It's cute, but how does he sleep through her crying?

For the love of God, shut up!

I roll over onto my side and drape my right arm over the bed to pet her on the head. "Do you need to go outside, girl?"

Pulling back the covers, I go to get out of bed when a warm hand reaches around my waist before my feet hit the floor. Apparently, he wasn't sleeping very soundly. He rapidly pulls me back down into the bed, straddles me then pins my hands down by my head.

"Going somewhere?" His dark brown hair is disheveled, but he looks scrumptious. He has a playful, youthful smile splayed across his face, and it occurs to me I don't know how old he is.

"I was going to let the dogs out, but first I want to know how old you are."

"Thirty. Why do you want to know?" He lowers his head to my neck and lightly kisses that spot right above my collarbone he likes so much. Then he moves to the right side and repeats.

"Just curious. And your sister?" The dogs can surely hold their pee. I don't want to move. His lips feel like velvet against my skin. The sensation ends too quickly.

"Thirty," he says as he chuckles. Releasing my pinned-down arms, he gets out of bed. I rise up on my elbows and watch his hot ass walk to the closet.

"Wait. . . Are you twins?" They look a lot alike, but I never thought they were twins, plus I know he called her his little sister. He walks back into his bedroom wearing a pair of sweat pants and plain, white T-shirt. The man knows how to rock the simple look.

"No. Nikki turned thirty a month ago. I'm exactly ten months older than she is." He walks over to my side of bed and reaches out to me. I place my hands in his and he pulls my naked self out of the bed. He's kisses the corner of my mouth before releasing me.

"I'll let the dogs out and start breakfast. You need to put some clothes on that pretty little ass before my dirty mind is fully wake," he says as he starts to head out the door.

"So when is your birthday?" I ask him as I search for my discarded clothes from last night.

He pauses at the door and turns to me. "June 20th," he says and I look up. No way. *Really? No freaking way.*

"What's with the dumbfounded look?" he asks.

"That is the same day as mine. Too cool," I tell him and head into the closet carrying my dirty laundry. I toss it on the floor and faintly hear him laugh before walking out of the room.

God, I'm getting more addicted to this man every day, and I don't want to leave. But I know I have to find an apartment if we are going to continue dating. Are we even dating? It feels like dating, but neither of us has clarified. Regardless, I have to leave this heavenly house. I haven't felt like I was at home in a place or in my own skin since I was a young teenager.

After I put my tank and sweats on, I head to the bathroom to pee and brush my teeth. I notice my phone lying on the bathroom sink. I don't remember placing it there, but I scoop it up and send a text to my mom, asking for her realtor's name. I haven't told her about my breakup with Luke yet. Hopefully, she won't think anything of it. The last thing I want to hear is how much she adores Dr. Lucas Carter.

After sending her a text, I wrap up my bathroom routine and head to the kitchen where I find Nick whisking eggs in a bowl. "I hope you like omelets," he says as I hop up on the granite island next to him.

"I love eggs cooked just about any way," I say as I cross my legs Indian-style. "Is there anything I can help with?"

"Yes, you can fix me a cup of coffee." I hop off the counter. There are two coffee mugs next to a Keurig single-cup coffee maker. I position one of the mugs into place, and pop in a K-Cup of Green Mountain Coffee's Nantucket Blend.

"How do you like your coffee?" I ask as I place the other mug under the machine and repeat the process with the second cup.

"Black with a little sugar. The sugar is in the cabinet in front of you." I take the sugar out of the cabinet and scoop a tablespoon into each cup. I stir his and place it on the island behind me. I take my coffee to the refrigerator and pour in a small amount of milk since I don't see any creamer. I walk the few feet back to the island, stirring my coffee. Nick sets the large omelet on the island countertop.

"I hope we're sharing that. There is no way I can eat it all." I take a sip of my coffee.

"We are." He chuckles. I love hearing him laugh. It puts a smile on my face. I've never paid attention to someone's laugh before.

Is that weird?

We finish the omelet in no time. I didn't realize how hungry I was, but then I haven't worked up an appetite in a long time.

"So what do you want to do today?" he asks, placing the plate in the sink.

I hear my phone beep with a text message. I grab it and it's my mom responding. She sent the name of her realtor and nothing else. No, "Hi, how are you," "I miss you," "I love you." That's my mom. I love her, but to say we are not close is an understatement.

"Whatever you want, but first I need make an appointment with a realtor for tomorrow so I can find a new apartment," I say as I shoot Vicky Smith, Mom's realtor a text telling her who I am and what I'm looking for.

"What?" I snap my head up from my phone when I hear the question. He's wearing an alarmed expression. "What the fuck is wrong with my house?" he asks, waving his hand about, indicating his home.

"Your home is great and I love it, but I don't live here. Nick, I don't even know what we are." I indicate the space between the two of us. "Are we dating or is this just casual fun for you?" I place my hands on my hips. I'm pretty sure we are about to have an argument. . .yet another common theme with this man. I can't recall one argument Luke and I ever had, but with Nick, it's been something every day.

"I'm sorry. I didn't mean to snap." He runs his hands through his hair as he's eyeing me.

"I—I haven't been someone's boyfriend in a very long time. Not since high school actually, and I don't consider that a real relationship."

Wow, he's thirty and has never dated. What's wrong with him?

I wrap my arms around his waist as he cages me in against the countertop. "You're right, we haven't talked about this. Us," he says as he lifts his right hand on the counter to move his index finger in between both of us. I don't interrupt him, but I continue to stare up at him.

"I don't exactly know how to do the normal relationship thing, but there is something about you. From the moment I laid eyes on you, I knew I wanted you. Wanted to get to know you. I want all of you and I want you here. I don't want a causal relationship. I want you as mine—as my girlfriend." He's waiting for my response. Is that what I want? I just got out of a long relationship. I know in my head this is moving way too fast, but damn it, I want him too.

"Okay." I hear myself saying. I have no idea what I'm agreeing to.

"Okay, you're staying?" His lips turn up into a smile.

"Okay, I'll be your girlfriend. I've never done a casual relationship before, and I don't want that. However, if that is what we are going to do, I still can't live here." I like the sound of being his girlfriend.

"Why the hell not?" His lips quickly turn down into a frown as he pulls his eyebrows together.

"Because normal people don't start dating and move right in together, that's why." What does he not get here?

"Maybe I don't want a normal relationship. Babe, I can guarantee you I'm certainly not the normal boyfriend type. I want what I want. It's really that simple," he says back to me.

No, he's certainly not normal, and apparently, he's used to people doing what he says. I try to push him back, but he isn't having it. He's not being forceful, but he's holding his position. What is it going to take to get through to him?

"Nick, if you want this to work," I say, moving my finger back and forth just as he did a moment ago, "then we need space, and we need time to get to know each other. We need to slow us down."

He rolls his eyes, not liking what I have just told him.

"Fine, I'll concede on the apartment if it's what you want." He pauses, but I can tell he isn't done with this conversation. "You can have your own space so long as you are here with me most nights."

"Thanks for the permission," I say sarcastically, ducking under his arm.

"Babe, I don't want to argue. Tell me what you want and I'll have a furnished apartment for you by this time tomorrow." He's following me out of the kitchen into the living room.

It's my turn to roll my eyes, but he can't see me doing so. I plop down on the couch. Nick comes up and sits on the corner. He reaches for me, pulling me into his arms with my back to his chest. He's making it difficult to stay irritated. He feels too good. I lay my head back against his shoulder. I don't want to argue either. I just want to relax in Nick's warm arms, but I don't need this man coming to my rescue. I'm perfectly capable of taking care of myself and I need to make him see that.

"I can take care of it, but I bet you're used to snapping your fingers and people do what you say. Am I right?" He wraps his arms around my shoulders, hugging me, and I realize I've never felt more safe and content in my life. What is this man doing to me? He'll have me dependent on him if I'm not careful.

He laughs. "Usually the people I deal with aren't defiant. They either know that I know what's best, or understand it's going to always be my way."

"Defiant?" I snort.

"Yes, and I can tell that you and I are going to have an issue with that. You are difficult at every turn." He inhales my hair and sighs.

"If you keep using words like defiant, then yes, we are going to have issues." I turn my face and body so I can snuggle in his arms. He chuckles lightly before placing a soft kiss on the top of my head. I could get used to being here. I like the way I feel tucked against Nick's body with his arms wrapped around me.

CHAPTER 13

After a lazy Sunday at Nick's house, the next couple of weeks seem to fly by. I don't remember the last time I was ever this happy. I conceded on the house search and I let Nick have his way when he brought me to a cozy beach-front property the following Monday. Much to my irritation, the house was perfect. It's going to cost me a fortune, but the beach is totally worth it.

The house is only about 2500 square feet, but who needs a big house when the ocean is your backyard? Not me. My house has three bedrooms and two and half bathrooms with an open floor plan. It's everything I could want; it's modern but still has a warm, homey feeling.

Somehow, I managed to close in five days. I'm pretty sure Nick had something to do with that, but I decided not to question it. I'm too in love with my house to think about the negatives or the craziness. The fact I landed a house in Mali-effin-bu for a cool two million dollars is a steal. Of course, that's after the three mil I depleted out of my savings account as a down payment. I'm a good photographer, but I'm not that high in demand to make those figures. The money came from an inheritance left to me when my father died. I wasn't able to use it until I turned twenty-five. This is certainly good use of all that money.

I spent most of the first two weeks picking out furniture and accessories. After waiting on deliveries, I spent the next week arranging everything. I did not concede on that end.

Nick didn't understand.

Part of the fun of a new house is picking out all new stuff. Every day something arrives, and it's like Christmas morning, opening presents. I don't remember the last time I had this much fun. When Luke and I picked out furniture for the apartment, he whined until I gave in to what he wanted.

Jenny worked for me this past Wednesday since the store will be closed for Memorial Day weekend on Saturday, so I've had the whole week off to get my home in order. I could have been an interior designer if I didn't love photography so much. I'm so proud of me. Nope, there is no shame in that. I'd shout it from the rooftops if I could. I love what I do and work damn hard at it. By late afternoon on Friday, every space is filled.

I'm hanging my last set of black-and-white photos on a bare wall in my living room when I hear a scratching sound at the door. I pull my head in the direction of the front door where I see Nick walking through. The dogs come running in, jumping on my oversized plush chair in the living room. Niko claimed that spot his first night here. The four of us have stayed the last two nights in my new home so far. I love Nick's house, really I do, but nothing compares to living literally on the beach. It's awesome. I wake up to the sound and smell of the sea.

"Need any help?" I ask as I step down from the step stool. Nick's arms are full with grocery bags. Instead of a Friday night out with just my friends, I talked them into a cookout at my new place. They readily agreed. The house is on the small size compared to the others in my neighborhood; however, I have a huge deck. I plan to make a lot of use out of it.

"No, we have everything. You relax, babe. You've been quite the busy woman this week and you've done a great job filling it with a lot of shit," he says as Nikki walks in the door, carrying more groceries. I roll my eyes at his comment.

"Damn, can I get you to do this to my house? Shannon, everything looks great." She looks in every direction as she walks to the kitchen, following her brother. This is the first time she's been back inside since the day I closed on it. The place was completely bare last week.

I follow behind them. "Did you two buy enough food?" I ask with a hint of sarcasm as I peek into each bag.

"Just shut up and put the meat in the refrigerator. You're not the one that has to cook all this shit for everyone," Nick says, taking out multiple bottles of wine and champagne out of a brown bag. He's not being an ass. He's smiling and jacking with me. I've learned, in the last couple of days, he does and says things just to get a rise out of me. I think the man loves to start arguments.

Luke has finally stopped texting me. I guess he's got the hint that we aren't getting back together after the last message I sent him. The fucker actually called my mother, who in turn called me, trying to plead his case.

Yeah. . .really.

Apparently, she didn't see the cheating as a big deal. After she found out my new boyfriend was the CEO of a multimillion-dollar publishing company, she changed her tune. Needless to say, I hung up the phone after a five-minute conversation and haven't bothered to call her back. I haven't even told her where I've moved to.

I never told Nick about the text messages Luke kept sending me. It would have been one more thing to make him flipping mad. I've been having a pretty awesome week and didn't need anything to piss him off. Our relationship is new and fresh. I don't want any more damn drama.

"Looks like you two have everything under control. I'm going to grab a shower before everyone starts to arrive." I walk out of the kitchen and head for our bedroom. *Your room, Shannon, not yours and Nick's. Slow down. You're starting to sound just like him.*

Walking through the bedroom into the master bathroom, I turn on the shower. I quickly shed my clothes and toss them in the overflowing hamper. Somehow, my closet has accumulated more of Nick's clothes than all the clothes I own, hence why the hamper is overflowing. He changes more times a day than Stacy, and she's a prima donna. I step into the shower and wash the day's dirt away.

Even though I've been working hard at prepping my house, I still feel like I've been a slacker at work. I haven't made an appearance all week. Mainly because Jeffery Chaney has been asking for an appointment with me all week from what Jenny has told me via our phone calls. Apparently, he is remodeling his office and wants to showcase my work. Nick is going to love this. I'm not looking forward to that conversation.

Once my hair is cleaned and I've shaved, I turn off the water and step out. After drying off, I wrap the towel around my body and go to the sink where it takes nearly ten minutes to dry my hair. This is why I like the air-dry method. Less time, but I don't have the option today. Not that I plan to style it. I'm more of the comb-through-and-go type.

I walk out of the bathroom into the closet and hunt for an outfit. No dress for tonight. I'm at home, and I want to be comfortable. I opt for a pair of dark blue jeans, my fitted Avenged Sevenfold T-shirt, and complete my ensemble with black Yellow Box flip-flops.

Perfect.

I finish up and head back in the bathroom to apply a light layer of makeup and I'm good to go. Why women feel the need to pile on tons of makeup is beyond me. All that shit makes me feel like I need to wash my face, so I opt for minimal.

As I walk back into the bedroom, I see Niko and Charmin curled up at the foot of our . . . I mean, my bed. Good thing I bought the doggy stairs for the bed, much to Nick's annoyance. Charmin would not have been able to get up there if I hadn't.

They aren't used to a lot of noise or people, so since they are in here instead of out there with Nick, I imagine people have started to gather. I notice the bedside clock reads 6:58 p.m. as I'm walking out of the room. Sure enough, more of my friends have filtered in.

As I walk out the backdoor, I see Nick at the grill cooking, and it smells wonderful. Jase is standing next to him talking and drinking a beer. Nikki, Stacy, Ben, and Kyle are hanging out talking in the lounge area of the deck. Katelyn is hanging onto Shane's arm with a beer in her other hand. Since when does she drink beer? Yeah, something is going on with those two and I mean to find out what it is.

I walk to where they are standing next to the railing. "And what are you two up to over here?" I ask, giving Katelyn a knowing look.

"Just talking," Katelyn says, returning my look that clearly says "Why the hell are you interrupting us?"

Shane breaks our stare. "I'm going to go hang out with my boys," he says and gives Katelyn a peck on the cheek. As he is walking away, she can't keep her eyes off his backside.

I snap my fingers in front of her face, saying, "Got it bad, do we?"

She rolls her eyes and takes a sip of her beer. "Like you're one to talk. You've been shacked up with dreamy eyes for over two weeks now. I wasn't sure you even remembered you had friends."

Touché.

"He must lay some serious pipe," she adds, and I bust out into giggles. *God does he ever.* Just thinking about his pipe makes my face flush scarlet red.

"So I hit that head on the nail, huh?" She snickers. I don't respond, but she already knows the answer. I snatch her beer and take a sip.

"What's up with you and Mr. Tall, Dark, and Oh So Sexy?" I ask as I hand her beer back to her.

"Girl, I don't remember the last time my girly parts have seen so much action." She can't stop glancing at him. I move beside her and we both lean back against the railing, staring at the men.

"That good, huh?" I ask as I reach for her beer again and take another sip.

"Fuck yes," she declares, snatching her beer back and downing the rest of its contents.

"Come on, let's go hang out with the others." We both pop off the railing at the same time and walk over to the seating area where Nikki, Stacy, Ben, and Kyle are still talking. Apparently, they are discussing Knocked Out when I take a seat on Ben's lap. Katelyn crunches in the middle of Stacy and Nikki on the couch.

"Did you know Nikki owns Knocked Out?" Ben asks me.

"No, I did not," I answer. That is cool. Perhaps I'll switch gyms if Nick doesn't mind. I saw a few people boxing when I was there a few weeks ago. I've been so busy with the house that I haven't been to a boxing class since I met Nick.

"You know Shannon boxes," Kyle chimes in talking to Nikki.

"Really?" Nikki says looking at me. She sounds excited. "That's awesome. Tomorrow you have to come up there and show me how good you are."

"Sure, but it's been a couple of weeks. I probably suck already." I doubt I suck, but no need to boast in front of a professional. I'm pretty sure she could kick my ass in less than five seconds.

"Shannon doesn't suck. She's been boxing since high school," Stacy tells her. Like she knows how good I am. None of my friends have seen me box before, so I'm not sure why she thinks I'm good.

"I only do it for a great workout to stay in shape," I lie to all of them. Really, I do it so I don't feel helpless and weak again. That's not something I ever want to face again. I shut that awful thought out of my mind and get off Ben's lap when I see Nick walking in my direction. I meet him halfway.

"Beer?" he asks, holding a Rolling Rock out in front of me.

"Yes. Thank you." I happily take it and down half the bottle. There are just some things that should stay buried deep in the past.

The rest of the night goes great. The food is outstanding and my friends are getting along great with Nick's. Things couldn't be more perfect than in this moment.

CHAPTER 14

"*P*lease, never let me drink that much ever again," Nikki begs from the back seat of Nick's car where she is lying across the seat, covering her eyes with her arm. She got a little drunk last night. . .well, a lot drunk last night. After Nick took me to the amateur fight night to watch one of Jase's fights, the four of us went to Club Blue where Nikki got sloshed. Jase won the fight; so apparently, she wanted to celebrate for her man. I don't think she is in much of a celebratory mood now.

We are on the way to Nick and Nikki's parents' house in Pasadena for a Memorial Day dinner. Perhaps I'm a little nervous, but really, I just want to get this part of dating out of the way. Maybe that is why I agreed to come with them as quickly as I did last night. How bad could meeting the parents go?

Nick made his mom sound like an angel, but the way he and Nikki described their dad, you would think the man was the devil himself. My dad died when I was very young, so I never really had a father figure in my life. I've never been able to relate to other friends and their relationships with their dads. I have a few memories of the man, and luckily, all are good, but when it comes to the fatherly authority, I'm clueless. I was never grounded while growing up like all my friends were for breaking curfew or bad grades. I was never the bad kid, but my mom didn't have a clue what was going on in my life. I could come and go as I pleased as long as I stayed out of trouble. Most kids would dream of a life like that, but really, I longed for attention from my mother.

"Why you got wasted last night when you knew we were coming here today is beyond me. You know Dad's going to say something about it and that's going to piss you off," Nick tells his sister as we pull into a driveway of a massive two-story house. If this is the house they grew up in, I understand why Nick doesn't like big houses. This place is huge and could easily be in an architecture magazine. I hate it immediately.

Nick turns off the ignition and grabs my forearm as I'm reaching to open the door. "If you feel uncomfortable in the least bit, just say the word and we'll leave."

He has an apologetic look on his face. Surely, his dad isn't that bad. "He's serious, Shannon. In fact, the sooner we leave, the better for all of us. These gatherings never end happy," Nikki chimes in as she is righting herself.

"Okay, but I'm sure it's not going to be that bad. Surely, I can get through a few hours in your parents' company," I say as I open the door.

"It's not our parents who are the problem. It's just our dad," she adds as I'm pushing the seat forward so she can get out. The three of us head for the front door. Nikki leads the way and I'm holding Nick's hand as we all make it up the steps to the house. Nikki doesn't bother knocking and walks right in.

The first thing I notice off to the side of the foyer is a large formal dining room with the largest table I've ever seen. Yes, I definitely dislike this house, but it hits me that it's not the house. Something just isn't sitting well with me. You know that feeling you get when you are in the wrong place and all your senses are screaming at you to leave—to get the fuck out? That's the feeling I'm having at this very moment. The hairs on the nape of my neck and arms lift, prickling over my skin.

I push the feeling out of my mind as we make our way through the foyer and enter the kitchen. I'm sure it's just my nervousness at meeting his parents for the first time.

"I thought I heard you guys come in the door," a petite, older woman with dark hair says. She has a wide smile on her face as she embraces Nikki in a hug. She must be their mom. She has the same stunning blue eyes Nick and Nikki have. Nick releases my hand to give his mother a kiss on the cheek.

"Food smells great, Mom," Nick tells her as he reaches for me. "This is my girlfriend, Shannon," he says as I'm pulled in front of his mother. She smiles again and pulls me into a hug.

I feel awkward. Isn't it customary to shake hands in these circumstances? I know she's only being friendly, so I return the embrace and force a smile when she releases me. I don't care for the touchy-feely types.

"I've heard so much about you over the last two weeks. It's great to finally meet you. Nicholas has never brought a girl home before," she says, eyeing her son in a loving, motherly way. "I'm Elaina Lewis, but please call me Elaina. I hate all the formal stuff."

"Lewis?" I question, looking at Nick. He didn't say he had a stepdad. The way he spoke about the man, it gave the impression his parents were married to each other.

Nick shrugs. "I'll explain later, but I decided to go by my mother's maiden name a long time ago. I had it legally changed when I turned twenty-one."

"And you?" I ask turning to Nikki. She shrugs the same way as her brother, as if it's no big deal.

"I've always done everything Nick does since I can remember, so when Nick did it, there was no questioning that I would do the same." She walks to the refrigerator and takes out a bottle of water. Do they hate their dad that much that they don't want to share the same name? Surely, the man can't be that bad. Right?

Nick tightens his hold on my hand, causing me to look up at him only to find his face is set in an expression of anger. His nostrils begin to flare. He's looking behind me, and as I turn to see what's caused his change in mood, I hear a shrill voice. A voice I'm all too familiar with, a voice that I have never been able to forget. This can't be happening. Please God, tell me this is a nightmare and I'm going to wake up any minute now.

"It's about time . . ." He stops mid-sentence when his eyes met mine. He wasn't expecting me, and I certainly wasn't expecting to ever see this monster again. "Shannon." It's not a question, but a statement. He knows exactly who I am and what he did to me.

My heart starts to race. The thumping echoes in my ears as each beat bounces off my chest bone. I take a step back on reflex, only to back into Nick's hard chest. My body freezes. I'm rooted to the ground when it hits me. Lewis, his mother's last name is Lewis. She is married to James Lewis, Judge James Lewis. Oh God, no. No . . . no . . . no . . . no . . . no. He's Nick's father. This isn't a nightmare. This isn't some sick joke someone is playing on me. This is real. Beads of sweat start to form across my forehead and on the back of my neck.

"You know my father?" Nick questions, jerking his stare from his dad down to me. His eyebrows are knitted inward. He's somewhat shocked. I think his mother and sister are too. How do I explain this? I think I'm going to be sick. A wave of nausea washes over me. I swallow, trying to keep the vomit I feel rising up in my throat at bay.

"I . . ." There are no more words I can get out. They are lost in my throat. I don't know what to tell him. I don't know what to do. I can't take my eyes off the evil monster standing before me. I want to run. I have to bite down on my bottom lip in order stop the tremble I feel forming on my lips.

The bastard smiles and then breaks eye contact with me to answer Nick's question. He knows what I could say even though I won't, but he isn't going chance it.

"Shannon used to work for me back when I was an attorney. If you would have ever come by my office, you would have known that." He turns his eyes back to me. They are sinister, cold gray eyes. "What's it been now—ten years?"

"Y-yes," I finally choke out. It comes out as almost a whisper. *Get control of yourself. Do not let the sick fuck see your fear. Don't give him that satisfaction again.* I take a silent deep breath and exhale slowly, calming my bubbling anxiety.

"Small world, I guess," Nick says as he tightens his hold on my waist. His tone is clipped, and he's not happy to learn this fact. If he only knew the rest . . . Something I've never told anyone. I don't know if I can tell him, either.

Nick's mother is looking between her husband and me. She has a strange look on her face, as if she is trying to figure out the pieces of the puzzle. I doubt anyone would figure out what that man is capable of. Everyone I knew who worked for him adored him. I remember people used to say what a wonderful man he was and how caring he was for other people who had been misjudged.

"Why don't we all gather in the dining room for dinner?" his mother suggests while leading Nikki in that direction. Judge Lewis gives me a sinister look and turns, following his wife and daughter. Nick turns me to face him. I try for a weak smile.

"Are you okay? As soon as my father walked in the room, your face paled and you looked like you wanted to pass out." He's holding both of my wrists and rubbing his thumbs over the surface of my skin. Somehow, it has a calming effect on me and I relax a little. Well, as much as I possibly can in a situation like this.

"Yes. I was a little shocked at first. I wasn't expecting my former boss to be your dad." He's searching my eyes. It looks like he is trying to decipher if I'm telling him the truth. It's partly true. I was shocked.

"Are you sure? We can leave if you're uncomfortable."

Just tell him you want to leave. He's giving you an out. You should take it and run like hell.

Instead, I snap at him. "Nick, I said I'm fine, so drop it." Fuck.

I instantly regret snapping at him. I shouldn't take this out on him. I haven't had these feelings in a long time. I didn't know how to deal with them then and I still don't.

"Fine, but I can tell something is bothering you and you are going to tell me later," he says as he pulls me to the dining room. His family is already seated. Nikki has a sour look on her face. She is staring straight ahead at a wall while her dad is talking. I think he is reprimanding her, but I'm not sure. We come in on the tail end of the conversation.

"Finally, what took you both so long?" Nick's dad asks. He's looking directly at me. No, fuckface, I didn't say a damn thing to him.

"Shannon and I were having a conversation." Nick sounds annoyed as he takes a seat.

Elaina is still looking at me the same way as before in the kitchen. Does she know what her husband is capable of? Do they all? Surely, they wouldn't be sitting at a dinner table with him if they did.

Taking my napkin off the table, I place it in my lap. I begin to gather food on my plate, starting with Beef Wellington and ending with a spoonful of roast potatoes. I have no appetite, but I'd rather stuff my mouth than talk or look at the man sitting at the head of the table. I can feel his eyes on me every few minutes. It makes my stomach turn and chest tighten.

"Nicolette, can't you wear clothing to my house that covers up those awful tattoos? You used to be so beautiful. I don't understand why you enjoy embarrassing me." Nick's father's comment brings my attention away from my food. God, did he just say that to his own daughter?

"I'm going to wear what I want, Dad. If I wanted to cover up the art on my body, I never would have gotten them," she responds with a tight lip before shuffling a forkful of food into her mouth. Nick takes a deep breath, and then slowly blows the air out as if he's trying to calm himself. He looks like he wants to say something, but doesn't.

The inked artwork displayed on Nikki's arms isn't as visible as the first day I met her. The tail end of one tattoo is poking out of the short sleeve of her shirt and she has a small tattoo on each wrist. On her right wrist, the name "Jason" is spelled out in black ink, ending with a line wrapping around her wrist to draw the shape of a heart on the inside. It's colored in with deep-red ink. On her other wrist, small hearts travel around her skin like a bracelet. They also wrap around to the inside of her left wrist, which has a date scripted. I have no idea what the date represents. Other than those, nothing else is visible. She looks stunning. Even when she has all her ink on display, she is beautiful, probably even more so with all the color.

The dinner is nothing like I expected before I arrived. No one has said a single nice thing since we sat at the table. Judge Lewis finds a way in every discussion to criticize either Nick or Nikki. I can tell Elaina doesn't like it, but she never interrupts her husband, nor does she defend her children. *Way to be a great mom!*

"Thank you for dinner, Mom, but we have to be going," Nick says as he pushes himself back from the table. *Hallelujah!* His sister follows suit immediately, looking relieved to be getting out of here. I can't blame them. Hell, I wanted to run out of here an hour ago.

As I stand up from the table, I cut my eyes to Nick's father. He's sitting back in his chair at the table and drinking a glass of wine. He looks right at me, over the rim of his glass, every time he takes a sip. Nikki doesn't speak to her father after she tells her mom she'll call her next week. She quickly exits the room and I follow her as quickly as my feet will take me. Nick doesn't linger and we all make our way back to his car. As I sink down into the passenger seat, I look over at Nick. He looks like he's brooding.

On the drive back, Nick heads to Knocked Out to drop Nikki off. The way he's gripping the steering wheel I think it's going to break. If that doesn't happen, his speed is sure to get us in an accident. I think it's safe to say he is royally pissed off. He looks like he wants to smash something. I hope it's not the car.

"Nick, maybe you should drop Shannon off first and come with me to Knocked Out," Nikki says from the back seat. She has been staring at the back of Nick's head while biting her nails for about twenty minutes.

"Drop it, Nikki. I don't want to hear it," he says through clenched teeth. "I'm taking you to Jase, and then Shannon and I are going home."

"I don't think that's a good idea," she snaps at him as Nick pulls into the parking lot of the gym. He doesn't park in a parking spot. Instead, he pulls up to the front door, throwing the gear shift into park as Jase is descending the stairs.

I open my door and step out, pushing the seat forward so Nikki can get out. She doesn't move and sits back, crossing her arms in front of her. Nick whips his head around to face his sister. "Get out of the car, Nikki."

"No, not until I make you see I'm right, and you know I'm right, Nick. I know what you do when you're this mad. Do you want Shannon to see that side of you?" Does she mean it gets worse than this? Jase has come to stand next to me by the door.

"Jason, you need to get your girlfriend out of my car, now." Nick has turned back around in his seat, looking straightforward. He is ignoring his sister. She doesn't strike me as the type to be ignored.

"Man, why don't you and I go work this out? Nikki can take Shannon home, or fuck, let Shannon take your car and we'll take you home later after you cool off," Jase tries to reason. He crosses his arms across his chest, concern displayed on his face. He obviously cares a great deal for his friend.

Nick and Nikki are staring at each other through the rearview mirror, neither wanting to give in to the other's demands. Nick is the first to break their silence. "Get the fuck out of this Goddamn car. NOW!" he yells.

"FINE!" she yells back as she throws her hands in the air. She leans forward and pulls herself up and out of his car. She takes Jase's hand and looks dead at me. "If you need anything— anything at all—please call me, okay?"

"Get in the car, Shannon," Nick spits out, still looking forward, ignoring his sister. I nod an okay to her and then descend in the passenger side seat, pulling the door shut.

Nick floors the accelerator just as I hear the clicking sound of my seat belt, letting me know I'm secure. I'm not sure if secure is the right word for what I'm feeling right now. Nick is beyond mad, and probably shouldn't be driving. I don't offer to drive. Something tells me that would not be the right thing to ask at this moment. I'm not sure what the right thing to say right now is. This is all pretty new to me. Last month, my life was pretty drama-free.

We ride in silence a little longer until Nick turns off, heading in the direction of his house. I only live about three miles from him. "Why aren't we going to my house?" I ask.

"Trust me. It's best to go to mine." He doesn't clarify, and there is no calmness in his voice. He looks like he could snap at any moment. I guess his sister just doesn't want me to see this side of him. I can understand, but really, if I'm dating the guy, then I need to see every side of him.

"But the dogs are at my house," I remind him.

"I know they are and I fed them this morning. They will live through the fucking night." He is getting irritated at me. I haven't done shit to him and he's getting irritated at me.

Just great.

His dad pisses him off and he takes it out on me? I don't think so. I cross my arms over my chest, but remain silent for the remainder of the ride.

He pulls into his driveway and stops abruptly. Exiting the car, he slams the door and heads for his house. He doesn't wait for me, but I follow a few paces back. He flings the door open and it hits the wall. Yeah, I'm sure that made a mark.

Walking into the kitchen, I see him pouring a glass of amber liquid. He tosses it back in one gulp and pours another. He repeats until he refills his seventh glass. Wow. Really? This is how he's going to handle things?

I stand in the entryway, watching him. He stands at the granite island with his palms cupping the edge, staring out the window to the backyard. I don't think he is looking at anything in particular. He looks lost in thought. He continues until he has finished off number seven. When he sits it back on the counter, he turns his head and stares at me.

That lost look turns to heat and lust. His eyes are a darker shade of blue than the normal flames I love so much. They are sinister, but not in a scary way. It's like he has his eyes on a prize and will stop at nothing to possess it. I'm pretty sure that prize is currently me. I know exactly what those eyes are telling me and it's almost a welcome sight. I know Nick can take my mind off the last few painful hours. I don't want to think about the past and I certainly don't want to think about his father. I want him to take my thoughts away, or at least redirect them.

He pushes himself off the counter to walk up to me. He's looks down and gazes into my eyes. Grabbing me by the waist, he backs me up against a wall. He's so close I can smell the alcohol on his breath.

Without moving his hand from my waist, he yanks my blouse out from where it's tucked inside my skirt. Nick moves both hands up to the top of my shirt and rips it open. He looks like a hungry wolf about to tear his prey apart.

After he pushes the shirt off my shoulders, I move my hands to hold onto his hips. I won't lie. This is so hot right now. I know in the back of my mind I should stop this. He isn't in the right state of mind, and could take things too far. My mind needs to shut the hell up and enjoy the ride because my vagina has other plans. She wants every bit of what this man is about to give her.

I go to lift his shirt off and he stops my hands. He shakes his head and I drop my hands to my sides. He runs his right hand up my bare skin until he reaches my hair. He grabs a handful and fists it in his hand, yanking forcefully, pulling my head back slightly. With his other hand, he runs it up my lower back until he reaches my bra. He unclasps it and pulls it from my arms, throwing it to the floor. He brings his free hand to my hip and presses himself into me. I feel how hard he is, but he doesn't rush things.

He's cupping my hip hard and I'll probably have a bruise tomorrow, but the way this girl is pooling with moisture down below, frankly, I don't care right now. He pulls my head, smashing his lips into mine. He's seeking entrance, and I part my lips, letting him devour my mouth.

Releasing my hair, he runs his hand down my body until he reaches the hem of my skirt. Grabbing the bottom, he pushes it up until it's bunched around my waist. He leaves it there, and with both hands, moves to my panties where he rips them off in a matter of a few seconds. He parts my legs and enters me with two fingers. I release his bottom lip I had been softly biting and gasp.

"I like how wet you get for me, Shannon. Has anyone else ever made you feel the way I do?" he asks.

I can only shake my head. He removes his fingers and brings them to my mouth.

"Taste how hot I make you," he says, pushing his fingers into my mouth. I suck them dry. With hooded eyes and a sinister grin, he could be a demon and I'd do anything he told me to right now.

Consequences be damned. I want him as badly as he wants me. No one has ever made me feel the way he does. Safe. Wanted. Good. Bad. Beautiful. Sinful. Content . . . Whole.

"Who owns you? Who owns this?" he asks as he's cupping my vagina roughly. Did he just use the word "own" while referring to me? Oh fuck! But honestly, I don't care what he said as long as he doesn't stop making me feel this way.

"Answer me, Shannon," he shouts, putting those same two fingers back inside me.

Oh God.

"You do . . . oh, God!" I'll say anything he wants to hear, as long as he doesn't stop loving me like this. *Whoa. Love? Where did that come from?*

"Baby, this has nothing to do with God. This is all me, and you are all mine." He removes his fingers and hoists me up, wrapping my legs around his waist. His hand is back in my hair, fisting and yanking my head back. I'm pressed against the wall and he's kissing, biting, and sucking my neck, down to my shoulder then to my breasts.

I don't hear him when unzips his pants, but when he lowers me a few inches, I feel all of him as he slams inside of me. Fuck! He doesn't give me chance to adjust as he pulls out and slams forcefully back inside. As much as it hurts, it hurts so good.

He takes a step backward as he is exiting me, and when he enters again, my back is slammed into the wall behind me. Yeah, that didn't feel exceptionally good, but the heat running through me before makes up for it. I know when I wake up I'm going to have several battle wounds.

He continues his exiting, stepping back and then entering, slamming me into the wall a few more times. Somehow, I'm still managing to build to an explosive climax. I feel myself nearing the end as I feel him start to pulse inside of me. The waves start to pour over me and I hear him grunt. I know he's coming with me. He slams into me harder this last time; I'm shuddering in his arms.

"Ahhh," I scream, but not because of the pleasure raining down on me. I've just felt something crush into my back and it hurt like hell. What the fuck was that? It's still poking me in my ribs and I need Nick to release me. I push at his shoulders. He removes himself from inside me and releases my legs from around his waist. He takes a step back and I almost fall to the floor. I'm in so much pain. I don't know what just happened. He turns and heads for his bedroom and I'm left bending over to the floor. I don't think he realizes the pain I'm in. He's just walked away.

I sit on the floor on my hands and knees for several minutes, trying to catch my breath. It isn't easy to breathe. I feel like I've been kicked in the ribs, and with every breath, there is pain. So much, pain that I don't want to breathe, but not breathing isn't an option. The lights are off so I can't see what Nick slammed me into. I know he didn't do it on purpose. We were both caught in a moment of lust, desire and passion, but fucking hell, why did it have to end with me on the floor hurting and Nick nowhere to be found?

I finally stand up. The pain is still there when I make it to Nick's bedroom. The lights are off, but there is a little light from the window shining in. Nick is lying in bed asleep. *Perfect. When I need you, you can't help me.*

CHAPTER 15

"What the fuck!" Nick's voice booms through the room. When I drag my eyes open he's walking back into the bedroom, a puzzled look on his face. Turning my head to the side, I glance at the clock on the nightstand to see what time it is. It's only a few minutes past six in the morning—way too early for me.

"Babe, how did the stereo control panel on the wall get broken?" His question brings my attention back to where he's standing in the doorway. Nick's dressed in a black suit with a blood red-colored shirt underneath. He looks like himself again—more pulled together, in control, and sexier than sin. Everything from last night comes back to me. The hot sex, the pain . . .

Goddamn the pain. Mother fucking shit, I ache all over.

I'm lying in the bed on my stomach with the covers trapped over my back. "You did, or w-we did," I say, wincing from the sharp pain on the right side of my back where my ribs are located. God, I don't want to move, but I have to get to work. I have been neglecting my job for far too long since moving into my house.

Nick eyes his hands, front and back like he's expecting to find cuts and bruises. Finally, his blue eyes snap to me, his expression even more confused than before. I start to push myself up, my hands pressing into the mattress, but hell, it hurts.

"How did we . . . Shannon, what happened to your back?" When I look over my shoulder, he's clutching the doorframe so hard, his knuckles are white. The way his eyes are bugging, I suspect out activity last night left a mark. Go figure. As much as this hurts, there would be a mark. Damn, and I bet he's going to flip worse than when I had a bruised shoulder.

He stomps forward, coming straight for me. Scooting to the edge of bed, my feet have barely touched the floor when he gently pulls me into a standing position, and then nudges me to turn, showing him my back. I peek over my shoulder, but Nick's gaze is fixated on my bare flesh instead of my eyes. After several heart beats, he glances to door where he just entered. I can see the wheels turning, it's dawning on him what happened.

"Oh, Christ, no." He closes his eyes briefly, but when they reopen, there is so much pain reflecting back at me that it hurts my heart. I know he technically did this, but it wasn't on purpose.

"I'm . . . su-sure it's not . . . as bad as it looks," I force through clenched teeth, knowing I'm doing a shit job at convincing us both. The pain increases as I talk, and really, I just want to lie back down. Going into work isn't going to happen.

"Fuck. What did I do? No. No no no. Why aren't you breathing normally? What did I do?" he repeats. Running his hand through his hair, his eyes are glued to my back. I know he waring with himself, and I've yet to really explained.

"Nick stop. Th-this isn't . . . your fault," I try telling him. He's not buying it. When he finally looks at me, I see so much torture in his beautiful blue eye that an ache starts in my chest.

It was a freak accident. No one is to blame.

"The hell it isn't. Look at yourself. You have a bruise the size of my head, and there's dried blood from scrape marks. You can't even breathe. I'm taking you to the hospital." He releases me. Turning away, he steps to the dresser drawer in the corner of room, opening one of the middle drawers.

"I don't need to . . . ahhh . . . go to the hospital." I probably do, but I hate it when he gets all demanding like this.

"Yes, you do, and you're going. You could have a cracked or broken rib. Oh God, baby, I'm so sorry." He walks back over to me with my clothes and helps put each piece on me, even my socks and tennis shoes.

"Please stop apologizing. If it makes you feel better, the sex was hot," I say, trying to lighten the mood—or his mood rather—by admitting the truth. It was hot . . . up until the moment the pain started.

"No, it doesn't. Fuck. Wrap your arms around me. I'm going to carry you to the car," he says as he wraps one arm around my waist, and with the other he lifts my legs off the ground. Then he totes me out the front door, not even bothering to lock up after he exits. Once he deposits me in the passenger seat he rounds to the driver's side.

Before he cranks the car, he pulls his phone out of his suit jacket and presses a button to make a call.

"I won't be in today. I have two meetings this morning. Handle them." I can't hear the other end of the conversation.

"That's none of your goddamn business, Teresa. Just handle the fucking meetings." He hangs up, not waiting for a response.

"Nick, I can drive myself . . . to the doctor. You don't have to miss work because of me." I take a deep, needed breath that hurts like fucking hell. *Shit.* "I'll be fine," I reassure him as he starts the ignition.

"Yes, I do," he says, snatching up my left hand, bringing it to his lips. Closing his eyes, he kisses the back of my hand softly before returning it to my lap. Finally, he puts the car in reverse and backs out of the driveway.

The ride to the hospital is longer than I expected. Morning traffic is a bitch. It took us forty-five minutes to get here. To my horror, he brought me to Huntington Memorial. *Great.* But at least I know Luke won't be here this early, though I could still run into someone I know, like my ex-best friend, who's a nurse. I still can't bring myself to speak to her. I know I should hear her out, if nothing more than to have closure. Allison and I will never be friends again, but I do need to have it out with her so it can be over. Right now isn't the time or the place, though.

Nick exits the car and comes to my side as I'm opening the door and pulling myself out. He doesn't ask, just simply lifts me into his arms and carries me inside. I let him even though I can walk. My legs aren't broken or bruised. I realize he needs this from me, so I keep my mouth shut and let him have this.

Once inside, he places me down on a cold plastic chair and

then heads to the registration desk to sign me in. I'm glad he picked out jeans, but I wish I had thought to bring a sweater. Hospitals are always too cold.

There is only one other person in the waiting room. I view that as a good sign. I remember Luke used to bitch a lot when the waiting room was full and he didn't get a break between patients.

Apparently, he got enough breaks to get involved with my best friend. In hindsight, I guess she spent more time with him than I did. Still, it stings when I think of what she did.

Nick walks back, taking the seat beside me. Lacing his left fingers with my right ones, he face is torn between guilt and anger. His body is stiff and I watch as he takes a deep, slow breaths like he's trying to calm himself.

"You know I would never intentionally hurt you, right?" he asks, but doesn't turn his head to face me. His stare is straight ahead, out the front door; though, I doubt he's actually looking at anything in particular.

"Yes, I know you would never hurt me on purpose," I tell him, apply light pressure to his hand. He brings mine up to his lips for the second time this morning, kissing it tenderly before releasing it.

He's taking this way too seriously. Leaning forward, he rests his elbows on his knees and places his head in the palms of his hands. "Stop beating yourself up," I tell him.

My breathing isn't getting any easier, but I push through the pain. I don't want him to think it's worse than it is. I know I'm the one in pain and he is the one who caused it, but he's being way too hard on himself. It was simply an accident following bad circumstances.

"I can't," he says as he lifts his head from his hands. Before I can tell him that he is being ridiculous, my name is called. Nick stands up first, taking my hand once more to pull me up from my seat. We both follow a lady through a set of double doors.

"I have to make a phone call," Nick tells me as I'm about to enter a small room where all my vitals will be taken. I nod, letting him know I heard him. He walks away from the door and down the hall.

"Please take a seat, Miss Taylor," an older blonde nurse instructs me. Her hair is pulled back into a tight bun, and she is already holding a thermometer in her hand. I take it from her and place it in my mouth. I hate it when nurses try to hold it in people's mouths for them. It makes me feel like a kid and I don't like it. After a few seconds, it beeps, and I hand it back to her.

"Please tell me what brought you in this morning?" She looks up from the small computer she is standing at. I haven't thought this out yet. What do I tell her? I know this looks bad. Domestic abuse is probably going to be her immediate thought, even though it's far from the truth.

"I need to have my ribs checked out," I say as I look up at the woman standing in front of me.

"What's wrong with them?" she asks, typing something into the computer. I assume she's typing everything I'm telling her into an electronic patient record.

"They are bruised, and I'd like to make sure they aren't broken." She continues to type, not addressing what I have said. She turns, facing me with a tight smile as Nick walks back into the doorway. She eyes him but doesn't look like she thinks anything negative. I'm not sure why I assume people will immediately think abuse. Maybe I'm wrong.

"Please follow me. I'm going to put you into an exam room to wait for the doctor." I immediately stand and follow her out.

Nick grabs my hand again and walks beside me, both of us following the nurse. The room isn't far. Nick releases my hand as I enter the room and I take a seat on the examination table. He comes to stand beside me, wrapping his arms around my waist and leaning his forehead against the side of me. I welcome his warmth. I think this room is colder than the waiting room.

"Had I listened to my sister and this wouldn't have happened. I'm so sorry, Shannon." I turn my face and upper body to face him. Placing my hands on his shoulders, my face only inches from, I look Nick in the eyes.

"Do you remember anything from last night?" I ask him, as I stare into his intense blue eyes.

"Not particularly. Certainly not hurting you," he says as he closes his eyes.

"Well, I do. And what I remember the most is the way you made me feel. God, Nick, it was . . . it was great. I've never felt more wanted in my life." I bring my lips closer, to meet his, placing the softest kiss on his lips. He barely kisses me back before he pulls away.

"Then I hurt you. Don't sit there and tell me you don't remember that. Where was I when you were in pain?" he asks, his brows knitted together, his blue gaze revealing too much worry and stress.

"Stop, dammit," I say back to him.

"No. I can't believe I—"

"Shannon?" We both look at the door to see who interrupted

us. Nick tightens his grip on my waist. What the hell is he doing here? This, I do not need.

"Is there another doctor on call this morning?" I ask through clenched teeth.

Luke ignores my question as he enters the room.

"What happened? Are you okay? I saw your name on the board just now." He looks at me with concern written all over his face, the doctor in him coming out.

"Do not come any closer to her," Nick growls, his jaw tight, once again firming his hold on my waist. Luke pauses only for a moment to look at him. I take a quick breath, which causes a sharp pain. I bite my bottom lip to stifle the cry that wants out of my mouth. Nick's hold is a little too secure, so not only do my ribs flame with pain, but so does my waist.

Nick doesn't register my discomfort. He is too busy giving Luke a death stare.

"What did he do to you?" Luke asks as he focuses on me, stepping closer.

"Nothing compared to what I will do to you if you step an inch closer to her." Nick's voice is full of anger. He looks like he's seconds away from snapping. The veins in his neck bulge against his tanned skin.

"Don't make me call security," Luke responds in Nick's direction.

"Lucas!" someone reprimands from behind him. The three of us turn to the door. It's Luke's boss, Dr. Marc Thornton. I remember him introducing himself to me last year at a Christmas party for his staff. "Go check on the patient in exam room 4." Luke hesitates, glancing back in my direction. "Now," Dr. Thornton demands with a raised voice.

I don't remember the man being this stern and assertive. He came off pleasant and nice during the short conversation I had with him. Luke huffs out a puff of air as he walks out the door, and I'm left staring at the tall, lean man with a light chocolate complexion and deep brown eyes.

"What took you so long?" Nick asks him. Pulling back, I eye Nick with confusion. Dr. Thornton closes the door behind him.

"I was asleep when you called, Nicholas. I got here as quickly as I could." He walks farther into the room and turns his head to look at me. "It's good to see you again, Shannon." His smile is warm but doesn't reach his eyes. The longer I stare at him, the more I can see that his sleep was very much interrupted. He's Luke's boss, so I know he is the attending that normally covers the night shift staff.

"You know Marc?" Nick asks me, and I turn to look at him.

"He's Luke's boss, so yes, we have met," I answer. I wish he would release me. I don't know how much longer I can ignore the pain he's causing by holding me so tight.

"Nicholas, why don't you take your hold off of her? She doesn't look like she is enjoying it," Dr. Thornton tells him, as if reading my mind. He's a doctor, so he's probably good at detecting someone in pain.

"Fuck, baby, I'm sorry," he says as he lets go of me and takes a step backward. Dr. Thornton raises his eyebrows at Nick. The word "baby" endearment definitely didn't slip by him, and it makes me wonder if Luke has told anyone the two of us aren't together anymore.

"I'm fine, Nick. Stop saying you're sorry, please." I've about had enough of that.

"Why don't you let me be the judge of your health? Nicholas thinks you need an X-ray. Care to tell me where and why?" He crosses his arms over his chest like he already knows he isn't going to like what I'm going to tell him.

"The right side of my back hurts with every little movement, I need to see if I have any fractured ribs." I keep my answer short and don't plan on going into any details. Dr. Thornton cuts his eyes at Nick before looking back at me. Apparently, my short answer isn't good enough for him.

"What happened that makes you think you may have fractured bones?" His voice is calm, not giving anything away. I take a deep breath that hurts like hell and give him an honest answer.

"Rough sex gone bad?" I smile at him, hoping someone is going to laugh. They don't.

"Shannon!" Nick shouts and looks at me in disbelief, like he can't believe those words came out of my mouth.

"Well, he asked," I say pointblank, crossing my arms across my chest. Wow. That hurts. I wince in pain. Shit. Why the hell did I do that? I quickly drop my arms to my sides.

"Yes, I did," Dr. Thornton remarks, finally cracking a small smile. Nick rolls his eyes at me and I sigh.

"Remove your shirt, please," he instructs, putting on a pair of blue latex gloves. Nick helps me out of my shirt. Changing clothes is going to be a bitch if my back doesn't heal quickly.

Dr. Thornton comes to stand on my right side. He gently

touches the area of my back that is bruised, pressing his fingers into the skin around my ribs to feel around. Even though he is only applying a small amount of pressure, it still hurts.

"So, when did you learn about Lucas's indiscretions?" he asks as he finishes touching my back.

"You knew?" I ask, my anger flaring.

"Darling, everyone knew. I'm just surprised it took you so long to figure it out." He turns away from me, removing his gloves and tosses them in the trash. I wonder if he knows how long it went on, but then, honestly, I don't care. That part of my life is over. I can't change it, but I can move past it.

"Are you going to do the damn X-ray now?" Nick asks, changing the subject, clearly not liking the topic of my conversation with the doctor. Dr. Thornton rolls his eyes this time.

"You don't have any broken ribs, but I'll send you for an X-ray to see if any are fractured. You can put your shirt back on." He turns to walk out of the room and pauses as he puts his hand on the doorknob. "Step outside with me, Nicholas," he says, not looking at Nick. I'm almost finished pulling my shirt down when I look up at Nick, then the doctor.

Something tells me this is about me. I'm not going to be discussed behind my back. "If it is about me, then I would appreciate you saying whatever it is you have to say in front of me." I glare at the doctor. He shuts the door. He had only begun to open it when I spoke.

He faces me, his eyes holding my stare for the briefest of moment, then his dark eyes cut to Nick. "She's a feisty one, isn't she?" he says as he crosses his arms over his chest and leans back against the door.

"Defiant is what I call her." I shoot Nick a deadly stare, which only elicits a smirk from his lips. "She doesn't like it when I say that."

"Fine," Dr. Thornton says as he pushes off the wall, placing his hands on his hips. "What the hell, Nicholas?"

"Hey!" I yell as I jump off the exam table. I shouldn't have done that. The pounding from my feet hitting the ground sends a sharp pain through my back. Nick stares at the doctor, but doesn't say anything. Neither of them acknowledge me as they continue to stare at each other.

"Since when do you go around injuring women? When did you become like your father?" At the mention of Nick's dad, my eyes widen, and I tense. Luckily, neither of them notice. Nick's face turns lethal. It's a look I've never seen on him. Quite frankly, it's a little scary.

"I'm nothing like my father, Marc," Nick bites out, his voice a low, strained growl. No, Nick is definitely not like that evil monster. A cold shiver runs down my spine as a horrible memory enters my brain. I push it back out just as quickly as it entered.

"Stop, both of you," I say, but I'm looking at Dr. Thornton when I say it. "This was an accident—nothing more." I note that I sound like most battered women when defending their man, but in my case, I'm defending a man who isn't an abuser. I may have only known Nick a few weeks, but I know he wouldn't intentionally hurt me. Ever.

"A nurse will be in shortly to take you for a scan," Dr. Thornton says before exiting the room. He doesn't acknowledge my response, and to be honest, I don't care what he believes. I only care what Nick believes about himself. I turn and wrap my arms around Nick's waist, placing my head on his chest. His heart is beating rapidly.

Before I can reassure him that I'm fine, the door opens behind me. I turn to see who it is, and the same nurse who took my vitals is standing in the doorway waiting on us. "Please follow me, Miss Taylor," she says before walking back out the door.

We follow her, Nick a pace behind me. He doesn't hold my hand like he did before. Again, the walk is short, and I'm ushered into another small, cold room. There is a tech standing beside the machine waiting for me. Nick remains outside the room.

The tech is a young man, probably a few years younger than me, with sandy-blond hair and small blue eyes. He gestures for me to sit on a table and I do as he asks. "Before we begin, I have to ask if there is a chance that you could be pregnant." He looks up at me, waiting for a response.

"No," I answer, looking confused. *Do I look pregnant?* Surely not.

"Sorry. It's a standard question. I have to ask all females before they get an X-ray."

"Okay." I'm sure that is something most people know, but this is my first X-ray. I went through my entire childhood and teenage years without any physical injuries. For someone as clumsy as me, it's a miracle.

He leaves the room to stand behind a closed-in wall. From there, he speaks to me through an intercom system.

"Please be as still as you can," he requests, and before I know it, the entire process is over and I'm getting off the table and walking to the door.

When I exit, Nick is leaning his back against the wall, his hand cupping the back of his neck. He looks tense and stressed. I hope he gets over this soon. It's going to eventually start getting on my nerves. I can only tell him I'm fine and that it was an accident so many times.

Dr. Thornton is walking out of the same room I came from. I had no idea he was even in there. I guess he was behind the same wall the tech was behind when he was taking my X-ray. He comes to stand in front of me.

"Your ribs are bruised, but there is nothing on the X-ray to indicate a fracture. A hairline fracture is possible since you are having a little difficulty breathing, but all is clear on the X-ray. You are free to leave, but I recommend resting for a few days. It will help them heal quicker." He looks over to Nick, who is pushing off the wall.

"Thank you, Marc," Nick tells him as he reaches out to shake the doctor's hand. He seems calmer, but his eyes reveal it's only for show.

Dr. Thornton takes Nick's hand and they shake briefly. "Any time, but that doesn't mean I want to see her back here again." His voice is strong, and I hear the underlining meaning behind it, which causes me to roll my eyes.

Nick reaches for my hand, lacing our fingers. "Let's get you home."

CHAPTER 16

inally, we get back to my house after Nick insisted on stopping by the pharmacy first. Once Nick and I enter my house, Charmin runs over and jumps on my leg. Niko looks up from the oversized plush chair but doesn't bother to follow Charmin. He lowers his head back down and closes his sweet eyes.

Nick takes my elbow, gently tugging me down the hallway toward my bedroom. Doesn't he know rest does not mean I have to stay in bed? Just before entering my room, I pull my hand from his grip. He immediately stops and turns giving me a "what the fuck" look. "I'm not getting in bed," I tell him.

Yeah, this is probably one of those defiant moments. *Get used to it, buddy.*

"Yes, you are. You heard Marc. He said you needed rest, and I'm going to make sure you get it." He waves his arm through my room, gesturing for me to go in. This is not the part where I play the compliant "good girl" and do what I'm told.

"Rest doesn't mean I have to get in bed," I say, putting my hands on my hips. "He never said bedrest."

"Yes, it does. Now, get in bed," he orders. I cut my eyes at him. If he thinks barking orders at me is going to get me to do what he wants, then he is sorely mistaken.

"No. Stop being an ass, Nick," I holler.

"Fine." He sighs. "Let me at least wrap your ribs. It will help. Trust me," he tells me, and I arch my eyebrow. "I've had broken ribs before." He shrugs like it should have been obvious.

"Oh," I respond, and he finishes pulling me into my bedroom.

"Sit on the bed and take off your shirt." I follow his orders, but not before rolling my eyes behind his back.

"I don't have anything to wrap them with," I tell Nick as I take a seat at the end of my messy bed. I hate that I left my house without making the bed first.

"Why do you think we stopped at the pharmacy?" he questions, holding up the bag.

"To fill my prescription of pain medication, which by the way, was a waste of money. I'm not taking them."

"That too, and what do you mean you're not taking your medicine? You are hurt. You're in pain." He's giving a 'are you arguing with me about this?' look.

"A little pain is nothing I can't handle. I don't hurt enough to justify medication." I pull my T-shirt over my head. I have to bite down on my bottom lip so I don't give away just how much that movement bothers me. I gently lay the shirt down on the bed beside me.

"Arms up." He gestures as he removes the ACE bandage from its wrapper. "The point of the pain medication is so you *aren't* in any pain. You're taking the pills. End of discussion, woman." I comply and raise both arms above my head a little too fast as I glare at him. The movement causes shooting pain and I want to curse. Nick is starting to get on my nerves.

"You're right, end of discussion. But I'm not taking the pain pills, so let it go." He cuts his eyes up to mine as he wraps the bandage around my body several times before securing it.

Wow, that's tight.

He huffs. "Why do you have to argue with everything I say?"

"Why do you think everything is going to be your way?" I retort, ignoring his question. I pull my T-shirt back on and over my wrapped ribs. Actually, the bandage does help. I should probably be thanking him at this point.

"Just get your ass in bed, Shannon," he says through clenched teeth while staring down at me. I stand up in front of him, causing him to have to back up a few steps.

"No. Don't you have a job to go to or something?" I ask as I'm walking out of the bedroom.

"For the love of God." He sighs. "You are the most stubborn woman I have ever met," he continues, falling in step behind me as I walk out the door. I turn on my heels, causing him to abruptly stop before he collides with me.

"No, Nicholas Lockhart, I'm not stubborn. I'm just not going to follow your orders because you think you're right, or you think you know what's best," I say, pointing my index finger into his chest.

Damn, he's irritating the hell out of me right now.

"Don't poke me in the chest like that again. I don't like it," he gripes.

"Yeah, well, I don't like being ordered around," I holler back at him.

"Fine, I'm going to work. I have a 6 o'clock meeting tonight, so I won't be home until late," he says as he walks past me in the hall.

"Why don't you just stay at your house tonight? I think we could use a night apart," I spit out, instantly regretting my words. He halts, but doesn't turn around to face me. After a second, he continues through the hall before I hear the front door slam. Why did I have to be such a bitch? I didn't mean that.

Way to go, Shannon. He's only been trying to help you all morning.

"Arghh," I scream out loud, frustrated with myself. I walk out of the hall and into my living room. The dogs are both on the oversized chair, staring at me.

"Stop looking at me like that," I tell them and head into the kitchen. I don't need his dogs making me feel worse. I walk over to the cabinet, pulling out a glass and fill it with water. I take a sip of the refreshing cool liquid. It feels great going down my throat.

Needing a distraction from my harsh words to Nick, I grab my water and my Kindle off the counter to head out to the deck. Reading will help relax me since Nick wants me to rest.

Taking a seat on my chaise lounge, I sit my glass of water on the table and turn on my Kindle. I begin reading *The Dark Prince* by S. L. Jennings. It's the second book in her series. The first one blew my mind, and I can't wait to start reading this one. A little supernatural is what I need to get my mind off reality.

By noon, I've been reading and relaxing on my glorious deck for the past hour, looking out at the ocean. My ribs still hurt like a bitch, but I'm becoming accustomed to the breathing and not moving in certain ways. Turning my Kindle off, I sit it on the table and get off the chair to walk into the house.

When I locate my phone, I notice that I don't have any missed calls or text messages from Nick, but I do from his sister.

Nikki: In the mood for company?

Something tells me she has spoken to her brother. I sigh then shoot a text back to her.

Shannon: Sure. Can you bring Starbucks? I'm not allowed to leave. Sergeant's orders and all.

I set my phone on the kitchen counter, but she quickly replies, so I picked it back up.

Nikki: Of course. Be there in 30!

I place my phone back on the counter and walk out of the kitchen. I haven't collected my mail in a few days, so I walk out front to retrieve it. Once I'm back in the house, I shut the door, but don't lock it so that Nikki can come in.

I toss several magazines on the couch and take the rest to the kitchen. Standing by the trash, I toss anything that looks like junk straight in the garbage without opening it, while shoving the bills in a drawer until I can take them to Jenny to handle.

I grab my phone and walk out of the kitchen to go to the couch. I can at least look through a magazine while I'm waiting on Nikki to arrive. Really, I should call Nick to apologize. I just can't bring myself to do it. Maybe he is right. Maybe I am stubborn.

Getting comfortable in the corner of the couch, I bring my feet up, tucking them underneath me, then I grab one of the magazines lying on the cushion, replacing it with my phone. I'm about to open the magazine in my lap when my phone chirps, telling me I have a text message. I notice it's an unfamiliar number as I open the message.

Unknown: It's James. We need to talk . . . PRONTO.

I drop the phone in my lap and my body freezes. How did he get my phone number? I don't want to talk to him. I didn't want to see him yesterday, let alone ever again.

No.

Leave me alone.

I grab my phone again, looking at the message once more and hoping I imagined it, but no, I didn't. I bite the corner of my bottom lip to stop the tears at the back of my eyes. I won't do this. I won't cry again. Not over him.

I quickly delete the message and throw my phone in Niko's chair. The dogs must have gone outside at some point, because they are not on the oversized chair any longer. Having a doggy door leading out to the deck comes in handy.

Pushing the magazine out of my lap, I bring my knees up to my chest and hug myself, causing pain to pierce my ribs. I ignore it as images of my seventeenth birthday flash before my eyes.

It was the worst day of my life. The day my innocence was stolen. How can someone be so cruel, so evil?

"Shannon?" I hear over my left shoulder. I release my arms

from around my legs and look over to see Nikki walking in the door.

"Hey," I greet.

"I knocked. Did you not hear me?" she questions.

"No, sorry, I didn't," I respond as I get off the couch. Walking into the kitchen, she places a large, white paper bag on the counter. From the smell, I know she brought food. She hands me a Grande cup of coffee that I gladly take a sip from, wishing it had something stronger than just the coffee inside.

"Sergeant's orders," she repeats what I commented in text while taking the contents out of the bag out and handing me a white Styrofoam container. I laugh at her use of my joke from earlier.

"Thanks," I tell her while opening the container. It smells wonderful, making me realize how hungry I am.

"Nick told me you like fried chicken salad and that you probably haven't eaten." She hands me a fork. I take it and then open the small container of honey mustard and pour it all over my salad.

"I assume you know about our fight." I take a large bite of my salad.

"You would assume right, along with your trip to the ER this morning," she says as she begins pouring what looks like ranch dressing all over her salad.

"Does he think I'm a bitch?" I ask on a sigh. He has every right to. I shouldn't have been so determined to do things my way. Sometimes, I don't think before I open my big mouth.

"No, but I do." She laughs, but the tone suggests she is serious.

"Thanks for the honesty," I return sarcastically.

"Shannon, what kind of friend would I be if I wasn't honest with you?" She takes a bite of her salad as she waits for me to answer.

"The type who is probably biased, seeing how Nick is your brother." I'm cramming this food down like I haven't eaten in several days.

"I can't argue with that, but you aren't the one who had to watch him get his ass kicked this morning," she says with a sad look in her eyes; one only a sister would have.

What?

"Excuse me? What do you mean? What happened?" I spit out, dropping my fork. My appetite just vanished.

"Everything is cool now. He's fine," she tells me, not reassuring me at all.

"Explain, Nikki," I demand. My mind is jumbled and I feel slightly sick at the thought of Nick being hurt.

"He came in this morning before I got there. Apparently, he picked a fight with a guy he and Jase can't stand. I walked in during the middle of the fight. He was letting Carson beat the shit out of him. Nick wasn't putting up a fight. I could tell he was letting it happen. I stopped it immediately." She keeps talking, but I can't hear what she is saying over my thoughts. Why would he do that to himself? I don't understand.

It finally hits me and I snap my eyes to hers.

"Me. I'm the reason, aren't I?" It's not really a question. I already know the truth.

"Yeah, but don't think it's your fault, because it's not. That was all Nick and his fucked-up-ness." She finishes the rest of her coffee and tosses the cup in the trash. "I didn't know why he did it at first. It took me and Jase over an hour before he would talk."

I sit in the chair, staring at her, trying to figure out why he would do that. "Was it because of last night or the fight?" I ask. Surely not because I pissed him off.

"Last night," she says. "He's pretty pissed at himself for hurting you."

She looks away like it is painful for her to tell me. "Nikki, it was an accident. He's not at fault. He told you the truth, right?" I question, wondering just what he told her.

"Yeah, kinky sex with my brother. Please don't go into details. I don't need more images going through my head than what are already there." She has a disgusted look on her face; the same look Stacy gives me when I eat something she doesn't approve of.

"I have to go and see him. He has to stop thinking he hurt me," I say as I get up to search for my phone so I can leave.

"No!" Nikki says as she reaches for my elbow. "He would probably kill me if I let you leave."

"I need to speak to him. Plus, I said some things I didn't mean this morning," I tell her, pulling my arm away. I walk over to the chair to retrieve my phone.

"If you think he was bossy this morning, then try leaving. You haven't seen anything yet. Just send him a text to come here instead of going home tonight. Trust me, it's better this way." She crosses her arms like Nick often does when he is serious.

"Fine," I concede.

"Thank you. Now, I have to go." She snorts. "I'm supposed to report back that you ate and are resting."

I roll my eyes. "Whatever," I say as she walks out the door. I go back to the couch and decide to send Nick a message.

Shannon: I'm sorry. Please come home after work.

I hit send and then realize I said home, indicating our home, not mine.

Great.

I lie down on the couch, pulling a throw blanket over me, and then place my phone on my stomach. The more comfortable I become, the more tired I realize I am, my eyes already closing as I wait on Nick's response.

CHAPTER 17

I wake up, feeling rested but lonely. Then it dawns on me that I sent Nick a text before I dozed off. Yanking the cover off, I search for my phone, finding it tucked underneath me on the couch.

My mouth falls open as I look at the time. I've slept over five hours. I guess I was more tired than I realized. Nick hasn't responded to my text, which is weird. He always responds immediately. I type out a quick message and hit send.

Shannon: Are you ignoring me?

Five minutes goes by without a reply. It pisses me off.

Shannon: HELLO.

I realize that probably sounds bitchy and perhaps even the psycho texter that no woman wants to be labeled, but he should have answered me when I sent the first message. My phone chirps. *About damn time.*

Nick: I'm not ignoring you. I accept your apology.

That's it? Ugh. I quickly type out another message and hit send.

Shannon: Well? Are you coming over tonight?

I'm gripping my phone a little too tightly. Luckily, it's in a protective case so there is no chance of cracking it should I throw it without thinking.

Nick: No, I think you were correct. We need a little time apart.

"No, I wasn't," I say, pouting out loud. I was mad and lashed out at him. Does he not know women at all? It's what we do.

Shannon: No, I wrong. Please come over.

Nick: Not tonight. It's not a good idea.

What the hell?

Shannon: YES, tonight! I know about the fight.

Calm down, I mentally tell myself. I'm starting to get as irritated as I was this morning. I want to see him. I need to make sure he is okay.

Nick: My sister has a big mouth.

Yeah, Nikki's going to be mad at me for that one, but I'm *going* to see Nick tonight, so either he can come here, or I'll drive to him. I doubt he is going to like the latter.

I send him a quick text back.

Shannon: I'm getting into my car. I'll be at your house in 10.

I shouldn't be provoking a tiger by telling a white lie, but as long as the end result is getting him here, then I'm okay with that. My phone rings in my hand.

"Hello?"

"You had better be on the couch when I get there," he fumes, just before the line goes dead. I chuckle and immediately regret doing it. A sharp pain shoots through my ribs. I toss my phone on the couch and get up. I need to pee and brush my teeth before he gets home.

Dammit! I said it again!

Entering the bathroom, I pee first and then wash my hands. After brushing my teeth, I head back into my bedroom and crawl into my bed. I'm not tired, but my body does ache. Niko jumps off the bed as I turn on my back and position myself up against the pillows in the middle. He trots out the room and Charmin follows. Apparently, there is no love for me from those two.

Thirty-five minutes have passed and Nick still isn't here. What the hell is taking him so long? He didn't tell me he was on his way, I just assumed he was. As that thought clears my mind, I hear a door open and then close, followed by what sounds like plastic bags being set down on the counter in the kitchen.

Moments later, Nick enters the doorway to my bedroom. He fills it, his arms extending to the doorframe above his head. He's staring at me and I'm looking back at him. He's wearing the same suit from this morning, but his jacket is open, minus a tie, and the first two buttons from his shirt are undone. I'm reminded of the first night I met him at Quaint.

"Thank you for wrapping my ribs this morning. It helped," I tell him, trying to go for a sweet, appreciative look, when really I'm mad as hell at him. Not for this morning—I'm over that—but for getting himself hurt.

He releases the doorframe and walks into the room. When he gets to the bed, he reaches his hand out for me to take. Placing my hand in his, he pulls me out of the bed until I'm standing in front of him. He then tugs me forward in an embrace, wrapping his arms around me.

"I'm sorry I was a bitch this morning." I wrap my arms around his waist and look up, immediately noticing the cut above his left eye. Other than that, I don't see any other marks that would reflect he had been in a fight. His sister made it sound, or rather said, he was getting his ass kicked. He certainly doesn't look like someone who's come out on that side of a bad fight.

"I'm sorry I hurt you," he adds on a sigh.

"Nick—" I start to say, but he cuts me off.

"Well, I did injure you." He bends down and kisses me in the center of my forehead.

"Fine, you're sorry and I forgive you. If you let it go and forget about it, then I'll forget about your fight today. I won't even ask about it." That's a fair deal. He just needs to take it and move on.

He looks down at me with his eyebrows scrunched together. His expression tells me he's considering it, and then he takes a sharp breath and exhales. "That's a lot easier said than done." He releases me and takes a step back, looking at me, before his eyes glide down my body, and then rest on my side. He can't see my ribs, but I know that's what he's thinking about.

"My father used to abuse my mother in every way," he admits. I tense up at the mention of his dad, remembering the text message from him earlier today; the one I ignored and deleted.

"What?" I question, my eyes are wide. He obviously needs to

tell me this, but I'd rather not hear anything concerning that man.

"I've hated my father for as long as I can remember. Nikki and I had to watch too many times him hitting her, kicking her, saying things no one who loves their wife would say too many times." His eyes are red and he looks up like he's trying to hold back unshed tears.

"Nick, you aren't like him," I reply, attempting to reassure him.

"I know that, at least, I think I do, but . . ." He trails off.

"No 'buts.' You. Are. Not. Like. Him." My voice becomes a little ragged at the end. He isn't anything like him. I don't want him to ever compare himself to that fucked-up man.

He looks back down at me and blows out a breath of air. "I hope you like Chinese. I stopped and got dinner before I came."

I remember hearing a bag when he came in a few minutes ago. "Then let's go eat. I'm starving."

I walk past him and head out of the bedroom. "You ate lunch, right? My sister brought you food today, didn't she?"

"Yes. I just didn't finish all of it." Hopefully, he will leave it at that. But probably not.

"Why?" he asks, his eyebrows furrowed.

"Does it really matter?" I answer vaguely as I sit down on the couch. The plastic bag with food is sitting on the coffee table in front of me. Nick takes a seat next to me.

"Because Nikki told you about this?" he says, motioning to the cut above his eye. I nod and he clenches his jaw.

"Don't be mad at her," I say to him as I lean forward to grab the bag of food and begin pulling cartons out.

"Too late, but that's okay, because she is way overdue for a little brother-sister bonding time," he says sarcastically. I look over at him. He catches my confused expression. "You don't have siblings, do you?" he asks while grabbing a carton of Kung Pao chicken.

I grab the Sweet and Sour, digging in with a plastic fork. Nick gives me a questionable look. "What?" I ask him through a mouthful of food.

"You're supposed to eat that with chop sticks."

"Not me. I can't use those things," I tell him, pointing to his choice of utensils. They are too complicated for me.

"I could teach you," he offers.

"No, thanks. This fork works just fine," I say, and then take a hefty bite. The food is so good. This is comfort food for me.

"Whatever." He rolls his eyes. We continue eating in a comfortable silence.

Once our meal has been devoured, Nick gathers the trash and throws it away. I'm comfy on the couch, so I remain seated, but grab my cell phone when I hear the "pinging" sound, telling me I have a text message. Leaning forward, I retrieve it from the table.

James: I WON'T BE IGNORED.

I gasp when I read the display. Quickly, I swipe the screen to open the message. I know it's from Nick's father. It's the same number I deleted earlier. I quickly do the same, deleting the message from my phone like it was never there.

Go away, dammit.

"Is something wrong? Are you hurting?" Nick asks. I look up to him walking back into the living room carrying two beer bottles.

As he reaches me, he hands one to me and take it from him.

"No," I respond, then bring the cold bottle to my lips. I don't think one beer is going to be enough. I guzzle the liquid until I need air. Releasing the bottle, I swallow, and then take a deep breath.

"Easy there, killer. There is only a six-pack in the fridge." I don't think it's going to be enough either. I sit the half bottle of beer on the table and then crawl onto Nick's lap. He proceeds to take a sip of his beer, and then places it next to mine.

"Are we okay?" He nods as he places his palms on both sides of me, cupping my hips.

"It's been a really long day and I want to take a shower. Join me?" I quickly nod my head. I'm amazed at how at ease I feel when I'm in his arms. He scoots to the edge of the couch and I move my arms up and around his neck. Nick stands with me, and as I wrap my legs around his waist, he walks us both to the bedroom.

CHAPTER 18

Thursday morning arrives; although, not soon enough. It's been three days since my trip to the emergency room. Nick has kept a watchful eye on me, which includes making me stay at home. I haven't protested, but the last three days have sucked. Well, mostly.

If not for my friends and Nick's sister keeping me company, I wouldn't have lasted more than a day sitting around doing nothing. I like to read, but even that gets old if that's all there is to do. Don't get me started on watching television. The daytime TV schedule is the worst. I can't take all the soap operas and boring scripted talk shows. Who enjoys that crap?

Nikki has become as essential person in my life. I adore Nick's sister, and over the last few days, I've discovered we're a lot alike.

Luckily for me, she didn't kill me for outing her to her brother. She and I are doing a "spa day" at Serenity after my meeting with

Teresa Matthews this morning. I really need a few hours of being pampered.

The elevator doors open, and I walk out into the main lobby at Lockhart Publishing. Rachel is all smiles as I make my way over to her desk. "Good morning, Shannon," she says cheerfully.

"Morning," I greet her.

She stands, walking out from behind her desk. "Miss Matthews just wrapped up a conference call, so I'll take you to her office, unless you'd like to speak to my boss first." She gives me a knowing smile. Great. She knows I'm seeing Nick.

"No, I'm only here to meet with Teresa. I'm sure Nick is busy anyway," I say.

"Okay, right this way then." She leads me the short distance down a hall on the east side of the building. Rachel knocks lightly before entering the room. "Miss Taylor is here."

Teresa looks up from her computer and immediately pushes her chair back to stand. She's an attractive woman—early thirties, I'm guessing—probably only a year or two older than Nick. She has loose, blonde curls that stop right past her shoulders, and she's wearing a tight-fitting black dress that hits just above the knee. The top is a swoop neck that shows off her abundance of cleavage.

"Shannon, it is great to see you again. Please come in and take a seat." She gestures to the chairs in front of her desk. I walk up and plant myself in one the comfy chairs.

"How are you this morning?" I say, trying to be nice. I like Teresa, but to me, she comes off a little fake. I ponder if she's like this with all her clients?

"Well, and you?" she asks, sitting back down in her chair.

"Great, thanks. What things in my portfolio did you want to discuss?" I ask, getting to the point. I'm ready to get my hour-long massage on, so the faster we wrap this up, the sooner I'll be relaxing.

She turns in her chair, grabbing what I'm assuming is my portfolio on the counter behind her. She turns back around and lays the collection on her desk. Thumbing through a few pages, I see she comes to a group of photos I took downtown in San Diego of an industrial warehouse that had graffiti art sprayed on it. These are my favorite photos in the entire collection. To me, they showcase the artist's beautiful talent.

"I feel we need to remove these photos, replacing them with a couple"—she pauses for a beat—"of more tasteful pictures. Wouldn't you agree?"

Uhhh, no.

"How are these photos not tasteful?" I ask, in somewhat of a defensive tone, lowering my brow. I don't care. She has just criticized my work. It's not that I can't take criticism, because I can. Every artist could use a dose of constructive criticism from time to time, and I also know I'm not going to make every person happy with my work. I don't strive to do that either. However, to say these photos aren't tasteful is to say the artist's work I captured isn't tasteful. There aren't many people in this world that have that type of creative talent.

"These pictures show the work of a hoodlum defacing buildings. They don't belong in a book published by Lockhart Publishing." She is trying to match my defensive tone, which has pissed me off. Hoodlums? Did she really just use that term?

"Is Nick . . . olas in agreement with this?" I spit out too quickly. I don't know if she knows I'm in a relationship with him, and really, I don't care. I wouldn't use him to get my book published, but I do think he would have talked to me about this first.

"*Mister* Lockhart—" she emphasizes, confirming that she doesn't know about our relationship. "Trusts my judgment. I've been doing this for many years. I know what needs to be done, and I know when to make tough decisions. I'm not trying to upset you. I'm trying to steer you in the right direction with your book."

"Those photos are works of art and I want them in the published version of the book," I say, crossing my arms over my chest. I will stand firm on this.

"Shannon, our contract states both parties must be in agreement to move forward with publication. I'm not in agreement with these pictures. Do you not see what it looks like to have photos of buildings being defaced next to a photo of a saint?"

"No, I guess I don't see your point here," I reply, a little louder than I intended as I uncross my arms and begin to stand. "Perhaps we should terminate the contract if you aren't going to publish it as is?"

"What is going on in here?" A deep and strong masculine voice cuts in. It's a voice I'm all too familiar with. It's a voice I can't get enough of. Nick. My Nick.

Teresa plasters on a fake smile while rolling her shoulders back to enhance her cleavage. Really? Doesn't this chick know they can be seen without her poking her chest out? I roll my eyes, realizing what she is doing. She has a thing for Nick. It's so obvious.

"I asked a question," Nick says as he walks farther into the office.

"I'm glad you stopped by. I'm sure you remember Miss Taylor," she says, gesturing to me. "She and I are having a disagreement. Perhaps you can help me."

"What's the problem?" he asks, pointing the question at me. Before I can answer him, Teresa speaks up.

"I'm trying to explain to Miss Taylor that these photos don't belong in her book. I've asked her to replace them with better photos," she tells Nick as she is closing my portfolio and standing up.

"If Shannon wants those photos in there, then they stay. If there aren't any other problems, go ahead and send it off to publication." He turns to look at me with a smile. His smile fades when Teresa speaks again.

"Nicholas, did you not see the photos?"

"I've seen every photo in there. Teresa, do not make me repeat myself. Now, is this meeting over?" he asks her. She looks a little stunned, like she isn't used to him disagreeing with her.

"Yes." She crosses her arms over her chest, emphasizing her breasts even more.

"Good." Nick's smile is back in place as he looks at me. "I'm taking you to lunch. Where do you want to eat?" he asks me.

"You're taking a client out to lunch? Since when did you start doing that, Nicholas?" I look over, noticing Teresa has stood up and is placing her hands on her hips.

"No, Teresa, I'm not taking a client out to lunch. I'm taking my girlfriend out to lunch." Her jaw falls open.

I smile. *Yeah, bitch, he's mine.*

Nick takes my hand, pulling me out of her office. My mood has drastically changed in the last few minutes. "Where does my beautiful woman want to eat lunch?"

"Mint," I say quickly. "Nikki and I are meeting at Serenity at noon. Do you mind if I invite her to lunch with us?"

"Of course not. I'll shoot her a text to meet us there." He then takes his phone out of his pocket, saying nothing else.

CHAPTER 19

"So, do you know Nick's VP, Teresa Matthews?" I ask Nikki while I'm laid out naked on a massage table with only a towel covering my ass. Nikki is in the same position next to me.

"Yeah, I've met her a handful of times. Why?"

"I don't think I like her," I admit.

"Honey, are you the jealous type?" she teases.

"I don't know, maybe. I've never been in the past, but there is something about her that rubs me the wrong way. I mean, it's obvious she has a thing for Nick, but . . . ." I trail off, not sure what I'm really trying to say. Maybe I am being the jealous girlfriend type. I don't want to be the jealous type at all.

Nikki is being quiet, so I turn my head in her direction. She is looking at me and biting her bottom lip like she's trying to stop herself from speaking. "What?"

She releases her lip and takes a large breath of air. When she exhales, she says, "I'm not sure if I should tell you this, but—" she starts scrunching her eyebrows together.

"Spit it out. You can't say that and then not spill," I tell her.

"Nick got really drunk at his office Christmas party last year and fucked her." She is biting into her lip again like she's bracing herself for how I'm going to take this news.

"Oh . . ." I'm not sure what else to say to that. I turn my head in the opposite direction. I don't want her to see the look I'm sure is plastered on my face; a jealous one. I can't be mad and I'm not. Nick and I have only been dating for a month, and that happened close to six months ago.

"Shannon, I'm sorry. I have no filter. I tend to say whatever pops in my head."

"No, it's okay. I'm sure Nick slept with a lot of women before me. He'll be thirty-one in a couple of weeks, after all." I turn back to face her. I don't care how many sexual partners Nick has been with, but her? Ughh . . .I don't like knowing this.

"If it makes you feel better, you're the only repeat," she says, and I don't think she's joking. Am I dating a manwhore? Probably. Even I hopped into bed with him after day two of meeting him.

I give her a weak smile. "Repeat, huh?"

"I'm serious, and it's a bit weird. I never thought I'd see the day my brother let himself fall in love." She beams.

"I wouldn't go that far. We've only just met, you know," I joke, but feel a ping in my chest. Certainly, we don't love each other. Not yet anyway. Love takes time to grow and form. Nick and I have known each other two fucking minutes, and didn't I just end an engagement? Do I want to be serious this quick? *News flash, Shannon, it's a little late for that. You already are serious with this man.* We've only slept apart two nights since meeting, and that was only because he had to go on a business trip to Las Vegas.

"Hello?" I look up to find Nikki waving a hand in front of my eyes. "Where the fuck did you just go? We were talking and then you just zoned out."

"Sorry," I tell her and change the subject. Enough about Nick and the subject of love. "So, how long have you and Jase been dating?" I ask as I feel the warm, soft hands of the girl giving me a back massage start to knead the tight muscles below my shoulders. *God, that feels so good.* This is much needed after the month I've had. The message therapist is careful and stays away from my tender ribs and the center of my back area.

"Um . . . that's complicated," she sighs out. "It's not an easy answer I guess is what I'm trying to say." She looks away.

"Meaning?" I ask, not understanding. I asked an easy enough question. She turns her face back to look at me.

"Jason and I are complicated, or well, I am—complicated, that is. Jason is pretty normal and great, actually." She leans her head from side-to-side, cracking her neck. "We started dating when I was fifteen and he was sixteen." There's a small smile across her lips. She is obviously in love with her boyfriend.

"Wow, fifteen years. That's amazing," I tell her, but her smile fades at my enthusiasm.

"It's been fifteen years, yes, but we haven't been together a solid fifteen. There have been others in between." She sighs, then adds, "For both of us."

"Oh," I respond, not sure what to say. Her face has saddened, but I don't know her well enough to say something that will cheer her up. "Everybody needs experience, right?"

"Not when you know it's the right person. When you know the person that you're with is the one you're meant to be with, you gain experience exploring each other, not accumulating multiple bed partners. I've known Jason was my forever since I was a kid."

Damn. Nikki surprises me at every turn. She is so different from anyone I've ever met. She's young, but wiser than I would expect a thirty-year-old to be.

"When people find out we have been together for as long as we have, the question that follows is always, 'when are you getting married' and even often times 'don't you want kids?'" she spits out like it's a bad taste in her mouth.

"So, you and Jase don't want to get married?" I ask for clarification.

"Oh, Jason wants to get married," she states matter of fact.

"But *you* don't want to get married or have kids?" She looks up at me like a deer caught in headlights. Her hesitance to answer mean I'm missing something here.

"Nick doesn't want kids either," she huffs out, not really answering the question, but giving me more information than I think I want to know. Nick doesn't want a family. Not that we are anywhere close to that type of relationship at this stage. I certainly don't want kids now. I have a career and I'm content. The mommy bug hasn't bitten this girl . . . yet. But one day I want a family. I'm sure of that.

Over the next two hours, I', going to put what Nikki has

revealed out of my mind while we are pampered with facials, manicures, and pedicures. I don't get my nails painted because I can't stand it when the polish starts to chip, but I love the color on my toes. I'm going with a French pedicure, but with a black tip instead of white. Once my feet dry, Nikki and I will depart and I'll head home.

I know I should think over the things I have learned today in regard to Nick, but doing that will only hinder my good mood and welcome stress back into my relaxed body. No, thank you. I can mull over that later.

CHAPTER 20

The following afternoon, I'm back at work and settling into my routine again. I've missed my sanctuary and having something to actually do. I gave Jenny the day off, so I'm out front working behind the counter today. I actually like these days like today, even though I'm on my feet most of it. I'm never bored because I'm usually rearranging framed pictures and adding new ones so the place consistently looks fresh and alive. Next week, I'll start planning the next collection. I'm thinking Las Vegas.

"Dammit!" I yelp after tripping over a brown box lying on the floor behind the front counter. I grab the glass countertop so that I don't hit the floor, but not before the corner of a large picture frame stabs my knee.

"Shit," I spit out. That hurts.

"Is that the language you want your customers to hear?" My

head flies up and I freeze when our eyes meet. How do people not see the evil in this man's eyes? Thank God Jenny isn't here. I wouldn't want her here right now. But then again, I don't exactly want to be alone with him. I close my eyes briefly and take in a calming breath. He's still standing on the other side of the counter when I re-open them.

Fuck.

"Leave. I have nothing to say to you." I try for assertive, but already know I've failed. My voice is breathy and anxious.

"Well, I have plenty to say to you, so no, I won't be leaving yet. You've ignored me long enough, so I had to come to you," he tells me as he walks up to the counter. I instinctively back up, but there is a wall behind me, so I don't get more than a foot or two away from him.

"What do you want?" My bottom lip trembles, but there's no controlling it, so I bite down on it hoping to calm myself. I want to flee, but I won't get very far if I try to run. I'm still within reaching distance from him now.

"You and I didn't get to catch up last weekend."

He has a sadistic smile on his face. I won't show weakness to him again. "We have nothing to catch up on. Now, get the fuck out of here!" I demand.

He reaches over the counter and grabs my arm, pulling me close to him. He has a firm grasp on me, but not so much that it will leave a mark. I inhale sharply, which causes an intense pain to shoot through my ribs. They are mostly healed, but every time I take a quick breath the pain lets me know it's not completely gone.

"Do I need to teach you a lesson, Shannon? A lesson in respect, perhaps?" His gray eyes are cold. My body tenses, afraid of what he's capable of doing. My mind flashes to the last time he said that.

"No," I plead. So much for not showing him how weak I really am.

"Good," he says as his eyes soften a fraction. He pulls me even closer. "Now, tell me, what have you told my son about us?"

"Nothing. Please, leave me alone. Please go," I beg him.

"There's my little beggar. I've missed you," he says, his face only inches from mine, and then he plants a quick, hard kiss on my lips. Nausea hits me instantly, rolling through my stomach. I think I'm going to be sick.

I pull back, yanking my arm from his grip. Without thinking or considering the consequences, I slap him across the face with all the strength I have.

Oh, God, what have I done?

Pure evil appears in his features. I cover my mouth with my hand, shocked I let myself lose control like that around him.

"You'll pay for that, bitch," he says as he takes his right palm and rubs the area of his cheek that I slapped.

"No," I whisper, already looking around, searching for anything that might help me if he attacks. There is no way I can reach the front door without running past him. The only thing in my reach is the picture frame I hurt my knee on. Not much good it would do. "I'm sorry. Please, I've kept my mouth shut all these years. I never told anyone. I just want you to leave."

"Then why are you back? Why are you fucking my son? What

is it you really want, Shannon?" His eyes are blazing, and his lips are curved up in a snarl as he stares at me, waiting for a response. Does he think I'm with Nick to get back at him somehow? What would give him that idea?

"I-I don't want anything from you." The only thing I want is to never have to see this man again, but how will that be possible if I continue my relationship with Nick?

As if reading my thoughts, he smirks. "Maybe you need to reevaluate your relationship with Nicholas. I want you to leave him, because if you don't, then I promise you that you will be seeing a lot more of me."

And with that last statement, he backs up and exits the building, finally leaving me alone.

Break up with Nick? No, I don't want that. I enjoy Nick too much, and we're good together. I'm not ready to end things. I also don't want to have to see his father ever again. I don't want to relive everything that happened all those years ago. I back up and slide down the wall, ending on my rear with my knees pulled up in front of me. I wrap my arms around my bent legs and lay my forehead against my kneecaps, trying to think.

I won't walk away from Nick, but how can I stay with him and keep this secret? How can I expect him to be honest with me in our relationship if I can't be honest with him? As I take a deep breath, I hear the chime of the door. Someone just entered. I look up, cutting my eyes in the direction of the door and see Jeffery walking my way. I push myself off the floor. "Shannon, are you okay?"

Man, I must look awful if he can tell something is wrong. I

take another deep breath and plaster on a smile. "Of course. What can I help you with?"

His eyebrows knit together, as if he doesn't believe me. Oh, well. This is none of his business. "I've been trying to reach you for a few weeks, but Jenny has been telling me you've been unavailable."

"I'm sorry. I haven't been in." I hesitate, remembering Nick's call to him. That was so embarrassing, but I need to address it. "And I'm sorry about Nick."

"So, Lockhart." It's a statement rather than a question, I think.

"Yes," I say, confirming for him that I am seeing Nick if he was questioning that. His eyebrows knit together, and then he shakes his head. "What is it that I can do for you, Jeffery?" I ask, hoping to bring the conversation back to business.

"I'm making cosmetic changes to my office. It's located downtown in Pasadena. I want to contract you for fifteen to twenty framed photos." This is an amazing opportunity to get my name out to more people. Jeffery is the CEO of an architectural firm.

"Everything you've said sounds good." I beam at him. My mind briefly drifts to Nick. He's going to hate this, but business is business. There is nothing personal between Jeffery and me.

"I was hoping you'd say that. I'll have my assistant call you next week to set up a meeting." He turns on his heels, striding out the door. How in the hell am I going to break this to Nick? Neither of us really talks about work, so maybe I should keep quiet and not bring up the subject. I know that omitting something may seem like lying, and I guess in a way it is, but bat-shit crazy Nick hasn't shown his face and I'd like to keep it that way.

CHAPTER 21

The weekend came and went too quickly, as did my Monday afternoon scouting locations for the shoot Jeffery wants me to do. His assistant called me first thing this morning, giving me a few details before setting up a meeting with him. From our brief conversation, I learned Jeffery wants framed photographs of structures and buildings in and around Los Angeles to be used as artwork to fill his office space.

We're supposed to meet at ten Friday morning to discuss the project in detail. Until then, I want to have some ideas to lay out in front of him. There are tons of buildings throughout the city, so this project is not only going to be easy, but also fun.

It's been well over a month since I've shot any photos for professional purposes, so I'm itching to get my Nikon D4 back into my hands. It's a beauty. I haven't been inside Jeffery's office before, so I don't have any idea what the layout looks like. Come

Friday, I'll have a better idea what I'm going to do for his space.

Even though my day has been long, I'm not tired. But I am glad to be back home. Nick should be home in about an hour. Since the accident a week ago, this is the first day he hasn't been fussing over me or calling to check on me. I didn't realize how much I missed it until arriving home.

After putting dog food into each of the dogs' food bowls on the kitchen floor, I wash my hands before retrieving a bottle of water from the refrigerator. I go to take a swallow of the opened bottle when I hear the front door open, then quickly slam shut with a loud thud. The noise startled me, but I remember Nick is the only other person with a key. It can't be anyone else. I place the water on the counter and exit the kitchen. When I enter the living room, my eyes lock with Nick's. The look in his eyes is a mixture of anger, betrayal, and hurt. I recognize it. It's the same one I had when I realized Allison was the person Luke cheated on me with.

"Nick, what's wrong?" I ask as I make my way to him. I have an overwhelming need to feel his touch, to have his arms wrapped around me.

"Don't touch me right now," he says, forcing the words out as he puts his right hand out in front of him to halt me from getting any closer.

"No," I say, pushing his arm away and closing the distance between us. I grab his arms loosely and look up at him. "What's wrong?"

"I said don't fucking touch me!" he yells as he jerks out of my hold and takes a step back. His eyes are wide and his breathing is ragged. He's obviously angry, but why?

"What the hell, Nick, why are you mad?" I ask him, taking a deep breath. I'm not going to let myself jump to any conclusions. His dad couldn't possibly have said anything. Not when I can ultimately tarnish everything he is.

"Mad? You think this is mad? This is far beyond mad, Shannon. I want to rip your fucking heart out right now!" he screams at me. I gasp in shock and take a few steps back, hitting the wall behind me. Why would he say that? In the back of my mind, I know there is only one possible answer—his father.

"What do you think I did exactly?" I ask him as I realize he's already made up his mind. Whatever lie his dad told him, he believes. It's been three days since James paid me a visit and I've ignored his text threat over the weekend. I've deleted them as soon as I realized who they were from. I haven't ended things with Nick, so something tells me he's taken matters into his own hands. I'd be lying right now if I said I wasn't scared. Not of Nick, but of what is about to come out of his mouth.

"My father came to my office about an hour ago. What do you think he told me?" He isn't yelling, but his voice is still loud. It's . . . cold, almost like his father's.

"I don't know," I say, my voice low. Looking down, I close my eyes. This is bad. I can't believe this is happening this way. Nick's father is a lying bastard and he actually believes him, despite what he knows his father is.

"That's how you're going to play this? You don't know?" No, I don't know. I look back up at him as anger sets in. Anger toward Nick's father and anger at Nick for believing him, for not giving me the benefits of the doubt.

"No, I don't know what he told you. Why don't you just say it? Why don't you tell me what you believe?" I clench my fists together, hanging them at my sides.

"What I believe? I want you to tell me it isn't true. I want you to tell me you didn't fuck my father. Can you do that?" Yes, I could tell him that, because I didn't willingly have sex with his dad. He raped me, but instead of responding, I remain silent. I can't get the words from my brain to my mouth. "You can't, can you?" Tears pool in my eyes.

"Don't start with the fucking water works. There isn't anything you can do that will take it back. Nothing will change the fact that you had an affair with my father."

"No!" I yell, but no other words follow getting caught in my throat.

"Like hell you didn't. What else do you call fucking a married man?" I look down, remaining silent as more tears roll down my face. "No response." He snickers. He actually snickered at me. "Were you playing me this whole time? Were you only with me so you could blackmail my father again?" What? I snap my head up. What the hell did he tell him? "Don't look at me like that. I saw the invoices where my father paid your college tuition." I had nothing to do with that. I never wanted it. He did that to make sure I stayed silent.

Tell him, Shannon, I urge myself. *Tell him the truth.*

But I can't. Instead, I lower my head as more tears fall.

"Your silence is all I need. It speaks volumes right now. We. Are. Done." He punctuates every word and turns to leave.

I grab his arm, pulling back. "No!" I scream.

His eyes are cold and harsh. "You don't honestly think I'd ever touch you again, do you? After knowing you've been with him, the sight of you makes me sick."

He pulls his arm out of my grip and walks out the door, slamming it shut. He's gone. He left me and I still can't formulate the words I've wanted to say for so long. How can I want to tell someone—anyone—so badly, yet not be able to?

I slide my body down the wall to the floor, cradling my head in my hands. I cry like I've never cried before—loud, ugly cries.

CHAPTER 22

My life couldn't get any worse. I've lost the man I love because I'm a coward and couldn't tell him the truth. God only knows what he thinks of me right now. I wanted to tell him; really, I did, but I couldn't get the words out of my mouth. "Silence speaks volume" he told me, and I'm sure mine confirms any lie his father told him.

I want the bastard to die.

I've never wished dead on someone before; not even when he raped me ten years ago. Back then, he stole my virginity, but now, he stolen my life. Isn't that rich . . .

Now that Nick is gone, I've realized that I love him and the magnitude of how much. My heart feels broken. Nick wanted to rip it out of my chest, and he succeeded in doing just that. Today is no different from Friday night. It may even be even worse. It's now Monday morning. I should be at work, but instead, I'm wallowing in my own misery.

I'm pulled out of my thoughts when the doorbell rings. Niko is sitting next to me, curled up on the couch. I have no idea where Charmin is. Nick didn't take the dogs when he stormed out. I'm sure he wasn't thinking clearly, and perhaps, this is him coming back for them. The thought saddens me. Over the last four weeks, I've not only fallen in love with Nick, but I love his two dogs, too.

I throw the blanket off and finally get up. I haven't moved since I sat down last night and cried myself to sleep. I've cried myself to sleep every night since he left. I didn't know heartbreak could hurt so much. I guess that's why they say losing love is like having your heart ripped out of your chest and broken into a million pieces. There isn't enough glue in the world to put it back together.

I walk over the door and unlock it. It's not Nick. I let out the breath I didn't know I was holding. It's his mother, Elaina Lewis. There is something about the expression she's giving me. I don't think she hates me, but it seems like a look I would give someone if I felt sorry for them. I don't need anyone's pity. I need Nick back.

"Hi," I say as I step back, opening the door wide so she can step through. She does and sets her purse on the floor next to the door after she enters. She must not be staying long. Perhaps Nick sent his mom for his dogs, but I highly doubt it. She doesn't look like much of a dog person. I didn't realize it before, but his mom looks perfect. Her attire is pressed and pristine. Her makeup is flawless, and her hair is perfectly in place without a stray strand.

"I probably should have called you, but I wasn't certain you would be answering any calls. You look like you had a rough night." That's putting it mildly. It's been a rough few days.

I walk back over to the couch and sit in the same corner I was in before she arrived. Niko has since gotten off the couch and probably went outside through the doggy door Nick had installed to use his outdoor potty. It must be a great life to be a dog. Eat, sleep, and shit wherever you please. They don't have to worry about falling in love and having it ripped away from you.

"You don't look like you want to rip me apart, so why are you here?" I ask, so she'll get to the point and let me go back to the depressing misery that is my life.

"You thought I would be mad at you?" she inquires as she takes a seat and grabs my left hand in both of hers. Yeah, she definitely feels sorry for me.

"Why wouldn't you be? You already know your husband's side of the story, or Nick told you, but either way, it's still James's version." Why couldn't I have just told him? Would he have believed me if I had?

"I should have come to see you before now, but I didn't want to face the truth." What does that mean? Did Judge Lewis tell her before yesterday? Is she the reason he told Nick? I doubt it. He wanted to hurt me, and he knew taking Nick from me would be the best way to do that. He told me I would pay and I'm certainly doing that.

"What do you mean?" I ask her and pull my hand away. I'd rather not be touched right now.

She sighs deeply before responding. "The day you came to my house, I saw your eyes when you heard James's voice. You were scared. I knew in that moment he had done something horrible to you." She pauses for a brief moment, casting her eyes down, before continuing. "He forced you, didn't he?"

Shocked, I snap my eyes to hers as she's looking back up. Oh, my God. She knows? I don't know how, but she does. Someone else finally knows what he did to me. Someone else knows he *raped* me. I can't stop the tears from falling. I'm crying before it even registers in my head that I am. Elaina grabs me, pulling me into an embrace. I sob uncontrollably on someone I barely know.

"I'm so sorry, honey. No one should have to go through something that traumatic alone." She is holding me by the back of my head and rubbing my back with her free hand. I bawl in her arms for at least five minutes, maybe longer. I have this overwhelming feeling of relief, yet I'm terrified at the same time.

I lift my head, pulling out of her embrace, and wipe the remaining tears with the back of my hand. "Does anyone else know?"

She momentarily looks away, before bringing her eyes back to mine. "No, I didn't tell Nicholas, if that's what you want to know."

"Oh," I respond, taking a deep breath.

"Shannon, I know James should pay for what he did to you. Really, I do. No one knows better than I do what it's like to suffer at the hands of that man." She takes a large gulp of air before finishing, letting it out on a sigh. "But I'm here for selfish reasons. I'm here as a mother. Please, don't tell Nicholas."

"What?" I ask, not believing what I'm hearing. I want to tell Nick. Hell, I want to tell the whole world. Doesn't she understand what it's been like to live with this secret inside me? All these years of pretending like it never happened, but also never really being able to forget?

"A mother knows her child. If Nicholas ever finds out, he will kill his father. My son's life would be over. So I'm begging you to never see him again."

I gasp. A migraine starts to take form. Is she for real? "Get out," I say quietly.

I don't know if I'll ever be able to tell Nick what his father did to me, but his mother has no right to ask me not to. She has no business asking me not to see Nick again. I love him. I love him more than I've ever loved another person.

"Shannon, he's my son. I'd do anything to protect him."

"And I love him. I'd never do anything to hurt him!" I yell back at her. "I said, get out." She stands, not saying another word, and quietly retrieves her purse from the door. Before she exits, she gives me one last pleading look.

Once it's shut, I turn, pressing my back into the hardness of the wood and slide down. Niko is at my side the moment my butt hits the floor. He looks as sad as I feel. He lies down on the floor with me, placing his soft head into my lap. I'm amazed at how this animal knows exactly how and when to comfort me. I lower my head, placing it into my palms and begin to cry . . . again.

CHAPTER 23

I wake up on the couch as I have every morning since Nick walked out of my life eight days ago. I haven't been able to sleep in my own bed—the bed where he's had me on in every possible way I can imagine in the short time we have been together. Every time I go into my room, all I see is us and the happiness we once had.

I throw the blanket off and sit up. Nausea hits and the feeling that I'm about to vomit washes over me as my mouth fills with hot saliva. I leap off the couch and race to the guest bathroom. I wouldn't make it to mine.

Everything comes up just as the seat hits the back of the toilet. I break out into a sweat, hugging the porcelain god. Another wave of nausea come and I vomit again. I don't know how I have anything left in my stomach to rid of. I haven't eaten since yesterday mo ing and even then it was more nibbling than anything.

I faintly hear knocking on the door, but I'm too spent to get up and check. I don't know if I'm finished puking my brains out yet. My back aches and my head is throbbing.

Great!

A migraine is just what I need to top off the day, and it's still early. I wipe my mouth with the back of my hand, not caring that it's gross. I haven't showered in a few days, so what's a little more grossness going to hurt?

"Oh, my God, are you okay?" Nikki asks from the entryway to the bathroom. I look up from the toilet and turn my head as she enters the bathroom. She kneels down next to me and places her hand on my forehead. I attempt to throw up again, but apparently nothing is left, as I'm only dry heaving at this point.

Nikki stands up, and a few seconds later, I hear running water from the sink. The water doesn't run long before she is kneeling back down on the floor next to me. She rubs a cool cloth over my face. It feels good; much better than the back of my hand. She then reaches over me and flushes the toilet.

"Thanks," I murmur as I sit back on my butt against the tub. I'm zapped and I only just woke up. Less than two months ago, I had the flu. This feels worse.

"You look like pure shit. Get up! I'm taking you to see a doctor." She stands and reaches for my hands, pulling me off the floor.

I feel like shit too. "I don't want to go see a doctor. I just need to lay down," I tell her.

"You're going, but first you are showering and putting on clean clothes. You smell, and I'm around smelly people all day long. When was the last time you bathed?"

I think over that question. A couple of days? Surely, not longer than that, but hell, I don't know really. When was the last time my heart wasn't shattered and scattered on the floor, being trampled on? That's a better question.

"Fine," I concede, as I follow her out of the spare bathroom, before walking down the hall into my room, and then enter the master bath.

I start to pull off my top as Nikki starts the water. "I'm going to go feed the dogs. I'll be in the living room when you're ready."

She exits the bathroom as I'm entering the shower. The hot water hits my body like sharp needles. I yelp, but after a few seconds, the piercing feeling subsides and I start to feel better.

I wash my hair and use some of Nick's body wash to clean myself. It, along with a few articles of clothing, are all I have left that still smells like him. I'll take every little fix I can get. I miss him like crazy and my heart still hurts. The pain there continues to get worse with each passing day. I thought time was supposed to heal all wounds. How much time? That hasn't happened for me yet. It's only been one week, so maybe I haven't given it enough time.

I just want him.

I turn off the water once I have rinsed all the soap off my body. I step out and towel off, then brush my teeth for the first time in a couple of days. Gross, I know. It's hard to care about hygiene when you can't even get up. I do a quick blow dry through my hair. I don't have the energy to stand here for five minutes, so a lot of it is still damp.

Walking out of the bathroom, I head into my closet where I put on a clean pair of panties and a bra. I don't bother with getting a matching pair. No one is going to see them. I grab my black Nine Inch Nails T-shirt that says, "NIN" across the front from a hanger and pull it over my head. I toss the hanger on the floor and retrieve a pair of ripped blue jeans. They are my favorite, and I need every bit of comfort I can get right now.

Tossing a second hanger on the floor, I put each leg into the pants and pull them up. I button them and realize they are a little snug. Perfect! A side effect of my break-up and not eating is weight gain. The day just gets better and better.

I grab my socks and tennis shoes before sitting down, and then put them on. As I stand back up, I feel a little lightheaded, but not as nauseated as before my shower.

When I walk out into the living room I see Nikki at the kitchen sink. She is loading the dishwasher with all my dirty dishes. "Thanks, but you didn't have to do that."

I bend down and pet Charmin on the top of her head. I haven't been a good dog parent in the last week. They aren't even my dogs, which is probably the reason Nikki is here. Nick must have asked her to come get them.

"They're done now, so let's just go. Are you feeling any better?" she asks as she presses the start button on the machine. She is looking at me, but I can't read her. She looks torn and sad, like she wants to say something but doesn't at the same time.

"A little," I reply as she walks past me to the front door. I follow and close up behind me. She walks to her red Jeep Wrangler. "I wouldn't have pictured you driving this type of vehicle."

"Oh, this is Jason's truck. He took my car in to get serviced this morning. His truck is all right and all, but it does not compare to my Mercedes that Nick got me for my birthday," she replies excitedly as she walks around to the driver's side.

I climb in and shut my door. She does the same and starts the truck, before driving to a local medical clinic not far from my house. We go in and I sign my name on the sign-in sheet. I've never been here before, so I have to give them all my information before I take a seat to wait. The wait isn't long at all.

Nikki is quiet. She has been biting her nails since she got into the truck. I'm sure she feels somewhat uncomfortable sitting next to me. Nick likely told her everything; well, his father's version at least. It wasn't the truth, but she doesn't know that. God, what she must think of me . . .

"Miss Taylor?" My name was called. I get up and walk to the nurse standing in the door. Nikki follows me. My temperature and weight are taken first. My temperature is normal, but I've gained six pounds, which would account for the tight pants.

We then follow her to a small exam room where we will wait to see the doctor. After taking my vitals, the nurse closes the door behind her as she exits the room. I take a seat on the exam table and Nikki sits in one of the hard chairs in the room. She is looking everywhere but at me.

"You didn't have to come with me. I appreciate it, but it wasn't necessary. I can only imagine what you must think of me." I lie back on the table and throw my arm over my eyes. My life sucks right now. I don't know how I ended up here.

"Shannon," Nikki starts, "I-I don't think anything bad of you.

How could I?"

"How could you not?" I ask her. Before she can respond, the doctor walks in. It is a middle-aged man with dark hair that has just started to gray on the sides. He has a warm smile. I sit up as he takes a seat on a rolling stool.

"Miss Taylor, please tell me what brought you here today. How are you feeling?" he asks, and then waits for my response. I tell him about the nausea and vomiting. The way it came on without warning but is no longer present.

"Could you be pregnant?" he questions, and I'm caught off guard. I was expecting him to say that at all. I know I'm not pregnant. I've been on birth control since I was fourteen.

"No, sir. I'm on the pill," I tell him. Nikki's eyes grow wide, but she doesn't have anything to worry about. I'm not pregnant.

"When was your last menstrual cycle?" He is staring at me, waiting for my answer, the same as Nikki. I'm wracking my brain. It's not something I generally keep up with, but I'm pretty sure it was right before I met Nick. I haven't started again since meeting him. I look up at the doctor.

No, I couldn't be . . .

"About six weeks, I think." He's jotting a note down in a chart. My chart. No, there has to be another reason. I'm not pregnant.

"Let's do a urine test to be sure. I'll have my nurse come in and take a sample in a few minutes." He stands up and walks out of the room, leaving me sitting here not knowing what to do. Nikki isn't saying anything at all. If anything, she is biting her nails more.

"Would you please stop biting your nails and say something. Whatever it is, just say it," I tell her. I need a distraction from what might be about to happen. I've always wanted children, but I always pictured myself happily married when I had them, which I am currently not. I'm not even happily in love. I'm in love with Nick, but there is nothing happy about our situation right now. Our relationship is nonexistent.

"I know . . ." She pauses, hesitating. "Nick misses you. He's miserable without you," she says, making my heart constrict. If that were the case, why hasn't he come back? Why didn't he give me the benefit of the doubt instead of assuming? Granted, I didn't say anything. Maybe that's exactly what he was doing, but I couldn't.

The nurse enters before I can speak, handing me a small plastic cup with instructions on where to place it after I've filled it. I quickly exit the room, handing my business and I'm back in the room with Nikki within a few minutes, waiting in silence.

After a stretch of time, I ponder what's taking so long with the results. The waiting is killing me and making my nerves skyrocket.

Please, just come in here and tell me already.

"How long does pregnancy test take?" Nikki shouts from her chair. I want to do the same. Finally, a few minutes later, the doctor walks in. He doesn't sit down. I'm not sure if I should take this as a good or bad sign.

"The test was positive, Miss Taylor." He says something else, but I don't hear anything. "I'm pregnant" is shouting over and over in my head, making the outside world a blur.

"Shannon," Nikki says, shaking my shoulders. She is now standing next to me. I never saw her get out of her chair.

"Huh?" I ask and look up at her. She gestures to the doctor

and I turn my head to look at him.

"I was saying, you're likely around four to six weeks. I can't be certain until you have a sonogram. I would suggest scheduling an appointment as soon as possible with your gynecologist. You also need to start a daily multivitamin with folic acid. Your doctor will give you more information. You are now free to go now, Miss Taylor, unless you have any other questions?"

He hands Nikki a slip of paper as I hop off the counter. "No, I don't," I tell him as I follow Nikki out of the exam room and make my way to the counter where she hands the receptionist the sheet. My co-pay is collected before we leave.

I get in the truck and sit there. Reality is sinking in, but I don't know what to do.

"Is it Nick's?" she asks me. "I know you guys have been together for about that long, but Nick also told me you were engaged right before you two hooked up."

She starts the truck and pulls out. "Hooked up?" Wow. That makes me sound like a slut. I know she didn't mean it that way, but it wasn't the comment I needed to hear right now. "Yes, it's Nick's baby." I'm not going into the details of my relationship and how I hadn't had sex with my ex for months prior to me meeting her brother. What is the point?

I don't know what I'm going to do. The father of my child hates me. Hell, his sister probably does too, even if she is being rather nice to me. "You have to tell him. This will change everything. I was serious when I told you he misses you."

She is pleading with me. I have no intention of keeping this from Nick. He has every right to know. "Yes, of course, I'm going to tell him, but how is that going to change a damn thing? Do you not remember telling me he doesn't want kids? Please take me home. I just need to go and see him and figure all of this out."

I pull my seatbelt on as she is putting the truck in reverse. I sit quietly, trying to come up with what exactly I'm going to say. I don't have the slightest clue. When we arrive at my house, I step out of the truck mumbling a "thank you" before walking to my car. She pulls away without another word. LP is where I'm headed.

CHAPTER 24

My phone rings as I settle into the driver's seat. I rise up to pull out my cell from the back pocket of my jeans. Looking at the display screen, it's Teresa Matthews. Why is she calling me? I just met with her close to two weeks ago. That meeting didn't exactly go well. I contemplate not answering, but I'm on my way to LP anyway, so I answer.

"Hello," I greet into the phone.

"Hi, Miss Taylor, it's Teresa Matthews from Lockhart Publishing. I hope I did not catch you at a bad time." Her voice is high-pitched and she doesn't sound like herself; Not that I know her that well. I've only had a handful of meetings with the woman.

"What can I do for you?" I don't want to be on the phone with her, but at least she will distract me for a few minutes from thinking about what I'm going to say when I see Nick.

"I need to meet with you regarding a few details before the

book goes off to print. I was hoping you could come by." I hate her voice. I know I'm being a jealous bitch because she had sex with Nick. That fact bothers me.

"Sure, I can be there in about twenty to thirty minutes," I tell her, since I'm already on my way. I don't want to deal with her, but I might as well get it out of the way while I'm clean and dressed. After I leave Nick's office, I don't know how I'm going to feel. I don't want to go back into the self-pity state I've been in for a week.

"Great," she beams through the phone. She's a little overly excited. "Please come straight to Nicholas's office. I'll meet you there."

"Okay," I say, as she ends the call. I need to see Nick before I see her. I have to tell him our news. She can wait.

I arrive twenty-five minutes later, pulling into the underground parking garage. I take a deep breath before I exit the car. The clock on the dashboard reads eleven sixteen in the morning. When I lock up, I walk quickly to the elevator. I have to get up there so that I don't chicken out; not because I don't want to tell him, but because it's been over a week since I've seen him, and I don't know if I'll be able to not beg him to take me back.

The elevator ride up to the eleventh floor lags as my anxiety rises. There is no one out front when I step out. Rachel must be at lunch. The office is quiet as I make my way to Nick's door; not in an eerily way, but in a way that it feels like no staff is here. I knock lightly and try the doorknob. It's unlocked.

I swing the door open and go to walk in. I hear voices and look up. I freeze and cover my mouth so that I don't gasp in shock and horror.

Teresa's bare back is facing me. She is sitting up and is leaning back a fraction on Nick's desk. I can't see her face, but I know it's her and it's obvious she is naked. She's blocking my view of Nick. Neither have noticed me. They're fucking. I feel like someone just stabbed me in the heart and punched me in the stomach at the same time.

Oh God, I'm going to be sick.

I back out of the door and take off running. I can't stay here. I head for the east set of stairs and run down a few floors. I need a bathroom before I puke on the floor. I enter a door on the eighth floor. I don't know what company occupies this floor, but I find a bathroom as quickly as I can.

When I enter, I go into the first stall and throw up. Barely anything comes up. I know it's disgusting, but I cross my arms over the toilet seat and start crying. I feel my phone vibrating in my back pocket. I don't bother taking it out. I can't talk to anyone.

What if it's her? Oh, God, what if it's him?

I know I don't have a right to be upset, but I am. I'm not his girlfriend any longer, but this hurts worse than anything I could have ever imagined. I just want the pain to stop before it consumes me. I sit back on my knees and flush the toilet. The sobs have quieted down enough to stand up.

My phone vibrates again.

I exit the stall and wash my hands at the sink. I feel dirty. I splash cool water on my face and towel it off. I locate the elevator as I exit the bathroom.

I come out on the ground level and find my way to my car.

I feel the vibration of my phone again, but I leave it where it is for now as I crank my car and pull out of the parking spot. I spot Nick's car as I exit onto the road, tears pooling in my eyes, which makes it hard to see.

I turn onto the road in the opposite direction of my house. Without thinking, I head to Katelyn and Stacy's apartment as Poison's "Every Rose has its Thorn" starts to play through my speakers. I'm not going to call. I don't want to take the chance of talking myself out of it. I don't know if there is enough alcohol to take what I'm feeling away. I stop at a red light and bang my forehead on my steering wheel. God, I can't even have any alcohol.

I'm not blaming my baby, but damn, can a girl not get a break? The light turns green and I continue on my way, wiping tears from each side of my cheeks with the back of my hand.

When I reach their apartment, I park out front. Katelyn's car is here, so I'm grateful she is home. I'm not sure what I'm going to tell her. I've been avoiding my friends' calls for a few days now. Either they know or they have an idea of what is going on, because they haven't stopped calling me in the last few days.

I run up the stairs two at a time. I can't get to her door fast enough. I knock harder than I intend and wait. She doesn't take long to answer.

"Shannon? Oh my God, honey, what's wrong?" She takes one look at my blotchy red face and pulls me into a warm embrace. I rest my head on her shoulder. It's the comfort I've needed for a week. I regret not coming before now. I've been shutting my friends out, and it's not fair to them or me. I still have people who care about me, even if it's not the one person I *want* to care about me right now.

"I should probably go, Katie," Shane says as he's getting off the couch. Katie? Since when does she go by Katie? A moment ago I regretted not coming, but now I regret being here.

I pick my head off her shoulder and she releases me. I had stopped crying before I got out of my car. "No, don't go. I'm sorry. I didn't mean to interrupt," I tell him.

Katelyn intercedes before he can respond. "Shannon, you didn't, but even if you did, it wouldn't matter. You are my friend. Go sit on the couch and I'll bring you a glass of wine," she tells me. God, how do I explain that I can't drink?

"Baby, I'll call you later." I hear her tell Shane as he's walking out the door. Once the door is closed, she heads into the kitchen.

"No wine," I yell from the living room.

"Honey, I think you need it," she yells back.

Hell, here I go.

"I'm pregnant," I confess. There is silence for a split second, and then there's the sound of glass hitting the floor and breaking. I guess she wasn't expecting that.

"What?!" She comes running back into the living room. Her eyes are wide and she's in shock. Maybe I should have broken the news to her differently. "Oh. My. God."

"Yeah," I reply as she takes a seat next to me.

She takes my left hand, entwining it in hers, and squeezes. "Does he know yet?"

"No." I proceed to tell her what I witnessed in his office. By the time I'm finished, I'm crying again. I just want all of this to stop. My heart aches so much. How do I make it stop hurting?

"That's . . . odd," she tells me. "Shane told me Nicholas has been a mess. He's never seen him act the way he has in the past few days." I have no idea what that means, but I'm not going to ask her. She releases me and stands up. "I'm going to get you a glass of water. Stay put."

"And some aspirin, please," I say as I rub my fingers across my forehead above my eyebrows, where my migraine lingers. The intensity is increasing. I want to lie down and forget about today. I don't know if I'll ever get the sight of Nick having sex with someone else out of my mind.

Katelyn returns a few minutes later placing two pills into the palm of my hand. "It's Tylenol. I remember when my sister was pregnant that's all she could take," she tells me with a shrug. I pop the pills into my mouth and reach for the tall glass of water. I swallow a gulp and then hand her the glass back. "So, what happened? Shane swears he doesn't know, and you haven't been taking anyone's calls." She takes a seat on the other end of the couch, facing me with a leg tucked under her butt.

What do I tell her? Obviously, not the truth, but I opt for a semi-truth. "I used to work for Nick's father," I murmur. She crunches her eyes together. "Back in high school," I clarify, and then reach for my glass of water to take a long sip, using the time to sort out exactly what I want to tell her.

"Okay, so what does that have to do with you and Nicholas?" she asks when I take longer than I should to continue.

"Last week, Nick's dad told him something about me that wasn't true, and he believed him," I say, blowing out a breath I didn't realize I was holding in.

"What did he say?" she asks, her voice flat.

"Can we talk about it later? I have a migraine. I want to lie down." I feel bad for brushing off her question, but it's not like I'm going to tell her the full truth, and this is the easiest way to end the conversation.

She eyes me like she knows exactly what I'm doing. "Fine. We can talk later when your headache is gone. Why don't you go get in my bed? It's dark in my room."

With that offer, I stand up and head down the short hall to her room. Closing the door, I kick off my shoes and crawl into her bed. The mattress is soft and the covers are fluffy. The room is dark—pitch black to be exact—just like she said.

I shut my eyes only to open them a minute later. The throbbing in my head is pounding like the beat of a drum. I turn over onto my stomach and bury my head under her pillow. It doesn't help. I can't think beyond the desire to drive a knife through my skull. If only that would relieve the pain, I would certainly do it.

I flip over onto my back and stare at the ceiling. I can't see in this dark room. After an hour or so of repeating that process, I doze off.

When I wake up—I don't know how long I was out—but the throbbing inside my head is gone. *Thank you, Jesus.*

Grabbing the blanket, I rip it off and sit up. Walking carefully in the direction of the door, I open it. The light flowing down the hall from the living room is enough so that I'm able to see my shoes laying on the floor. I bend down, scoop them into my arms, and walk out, shutting the door quietly behind me.

As I make my way down the hall, I hear soft voices. It's Katelyn and Stacy talking in the kitchen. I make my way in their direction and pull out a chair in front of the bar that looks into the kitchen, hopping onto a cushioned stool. Both heads fly up like they've been caught with a hand in the cookie jar. I'm assuming I was the topic of their conversation.

"You're awake," Katelyn says.

"Obviously," I deadpan. "What's that smell?" I ask before she comes back with a smart-ass comment to my sarcasm.

"Spaghetti and meatballs," she tells me. "I thought you could use some comfort food."

"You know me too well." I smile. Spaghetti is one of my favorite dishes and one of the only meals I can cook. Hers smells better than mine. She comes from a large Italian family, so I can't be mad.

"Are you okay?" Stacy finally speaks. Am I okay? Not sure that's the right question to ask, but I know she's only trying to be nice.

"Peachy," I say with a force smiled. They both roll their eyes at me.

"You don't have to be a bitch," Stacy spits back.

I gape at her.

"Food's ready. Let's eat. I was about to wake you," Katelyn says as she opens a cabinet and removes three large, round, white plates.

I hop off the chair and make my way into the kitchen to fix my plate. I feel like I haven't eaten in days. Honestly, I'm hungry, and I need to eat considering there is now a child inside me. That's about as much as I let myself think about the little minion growing in my belly. I'll have plenty of time for that later, when I'm by myself.

After I pile a generous helping onto my plate, I grab a piece of warm garlic bread, adding it on top, before making my way to their dining table. We all three eat in silence, each one of us staring at the other every so often. This isn't the comfortable silence I usually have in the company of my friends. This is the silence where everyone wants to say something but no one does for fear of saying the wrong thing.

"How long was I out?" I ask, trying to break the silence among us.

"Five or six hours," Katelyn inform me over a mouthful of bread. This woman can devour bread. She loves it. I don't know how she stays slender.

We fall back into silence, which lasts throughout the rest of dinner. Once I'm done and all the plates are piled into the sink, I make a friendly exit. I want to go home. It's late and I'm aching all over. A shower and bed are what I need. Not to mention the dogs are probably starving. I don't recall feeding them this morning.

"You don't have to leave. You're welcome to spend the night here," Katelyn says as she pours a glass of wine for herself. It looks good. I can imagine the crisp, wet and cool liquid sliding down her throat as she takes a sip.

Damn her.

"No, thanks. I want to go home," I tell them as I give both a hug from my place at the apartment door. It's the truth. I'm just not so sure it's the escape I'm looking for.

CHAPTER 25

It's day nine without Nick. He hasn't even come back for his dogs. I'm not sure why. In a way, I'm somewhat thankful. I don't know how I would have survived our breakup without their comfort.

This is all so . . . unfair.

Had I known this was the kind of pain that comes from love, I would have avoided it and run the other way. Yeah, I'm lying to myself, but this is what I need right now. The moment Nicholas Lockhart entered my life, I was his; my heart was his. I just didn't know it that short time ago.

Yesterday, I walked into LP to tell Nick I was pregnant with his baby, but instead, I found him having sex with Teresa Matthews. That was the worst thing I've ever seen. My heart was ripped from my chest, causing a level of pain I've never known before. Everything his father took from me didn't even hurt as much as seeing . . . that.

I know he didn't cheat on me like Luke did. When he walked out of my house because I was too much of a coward to tell him the truth, I knew we were over. He told me we were done. But everything inside me belongs to him—from my lips, neck, and breasts, and the rest of my body and the heart inside it. Everything is his, whether he wants me or not. I belong to him, and Goddammit, he belongs to me.

I did this to myself., though I know that much. I'm hurting because I couldn't bring myself to say the words I spent so many years forcing myself to forget. Some things a person can't tell someone else no matter how much they want to. I couldn't get it out of my mouth. I couldn't tell him that his dad raped me.

And now, everything I never faced or dealt with ten years ago is crushing my future with the only man I've ever loved.

Isn't it ironic? I didn't know how much I cared, how much I loved him until I didn't have him any longer. If I could go back and do it all over, knowing what I know now, I can't be certain I would have made a different decision. I don't know if I would have told him. I wanted to—really I did—but I couldn't. How do you admit to a person your innocence was stolen by someone you should have been able to trust? So many years have passed, and I still don't know how to do it. How to talk about it. How to speak the truth that someone hurt me.

Tires screeching outside of house pulls me out of the eerie memory. For a brief moment, I hopeful it's Nick. I need him so badly. I want someone to take all the pain and hurt away. He is the only one that can.

I get off the couch to walk to the door when I hear someone trying to unlock it. Nick is the only other person with a key. My heart races. I'm five feet from the door when it flies open, causing me to suck in a deep breath. It's not him. It's the monster in every one of my nightmares.

Nick's father is standing in the doorway.

His gray eyes are blazing with a dark fire. He's angry, and he's holding a key in front of his chest so I can see it. "Spare key under a cushion? How stupid can you be?" he remarks as he tosses it to the floor.

I take a step back. "Get out of my house," I tell him, sounding weak, my voice barely audible. He steps closer to me and grabs my throat in his right hand, squeezing tight and hurting me.

"Telling my daughter wasn't smart, little girl. I told you that you would regret it if you told a soul." His grip tightens and he pushes my back against the wall. My head hits it from the force of his hand. It painful, but not enough to make me see stars.

"Stop," I beg. "I didn't tell her." I force out.

"You're a lying little bitch. She paid me a visit this morning and took a swing at me; her own goddamn father. It's all because of you!" I try to push him away, but it only makes him more forceful.

"Please. Leave me alone," I continue to beg and push at him with all the strength I can muster. If he hurts me, he hurts the baby too. I can't let him hurt my baby—Nick's baby.

"Keep begging, Shannon, because it only makes me harder. I haven't forgotten the first time I fucked you. You're the best piece of pussy I've ever had. I think I'll have you again before this is over."

No.

He releases my jaw, only to gather both of my hands, holding them in a vice grip with one hand above my head. I continue to struggle in his hold. With his free hand, he skims down my tank top, making me regret taking off my bra when I came home last night. His lips land hard on mine. A moment later, his hand is in the waistband of my shorts. Panic sets in. I can't think straight. If only I could calm down, I might be able to react, and put to use all those boxing classes.

He uses his knee to pry my legs apart. His hands slide farther down, into my panties. I shut my eyes as tight as I can possibly get them when he shoves a finger inside of me. It hurts from being dry, he shoves another in.

"Motherfucker!" he shouts. My hands are released and the groping stops. Niko's growl registers in my head, causing me to look down. He bit James. Niko continues growling and showing his teeth. He looks vicious; something I've never seen from him.

"This isn't over, my little whore," he says to me as he's backing out the front door.

He isn't eyeing at me. He keeps his gaze trained on the dog. When he's out of the entryway and gone, I run to it, securing it as fast as my fingers will turn the lock. I lean against the door, trying to calm myself. It isn't working. I take off, racing to my bathroom and turn the shower to hot. I have to get his touch off me. I can't have any part of him on me.

I strip and get in the shower, grabbing Nick's body wash and pour all that's left onto my bath loofah. I scrub every inch of my body. I can still feel is him all over me and inside me as I bathe every part of me.

I rinse all the soap off and turn off the water, before stepping out and towel drying off, not bothering with drying my hair. Opening the door to the bathroom, I walk to my closet and put on a pair of panties. I need something to comfort me and Nick's clothes are still here. I grab one of his white dress shirts from a hanger and slide it on.

Tears form in my eyes as I stand in the closet. I can't hold them back, and I no longer want to. They run down my cheeks as I slide down to the floor. I scoot backward into the back of the closet and continue to sob, wrapping my arms around my knees to hug myself. How I wish Nick were here to hold me.

I rock myself and continue to sob for hours, until there are no more tears remaining. I cried for all the times I never let myself cry in the past. Finally, I lie on the floor in my closet, spent and tired, and I let my eyes close, not wanting to move. The only thing I want to do is forget.

CHAPTER 26

I wake up to my name being called, or rather, yelled. I'm exhausted and still lying on the floor in my closet. I don't know how long I've been here, but I'm cold and my body aches.

"Shannon, where are you?" I start to breathe rapidly, thinking he's back to finish what he started earlier. Then it registers that it's Nick's voice. His tone is laced with panic. He's here and he's in my room. I look up to him walking into the closet. Blue intense eyes stare down at me. It's almost enough to start the waterfall of tears again. God, I've missed those eyes.

"What the fuck happened out there? Why are you lying on the floor?" he asks as he squats down, resting his elbows on his knees. The panic I thought I heard in his voice moments ago has faded. He pulls me off the floor with gentle hands, and I leap into his arms, almost causing him to fall backward. He catches us both by grabbing onto the doorframe.

I don't care what he did yesterday in his office with her. I need him. I need this. I don't care about the horrible things he said to me last week. Wrapping my arms around his neck, I begin to cry again. I didn't think I had any tears left, but apparently I do.

He wraps my bare legs around his waist as he stands up, and then exits the closet. He strides to my side of the bed and attempts to release me, but I shake my head and hold him tighter.

Sighing deeply, he heads out of my bedroom, instead carrying me down the hall into the living room. The shirt of his that I'm wearing is long enough to cover my panties and the tops of my thighs. "Jase, get her a glass of water, please," he requests, as he is walking over to the couch.

My face is hidden against his neck when I hear his sister's voice. It's shaky and a bit nervous. "Shannon, are you okay?" she asks me, but I can't respond. I'm not okay, but I'm better now that Nick is here. I can't bring myself to release him. If I do, he might leave. He can't leave me. Not again. I can't handle that.

Nick sits on the couch, bringing me down onto his lap with him. I unwrap my legs to place them on each side of his thighs on the cushions. He pries my arms loose from around his neck and shoulders, pushing me back so we are face-to-face. When I look at him, he isn't staring back at me. Something else has caught his attention.

"Who the fuck did that?" he yells. His eyes are wide and filled with alarm. He's looking at my throat, and I know from his stare, there must be a bruise from earlier. I start to tear up, burying my face back in his neck again. I shed more tears. When are they going to end? I don't want to cry; not over that worthless bastard, but I am, and I can't stop.

"Oh God!" Nikki's voice penetrates the room again. "He was here, wasn't he?" she asks, and I know it's directed at me. I remain silent and still as I keep my face buried. I hear something being placed on the table nearest the couch. I realize my throat is parched. Water would be nice right now.

Nick's holding on to me tightly. This is what I need. *Please don't take this from me,* I silently pray. "Who was here? Who are you talking about, Nikki?" Nick asks his sister.

She ignores him. "I know what he did to you. My mom told me. I'm so sorry, Shannon. This is all my fault. Oh God, did my dad . . ." She trails off, not able to finish her sentence. I shake my head from side-to-side, silently answering her. She knows. Nikki knows what he did. Someone else knows he raped me. My mind is reeling in all directions. The water I need is forgotten.

Nick's body goes ridged. He grabs my head with both hands, pulling me away from him. His eyes are wild as they grow wide. "My father did this? He hurt you?"

I nod as more tears slide town my cheeks.

"I'm going to murder him." His eyes are on fire and I know he's serious. I can't let him do that. His mom was right. No matter how much I want his father dead, I can't let Nick ruin his life, our life, our child's life. The sick bastard isn't worth that.

"No, Nick. You can't. I won't let you do that," I plead.

"The fuck I can't," he barks back to me.

"Shannon," Nikki starts, and I look at her. "You have to tell him. Forget what my mom said and tell Nick the truth. Please," she begs, gesturing at Nick with a nod of her head. "If you don't, I will."

I turn my face to the left, looking away from her.

"What's she talking about?" he asks me as he's guiding my face back to face him. I stare at him, not saying anything. I can't do it. I can't tell him. He's going to leave again if I don't, and I still can't say the fucking words. Just like the first time, I'm silent.

"Get out," he orders, but his demand isn't aimed at me even though he isn't taking his eyes off mine.

"Excuse me?" Nikki says.

"You and Jase need to leave, now. This is between Shannon and me." Nick pauses for a brief second. "Nikki, I'm not asking, so just go." Nick still doesn't break eye contact with me. I notice Nikki hesitating from my peripherals. She sighs, and then exits my house.

"Don't do anything stupid, man," Jase says as he goes to follow Nikki out the door.

"Jase?" Nick says, and it seems like a question, causing me to look at Jase standing in the entryway.

"I'll take care of it," he says, and then the door closes, leaving us alone. Even the dogs are nowhere in sight. He continues staring at me for several minutes, his mind working, but I have no idea what he's thinking.

He places his hands gently on each side of my face and pulls me closer until his lips are touching mine, causing my body to relax into the kiss. After a few seconds, I collapse onto his chest, breaking our tender kiss.

"God, I've missed that. I've missed you. I've been in fucking hell for over a week," he tells me as he wraps his right arm around my back and puts his left hand on my face, holding me to his chest. He takes a deep breath, expanding his chest beneath me, and then slowly exhales. "I'm a fucking idiot, aren't I?" he asks as he leans his head on the back of the couch and releases me to run his hands through his hair.

I push off his chest and stare at him. I don't know how I'm going to tell him, but I know I have to. I just don't know where to begin: the rape, the baby, the attempted rape again, or Teresa. This is all so messed up. There is too much shit we need to talk about.

"I'm sorry for everything I said last week. I didn't mean any of it. I was just so mad after he walked into my office and had such a smug look on his face. I knew I wasn't going to like whatever he was there to say. I didn't believe him at first. I swear I didn't. But he left, and . . . and the way Teresa made it sound so . . . believable."

So, I have her to add to my shit list. Bitch.

"Baby, I'm sorry. I am. I shouldn't have assumed, but you wouldn't say anything. Why didn't you say anything?"

It's now or never. "Nick, I didn't know how. I still don't. He . . ." I stop myself. This is too hard.

"Did he hurt you?" His voice is barely above a whisper. He pulls his head off the couch and drops his hands to my thighs. I momentarily tense up. I'm not hurting between my legs, but the memory of that monster pushing inside me is still fresh. Nick catches the change in my body. I nod. He fists the hem of his shirt that I'm wearing. "Shannon, I need you. I need you like I need the air I'm breathing right now. Whatever it is that you couldn't tell me last week, just say it. Just tell me already. Please."

He releases the shirt, moving his hands to hold me at my waist. I have to do this. I have to find whatever strength I have left and tell him everything. I have to do this for us and for our child. I just pray we have a future when it's all said and done.

"I'll try, because I need you, too. I love you." He stills, and I think he stopped breathing. "I know the woman isn't supposed to say that first, but I'm tired of not saying what I feel. The way I feel for you is crazy. It's heartbreaking. It's uncontrollable. It's love. I love you, Nicholas Lockhart."

"Jesus, you know how to cut a man down to his knees. I never knew I wanted to hear those words until you just said them. I've loved you from the moment I laid my eyes on you," he tells me, making my heart swell. I lean forward and kiss him on his lips. He takes control and deepens the kiss. I could do this for the rest of my life and be content. I love him so damn much. He releases my lips and leans his forehead against mine. "Whatever it is, we will get through it. I promise."

I believe him, and I'm ready to get this out. Nothing can stay buried forever. Secrets always come out, and no matter how much someone tries to forget, there are things in one's past that are too great or too tragic to forget. The only thing you can control is yourself. You have to be honest and hope that those you love are there to help you get past the heartbreak.

"I'm going to tell you everything, but first, you have to promise me two things."

I wait for his response.

"I promise. Whatever it is, I promise," he says.

"I need you to let me tell you everything without you saying anything. If you interrupt me, I don't know if I'll be able to finish." He nods in agreement. "Second, I don't want you to leave here tonight. I need you to stay with me, even if you get really angry."

Again, I wait for his response.

"I'm not going anywhere, baby. I promise. Just being away from you this past week nearly killed me. I'm never going anywhere."

I take a deep breath to prepare myself. I try to work it out in my head, but really, there isn't enough time, so I just spill everything before I lose the nerve to tell him. "I worked for your father when I was sixteen. I was still in high school. I was the file clerk and sometimes a runner. I worked in his office after school three days a week, and then every afternoon starting in the summer. I actually loved working there. Well, what I loved was the money, not the work. The work was boring; however, your father pays his staff well, so it was worth it at the time. It happened on a Friday. It was my seventeenth birthday. When I walked in the office, I immediately noticed how quiet it was. The receptionist wasn't at her desk and she was always there. The woman rarely left to take a restroom break. Your father's partner wasn't there either, nor were any of the paralegals. It was strange, but I was also pretty naive back then, so I didn't question it. I went directly back to the file room and started from where I left off the previous day."

I briefly pause to take a cleansing breath. So far, this isn't as bad as I thought it would be, but then again, I haven't told him much. Nick is holding onto my hips with both hands, and he's

N. E. HENDERSON

looking directly into my green gaze. He has this "where is this going" look plastered on his face.

I place my hands on his chest and continue. "I was listening to my iPod. I didn't usually do that. One of the paralegals had warned me that your dad wouldn't approve. He saw music as a distraction from getting the job done; however, there didn't seem to be anyone in the office, so I put my ear buds in and started to work. Honestly, I probably got more work done with the music than I would have without them. If I had been a little smarter, I might have actually checked to see who was and wasn't there when I arrived. About a half an hour later, I heard a sound, even with Papa Roach screaming in my ears. It was the sound of something breaking. It startled me and I froze in place for a moment. When I turned around, your father was standing in the doorway of the file room. He looked angry, but I think he became angrier when he noticed the iPod in my hand. I quickly set it on the filing cabinet and apologized."

Nick's eyes grew wide the moment I mentioned his father was angry with me. I close my eyes and I force myself to continue as the sick memory filters through my mind.

"Follow me to my office, Shannon," he said, and turned on his heels, walking out of the doorway. I followed behind him with my head hung. I knew I was in trouble. I assumed he was going to fire me.

I entered the office as he was removing his jacket. It seemed a bit odd. I noticed broken glass on the ground across the room. It was shattered, as if it had been thrown against a wall. I also noticed an open bottle of dark amber liquid sitting on the desk

256

behind his chair.

"Sit," he ordered with an icy, cold tone. The man wasn't a warm and fuzzy boss to begin with, but I had never seen this side of him. He walked to the desk with the alcohol and retrieved it. He turned around and looked straight at me. His eyes were just as cold as his voice, perhaps even colder, if that were possible.

I wasn't scared of him, but I was uncomfortable in his office— alone with him. I knew he shouldn't have been drinking at work, and I wished I hadn't taken out my iPod. I took a seat in one of the chairs facing his large, wooden desk and placed my hands in my lap.

"Where is everyone this afternoon, sir?" I asked him. I wasn't really sure what to say or do. I had already told him I was sorry. Wasn't that enough? What more did he want from me? I was seventeen for Christ's sake. Surely, I was allowed a mistake or two. It's not like I was a bad employee and broke the rules often. Before then, I had never been in his office, nor been in trouble, so I wasn't sure if the feeling I was experiencing was guilt for doing something wrong or something else entirely. I knew I didn't want to be in the same room with him. I wanted to run. Goose bumps formed and ran down my arms.

"I made them all leave a few hours ago. Do not say another word unless I give you permission to speak. Do you understand?" he asked. I was left speechless and wondering who the hell he thought he was. Apparently, my silence meant that I didn't respond quickly enough. "Answer my Goddamn question, Shannon!"

His eyes darkened. They looked evil, and I wondered briefly

if it was possible to be possessed by the devil himself. I learned later he wasn't possessed by the devil. He was the devil.

"Yes, sir." *My voice trembled, but only for a few seconds.*

"That's better," *he said, taking off his tie completely and holding it loose in his hand. He set the bottle down after taking another large gulp. He stared at me for a long time, like he was trying to hash something out in his head.*

"Get up and come here," *he demanded. I hesitated, but eventually did as I was told. I actually believed that maybe it would get me out of there a little faster. I'd never had sex before, but the look on his face was undeniable. He still looked evil, but his eyes were full of lust. A sickening dread filled my stomach.*

Somehow, I found the courage to speak. "Mr. Lewis, I'm really sorry. I will not do it again. I promise." *I told him as I walked to stand in front of him.*

"You're not half as sorry as I'm going to make you." *His voice was eerily calm as he grabbed my arm, pulling me to him. I tensed as he forcefully embraced me, then crashed his lips into mine, hard.*

I tried to pull out of his hold, but I wasn't strong enough. He moved his lips from mine, against my ear. "I'm going to teach you a lesson about following rules as I take your virginity."

He laughed.

My eyes widened and my mind screamed for me to run. "No!" *I yelled and tried to squeeze out of his grip. He laughed at me as he reached for my hair and yanked it back. I knew at that moment I was in deep shit; the deepest kind imaginable.*

"You have two options here. You can be a good girl and

learn your lesson, or you can be a bad girl and I'll make sure you regret every second of it. I will show you pain like you have never imagined." He bit down hard on my earlobe, causing me to yelp from the pain.

"Please don't do this. Please let me go," I begged him.

The sadistic bastard smiled down at me. "Begging is allowed. The more you beg, the harder my dick becomes," he said as he ground his erection against my hip.

"Please stop," I whimpered. I couldn't believe what was happening. Not to me, I thought to myself. I had no way out and no idea how to escape. My emotions finally caught up to my brain as tears clouded my vision.

"Bad girls must be punished, Shannon. This is your punishment. Next time, I doubt you will do something you aren't allowed to." He pulled his tie out of his pocket and grabbed both of my wrists. With the tie, he bound my wrists together tightly.

I tried to struggle free, but there was nowhere to go. He had me pinned against his desk; I struggled anyway. He then yanked my hair back for the second time, forcing my head backward. His eyes meet mine as a sinister grin spread across his face. It was too late. The pain, as he forced himself on me, was too intense, too painful, too sickening. My world and my body were ripped apart.

I wanted to cry out. To scream at him to stop, but my voice was lost.

I don't know how long it went on, but it felt like it lasted forever. It felt like I was falling into Hell. The more he pushed, the closer I got. The devil was right there with me, pulling me *into the fiery pit. I didn't know how much more I could handle. Finally, my hands became free of the binding around them.*

"Get dressed," he ordered. I obeyed as quickly as possible. I didn't want the chance of anything else happening to me or my body. Once I buttoned my shirt and tucked it into my dress, I scooted off the desk and nearly lost my balance as my knees buckled. A crippling pain spread between my legs. More tears fell, hitting the ground. I caught myself on the edge of the desk right before my knees hit the ground.

Standing back up, I wrapped my arms around myself, not knowing what to do. I looked at him, past him to the door. As if reading my mind, he said, "I wouldn't try to run if I were you."

He walked closer to me, and I tried to back up, but I couldn't. The desk was directly behind me. He grabbed the back of my neck, pulling me into an embrace. Any other embrace would have been warm and comforting. This wasn't one of those. He kissed my cheek softly, then moved to my ear.

I shivered.

"If you ever tell another soul about this, you will not live long enough to regret it." His tone was ice. I tensed, and my breath caught in my throat. "That is a promise, Shannon. Nod if you understand me."

I complied immediately.

He released me.

I ran before it registered in my head. I was opening my car door before I realized I'd made it. Once I was safely inside, I still didn't think. If I'd allowed myself to think, then I'd have lived it all over again. I never wanted to remember any of it. I wanted to forget about the Hell he took me to.

When I finish recounting all the horrible details to Nick, I'm crying on his chest. His shirt is soaked with my tears, and he has a death grip on the bottom, but I don't care. I can't control the tears any more now than when it happened ten years ago. I don't dare look up at him. I'm too scared of the expression that might be on his face. Does he believe me? Does he think less of me? Does he believe his father is even capable of rape?

"And today? What did he do before I got here?" I lift my head off his chest, and I meet a set of glassy, blue eyes surrounded by red. He's crying. Wet streaks run down each side of his face.

He believes me.

"He tried," I tell him as a lone tear falls, rolling down the right side of his cheek. His eyes close briefly. "He didn't, though. Niko bit him as he put . . . as he forced his fingers in me."

"Oh, God." Nick grabs me, pulling me closer as he presses his face in my neck. His body shudders as he cries harder. "I'm sorry. I'm so fucking sorry I let this happen."

"Nick, don't. This isn't your fault," I try to tell him.

"My own father raped you not only once, but twice, and I let it happen. You can't say this isn't my fault, because it is."

"He didn't today. Your dog stopped it."

"Not soon enough. He forced himself on you, in you. That's rape!" he yells out through his tears. I realize he's right. It is. He might not have put his penis in me, but he did rape me with his hand. My own tears begin to flow again. I close my eyes, put my face in the crook of his neck, and sob.

CHAPTER 27

y eyelids flutter open to the morning sun shining in through the bedroom windows. Looking down, I see two ink-covered arms wrapped firmly across my chest. Nick's arms are warm. My back is aligned with his front, and his right leg is draped over my hip. I'm cocooned in his embrace, feeling protected and safe. Relief floods my body, and I know it is because of the secrets I shared with him. I only wish I had done it a week earlier, but I can't change the past. I can only accept it and move forward.

I don't remember getting into bed last night, so I assume Nick brought me since the last thing I recall is lying across his chest on the couch, sobbing. We were both crying. I must have been too exhausted. I'm still wearing his white button-up shirt and my panties.

He tightens his hold around me, and then he places a light kiss on the top of my head. I take a deep, cleansing breath. It feels nice to have him back with me. His touch is comforting. It's my home. I never want to lose this again.

He releases his hold on me when I attempt to turn over in the bed, facing him. His eyes are red and bloodshot. He doesn't look like he's slept at all. There are no words that can describe the pain I see looking back at me. I've never seen Nick so distraught. There is also so much anger reflected back at me. It's not a good look on him, and I'm worried.

Shit.

How do you get over finding out your dad raped your girlfriend? "You didn't sleep, did you?"

He inhales a large breath and slowly forces the air back out of his mouth. "No, but I'm glad you did," he tells me. His voice is laced with sadness. He doesn't sound like *my* Nick, and I don't like it one bit. He feels distant even though there is no space between us. I won't let him pull away from me. I won't lose him again. I can't.

"Nick," I start, and then pause, trying to gather my thoughts. "You told me last night, before I spilled my guts, that we would put it behind us. Putting it behind us means we move past this— together."

He closes his eyes briefly. When he opens them again, he doesn't respond to my statement. He changes the subject instead.

"You're probably hungry. Get dressed. I'll cook you breakfast." My stomach growls at the mention of food, so I don't protest. I haven't eaten since leaving Katelyn and Stacy's apartment two nights ago. He rolls onto his back and then pulls himself out of the bed, walking out of the room without saying another word.

His silence is not good; far from it. I need to know what he's thinking. I force myself up and out of my bed. My body aches all over, but I make myself walk to the bathroom. After I pee, I quickly brush my teeth and then comb through my matted hair. Looking in the mirror, I confirm that I look like hell. I look the same way I feel. Don't get me wrong, I'm still relieved after everything I told Nick last night, but that doesn't make the pain or the memory go away. It's still there, and I know I'm going to have to deal with it. I'm going to have to learn to find a way to get past it and not ignore it. I've ignored it long enough, and I feel it was all wasted time. Time I could have used to heal.

Walking into the closet, I strip out of my worn clothes and put on my favorite Papa Roach T-shirt and some sweatpants. I remain barefoot and head to the kitchen to find Nick. I don't want to spend any more time without him. I've already spent enough time apart to last a lifetime.

The moment I reach the entrance to the kitchen, the smell of eggs hits me. My mouth fills with saliva. Nick turns as I cover my mouth and run to the hall bathroom. Just as I reach the toilet, Nick is at the door. He is at my side in no time, pulling my hair back just as I throw up all the contents of my stomach. How I have anything in there is beyond me.

"Are you done?" he asks, and I nod. He pulls me off the floor and walks me the two steps to the sink. I lean down, splashing water onto my face and rinsing out my mouth. After I turn the faucet off, he hands me a towel. The reality of my pregnancy comes back.

Shit. He doesn't know yet.

"Are you sick?" he asks as I hand the towel back to him. He tosses it on the counter.

"No, I'm not sick, but there is something else I need to tell you."

His eyes flash with what I think is panic. I've already told him enough shit to last a lifetime. "Okay," he says cautiously.

"I'm . . ." I pause, looking for the right words. Coming out and just saying it seems . . . I don't know . . . real, but then again, this is real. I'm pregnant and we are having a baby. I don't think either of us are ready for this.

Before I can continue, pounding sounds from the front, like a fist beating on my door. Panic washes over me and I leap into Nick's arms. What if his dad is back? Surely, he won't come here if he knows Nick is here.

"It's not him. Relax," he assures me as he cups my face in his palms. How can he be so sure? He places a chaste kiss on my lips before dropping his hands and grasping my left hand into his right. He just kissed the mouth that puke came out of. That has to be gross.

"Are you expecting someone?" I ask as he pulls my reluctant body from the bathroom and down the hall, leading me to the front of the house.

"No," he simply says. The banging continues until Nick yanks the door open. I cower behind him, but he doesn't release my hand. "What the fuck, Nikki?" he says, pulling me into his arms and tightly wrapping them around me. Relief fills me at the sight of Nick's sister.

"I've been calling you all Goddamn morning. Why haven't you answered any of my calls?" she huffs out with an irritated glare directed at her brother.

"My phone has been on silent since I went to bed last night. What is so damn important that you had to beat the Goddamn door down and scare the shit out of Shannon?"

She cuts her eyes to me and they soften. There is sympathy pooling in her blue gaze. "I'm sorry," she tells me, and then flashes her eyes back up to her brother. "I need to speak to you," she says, giving him a pleading look.

"So speak," he demands.

Nikki glances back at me. Whatever it is, she doesn't want to say it in front of me. I'm guessing it has to do with their father. I could use a cup of coffee right now, but I don't want to set foot in my kitchen. There is probably a lingering smell of eggs and I don't want to chance hurling again.

"Why don't I feed and water the dogs while she talks to you?" I try to take a step back out of his arms, but Nick's body stiffens. When I glance up, his eyes are wide.

"She doesn't know?" Nikki questions, giving Nick a disbelieving look.

Know what? What don't I know?

"Nick?" I question. My eyebrows pull together as I wait for him to tell me.

"For fuck's sake, Nikki," he hisses at his sister before looking down at me. "Um . . . I . . ." He's reluctant to tell me. This is bad.

"What is it?" I whisper. I look at Nikki, who is biting her bottom lip. I glance back up at Nick. Whatever it is, he's having a hard time trying to tell me.

"Niko is . . ." He pauses briefly, and my eyes dart around, looking for the dogs. They weren't in the bedroom when I woke up. They always sleep in our room. And then, he shocks me with, "He's dead," Nick sighs out. I gasp.

"What? No . . . he was . . . how?" That can't be right. That dog saved my life yesterday. What happened? I don't understand.

"I don't . . ." Nick starts to say as he runs his free hand through his dark hair. He looks sad. "Know," he finishes.

"I don't understand," I say as tears pool in my eyes.

Nick pulls me into his chest, hugging me tightly. "He was lying on the doormat in front of the door when we got here last night." Nick takes a deep breath and I pull my head off his chest. "I nearly had a heart attack until I found you, and when I did, you were lying on the floor in the closet. I didn't know"—he pauses, blinking rapidly—"that he was gone until Jase confirmed it last night when I brought you into the living room with me." Nick takes another deep breath and looks up at the ceiling.

"Where's Charmin?" I ask.

He looks back down, but it's Nikki who answers my question. "She's at my house," she answers. "She's fine."

"But how?" I ask. I still don't understand.

"My father," Nick says.

"How do you know that, Nick?" Nikki questions him, her tone accusatory.

What am I missing here?

Nick cuts his eyes at his sister. "Shannon told me Niko bit him yesterday." There is a quick pause before he continues. "I'm only assuming," he tells her as he throws his arms up.

"I can't believe this," I mumble. My stomach begins to churn again.

"Nick?" Nikki says in a low tone.

He looks back at her. "What?"

"I really need to speak to you." Again, her tone is low, but it's laced with something I can't figure out. She is pleading with him.

"For the love of God, what?" he yells.

"I don't think—"

Nick cuts her off. "Just spit it the fuck out already!"

"Dad's dead," she blurts out. I gasp again. My eyes snap to hers. She's biting her lip and looking at Nick. I look down, trying to gather my thoughts. Isn't this what I wished for? Now that it's real, how do I feel? I feel like the weight of the world has just been lifted off my chest.

"Good," Nick says calmly—too calmly—which is what catches my attention. Now, I start to wonder. My eyes flicker back to his sister. They are staring at each other as if having a silent conversation.

"Did you?" she asks, also calmly, and my mouth gapes open. How could she think that?

I speak before Nick has a chance too. "Of course, he didn't. He's been here with me," I say. "The whole night," I add for clarification. The expression on her face doesn't change as she continues to look at her brother. Nick remains silent.

No . . . he couldn't.

"How?" I add.

"He was beaten to death sometime last night or early this

morning. His body was found on the beach by a jogger," Nikki tells me before turning her eyes back on her brother. "Nick?"

"You heard her. I've been here. Besides, I rode with Jase last night. It's not like I had a way to leave." He turns, facing away from us, and then runs his hand back through his hair. "Is there anything else?" he asks as he starts to walk off.

"Mom," she adds, causing Nick to stop before reaching the kitchen. He turns back around. "She's freaking out. You didn't show up for your usual birthday breakfast this morning." She pauses. "What do you suppose she's thinking right now?"

Nick's eyes fall back on me. They are pleading like he's silently asking me for some type of forgiveness. But why? "Take me over there," he says, but I can tell it's not directed at me, even though his eyes haven't left mine. He can't leave.

"No, you can't leave," I say and quickly walk over to him.

"Nikki, go wait in the car," he commands, and she immediately follows his order.

I grab the bottom of his T-shirt for something to hold onto. "Nick, please don't leave, or at least let—"

"I have to deal with this—my mother," he says, but that isn't what his eyes are telling me. I think back to the pleading look a few moments ago. It doesn't sit well with me. He's planning to walk out the door and I don't think he plans to return.

"What just happened here?" I question, motioning between our bodies. I'm confused. Last night he said he missed me, that he loved me, and then . . .

Is what I told him too much?

"I need to walk away before I hurt you more." He grips my

upper arms, as if to hold himself back.

What is he talking about? Hurt me? He hasn't. "Nick, you haven't done anything, but you're about to."

He looks up at the ceiling. "Yes, I have. Everything that's happened to you is my fault," he states.

"No, it's not." I try to reassure him, but it comes out as a whine. What his father did to me—both times—isn't his fault. Nick isn't to blame. The blame is all on his father. I only hope that whoever killed him made him feel every bit of the pain I felt, and Nick's mom felt, before he took his last breath. I know the Bible says vengeance is the Lord's, but I can't help but wish I would have been the one strong enough to hurt him back.

"You're better off without me. That way, it will be easier to forget," he says, releasing me and taking a step back. My hands fall from his shirt.

"Maybe forgetting isn't what I want anymore. Don't walk away from this, from me. Please," I beg.

I still have so much to face. Just because it's out there and I've finally told someone, doesn't mean I've dealt with it. I know this. It's going to be a long time before I can truly put this behind me.

"I have to," he says as he makes his way to the door, with a sad voice.

"Nick," I whisper as he's opening it. He pauses before exiting. "I'm pregnant."

A loud gasp escapes his mouth, followed by Nick grabbing the doorframe. I can't see his face to gauge his reaction, but I quickly remember what Nikki told me. Nick doesn't want kids.

"Is it mine?" he whispers back.

"Yes."

Nick drops his head at my answer. After a few seconds, he proceeds to walk out the door, closing it behind him without even looking back at me.

He's gone, and once again I'm alone . . .

The conclusion happens in <u>SILENT GUILT.</u> *Find out now, what secret and why Nick harbors so much guilt.*

ALSO BY N.E.HENDERSON

SILENT SERIES:
Nick and Shannon's Duet
SILENT NO MORE
SILENT GUILT

MORE THAN SEIRES:
Can be read as standalones but not recommended
MORE THAN LIES
MORE THAN MEMORIES

DIRTY JUSTICE TRILOGY:
DIRTY BLUE
DIRTY WAR
DIRTY SIN

THE NEW AMERICIAN MAFIA:
BAD PRINCESS
DARK PRINCE
DEVIANT KNIGHT

STANDALONE BOOKS:
HAVE MERCY

BOXSETS / COLLECTIONS:
Silent Series
More Than Series
Dirty Justice Trilogy

ACKNOWLEDGMENTS

You, my reader, thank you from the bottom of my heart for reading my story. I am grateful you decided to take a chance on me. Please consider writing an honest review from the platform you bought this book from. Again . . . thank you so much. It means so much.

Joe, thank you for not ending this journey like you threatened to do so many times. I know my hours spent on the computer got on your nerves—a lot. Thank you. I love you.

Elizabeth, I can't even begin to say or describe what you mean to me without tearing up and being a crybaby. Thank you for everything. You are one of the most supportive person I've ever known. Telling you I love you is an understatement, but I love you so much.

Sabrina Hart, my first reader beta reader and friend, I'm so glad we met on Goodreads. Thank you for all the feedback and suggestions you made. I don't think this book would have seen the light of day if not for you. You encouraged me a lot and I'm so grateful. I love reading every story you write and I cannot wait for them to all get published. You are an amazing writer.

Amy Eye, you took the original edited version of this book and showed me how much I needed you sooner. Thank you for polishing this baby. Through the re-editing process I feel I've learned from you and for that I thank you.

ABOUT THE AUTHOR

N. E. Henderson is the author of sexy, contemporary romance. When she isn't writing, you can find her reading some form of romance or in her Maverick, playing in the dirt.

This is Nancy's debut book.

For more information:
www.nehenderson.com
facebook.com/authornehenderson
instagram.com/nehenderson
tiktok.com/author_nehenderson